MONUMENT ROCK

MONUMENT ROCK

LOUIS L'AMOUR

BANTAM BOOKS
NEW YORK TORONTO LONDON SYDNEY AUCKLAND

MONUMENT ROCK
A Bantam Book/May 1998

Library of Congress Cataloging-in-Publication Data

L'Amour, Louis, 1908–1988.
    Monument Rock / Louis L'Amour.
        p.   cm.
    ISBN 0-553-10833-6
    I. Title.
PS3523.A446M66   1998
813'.52—dc21   97-43622
                                                                       CIP

Published simultaneously in the United States and Canada

Bantam Books are published by Bantam Books, a division of Bantam Double-
day Dell Publishing Group, Inc. Its trademark, consisting of the words
"Bantam Books" and the portrayal of a rooster, is Registered in U.S. Patent
and Trademark Office and in other countries. Marca Registrada. Bantam
Books, 1540 Broadway, New York, New York 10036.

PRINTED IN THE UNITED STATES OF AMERICA
BVG   10   9   8   7   6   5   4   3   2   1

CONTENTS

MONUMENT
ROCK

A MAN NAMED
UTAH

The small glow of the lamp over the hotel register, shaded as it was, threw his cheekbones into high relief and left his eyes hollows of darkness. The night clerk saw only a big man, in dusty range clothes, who signed his name in the slow, cramped manner of a man unaccustomed to the pen. Hibbs handed him his key and the man turned and started up the steps.

As he climbed, the light traveled down over his lean hips and picked out the dull luster of walnut-stocked guns, then slid down to worn boots and California-style spurs. When the heels vanished, Hibbs waited no longer but turned the register and peered at the name. Without another instant of delay he came from behind the counter, cast one quick glance up the stairs, and bustled out the door.

The quick, upward glance did not penetrate the darkness. Had it done so, he would have seen the stranger standing in the shadows at the head of the steps, watching him. When Hibbs hurried across the dark street, the rider was at his window, looking down. The clerk disappeared into an alley.

It was a small thing, but the rider knew the wheels had begun to turn. Already they knew of his presence, and already he had gathered his first fragment of a fact. Somebody was almighty interested in his arrival, and that somebody had a working deal with the hotel clerk. Not much to know, but a beginning.

The clerk had hurried on for several hundred feet then turned and stopped by a window with three inches of opening. He tapped lightly with a coin, and at a cautious response, he whispered, "Hibbs, here. Gent just registered as Utah Blaine, El Paso."

"All right."

Disappointed at the lack of reaction, Hibbs waited for something else to be said; then, when it did not come, he added, "He looks salty."

"All right."

Hibbs walked slowly back to the hotel. His round, rather querulous face sagged with vague disappointment.

The man behind the darkened window rolled on his side and picked up a carefully prepared cigarette that lay on the table by the bed. When it was lit he lay back, his head on the bunched-up pillow. Against the vague light of the window, the cigarette glowed and he stared up into darkness.

How much longer dared he continue? The pickings were rich, but he was feeling the uneasiness that preceded danger. He had a bag full, no doubt about that. Maybe it was time to pull his stakes.

He knew nothing of Blaine, yet that the man had been

asked here was evidence that someone believed he was the man for the job.

Jack Storey had been tough and fast . . . a drunken miner named Peterson had been egged into shooting him in the back. Three other marshals had preceded him and they were buried in a neat row on the hill. The man on the bed inhaled deeply and knew he had managed well up to now, but his luck was sure to run out.

He had the gold taken from miners, gamblers, and casual travelers and only Hibbs knew who he was, only he knew the murders and robberies had been engineered by one man. And the clerk could be removed.

So he would quit at last. This was what he had planned when he first came west, to work at a quiet job and amass a fortune by robbery and murder—then he would quit, go east, and live a quiet, ordered life from then on.

From the beginning he had known there was a limit. So far he was unsuspected. He was liked by many. His whole plan had depended on the crimes seeming to be unrelated so they would be considered casual crimes rather than a series planned and carried out by either one man or a gang.

Yet it would be foolish to continue. Three marshals . . . it was too many. Not too many lives, just too many chances. Too many risks of discovery. No matter how shrewd this new man might be, or how dumb, it was time to quit. He would not pull even one more job. He was through. Putting out the stub of his cigarette, he turned over and quietly went to sleep.

A solid-looking man in a black suit and boots was sitting on the creek bank when Utah Blaine rode up. The new marshal's sun-darkened face had a shy grin that livened his features. "Hi, Tom! Mighty good to see you."

"Sure is!" The older man gripped his hand. "Long time since the old days on the Neuces."

Blaine started to build a smoke. "So, what're you gettin' me into?"

Tom Church dug at the sand with a stick. "I don't really know. Maybe I'm crazy in the head. We've had fourteen murders this past year, an' it worries me some. This here town was started by my dad, an' he set store by it. We've always had the usual cowpuncher shootin's an' the like of that, but something's different. No other year since we started did we have more'n three or four."

He talked quietly and to the point while Blaine smoked. Nobody in town showed an unusual prosperity. No toughs were hanging around town that couldn't be accounted for. Nobody left town suddenly. Nobody hinted at secrets. The murdered man was always alone, although in two cases he had been left alone only a matter of minutes. All the murdered men had been carrying large sums of money.

A half-dozen men carrying smaller amounts had left town unhindered; only two of the fourteen had made killings at gambling. Others had worked claims, sold herds of cattle or horses. All fourteen had been killed silently, with knife, noose, or club. Which argued a killer who wanted no attention. "This town means a lot to us. My boys are growin' up here, an' two of the men killed were good friends of mine. I think there's a well-organized gang behind it."

"Got a hunch you're wrong, Tom."

"You think there's no connection?"

"I think they tie up, but I don't think it's a gang. I think it is just one man."

"How's that?"

"Look at it. Nobody has flashed any money and nobody has talked while drunk. That's unusual for a gang. You know there's always one wheel that won't mesh. I'll get to work on it."

Tom Church got up and brushed off his pants. "All right, but be careful. We've lost three marshals in the last ten months."

It was to Utah Blaine's advantage that he did not make a big show of looking for information. He did not throw his weight around. He let people know that he thought the marshal's job was mighty easy if people would just let him be. And while he sat around, he listened.

Hibbs at the hotel might be the key. Hibbs had rushed word of his coming to someone, and Blaine had seen the street he went into. For the first four days Utah Blaine strolled about, rode into the hills, talked little, and listened a lot. He heard a good deal of gossip about conditions of the claims, who was making it and who wasn't. There was talk about cattle and cattle prices. Most of this talk took place on the worn bench outside the barbershop.

It was late on the fourth night that he received his first test as marshal.

Blaine was at a table in a back corner of the saloon when a wide-shouldered young man with red hair smashed through the swinging doors and glared around him. Obviously, he had been drinking, just as obviously, he was not so drunk that his speech was slurred or his reactions slow. "Where's that two-bit marshal?" he demanded.

"Over here. What's on your mind?"

The casual tone upset Red Williams, who was trouble-hunting. Nevertheless, he took three quick steps toward Blaine, and Utah did not move. "You're the marshal? Well, I hear we got to check our guns! You figurin' to take mine away from me? If you do, get started!"

Blaine chuckled. "Red," he said conversationally, "don't you get enough trouble wrestlin' steers? Why don't you fork your bronc and head on for home?"

Red Williams was disturbed. It was not going as expected. Instead of being a hard-eyed marshal who immediately started for him, this man talked like another cowhand. "You tellin' me to get out of town?" he demanded.

"Just advisin'," Utah replied casually. "If you figure to do a day's work tomorrow, you better sleep it off." He pushed his hat back on his head. "I call to mind one time when I rode for Shanghai Pierce. We was—"

"You rode for *Shanghai*?" Red's truculence was forgotten.

"Took a herd over the trail for him in 'sixty-seven," Utah said. "The next year I took one up the trail for Slaughter."

Red Williams swallowed hard, his stomach sick with sudden realization. "You . . . you're *that* Blaine? The one who stopped the herd cuttin' north of Doan's Store?"

"Yeah," Blaine replied quietly. "That was later."

"Wow!" Red backed up, suddenly grinning. "Mister, if that's who you are, this town is off-limits for my kind of trouble!"

Squaw Creek was impressed but not convinced. Twice Blaine quietly talked his way out of trouble that with any other marshal would have meant shooting. Days passed with no gunfights, no brawls, and surprisingly, no robberies and murders.

Once, sitting on the bench in front of the barbershop, he was asked about the killings of Van Hewit and Ned Harris, the two last murders before he took the job of marshal. He shrugged and replied, "I'll handle the crime that comes my way, but I say let the dead past keep its dead."

Before the saloons opened, the benches in front of the barbershop were the usual loafing place. It was there he stopped to gather what facts he could. "Nice idea," he commented. "Gives a man a place to sit and talk."

"Pickard's idea," they told him. "Built 'em for his customers to wait on."

Pickard was a man of medium height, smooth-faced but for a flowing mustache. Square-jawed and square-bodied, he was a friendly man, skillful at his trade, and a good listener. "Mighty fine barber," Tom Church said, "I'll be sorry when he goes."

"He's leavin'?" Blaine asked.

"Brother died, back in Illinois. Got to go back and manage the property."

It was their second meeting since Blaine's arrival, and Church was visibly disturbed. "The rest of the city council, the men who pay your salary, Utah, they're complaining. You've kept it quiet, or it's been quiet, but you've found no killer. I promised that you would."

"You don't catch a killer right away any more than you take a herd to Montana by wishin' it there."

He knew more than he was telling Tom Church. Things were beginning to add up. All the killings had been within five miles of town. All but two had taken place at night or early in the morning. The two had occurred at midday. Five men lived on that street into which Hibbs had gone on the night of his arrival. Childress, Hunt, Newcomb, Jones . . . and Tom Church.

Actually, it was a one-sided street. The houses faced south, which had them looking across the street at the cottonwoods that line Squaw Creek. Behind those cottonwoods were the back doors of the business buildings on Main Street. The saloon, barbershop, marshal's office, harness shop, and general store backed up to the trees.

Hibbs lived in the hotel and did not drink. He was an odd personality, not talkative, and yet he had a habit of always being around when a conversation developed. Unobtrusively, Utah Blaine watched him and waited, knowing his time would come.

Hibbs was never found near the barbershop. For a man so interested in gossip, this was interesting if not odd. Hibbs went to the barbershop only when he needed a haircut.

From the beginning Blaine had known that Hibbs was his key to the situation, yet while watching Hibbs, he had listened and studied the town, and one by one he eliminated the possibilities. The more men he eliminated, the more certain he became of the killer's cunning. He had left no loose ends.

Utah Blaine had learned, long since, how to apply simple logic to a problem. Men were creatures of habit. Therefore he must observe the habits of the possible suspects and watch for any deviation from the usual.

Opportunity was a consideration. Not more than a half-dozen men in town would have been free to move at the hours of the two midday crimes. Childress could not leave his store at the noon hour, and had a wife who insisted upon his being on time for supper. Hunt was a man who habitually drank his supper at the saloon, a convivial soul whose absence would have been noted and commented upon. So it was with most of the others, yet Pickard was a bachelor. He had means of learning, through the talk around the shop, of who had made strikes and who did not, and he could be safely absent at the hours of crimes. Moreover, the cottonwood-cloaked creek bed back of the shop offered an easy means of leaving and returning to town unobserved. All of these were logical reasons for suspicion, but none of it was proof.

On the morning of his tenth day in town, Utah went to the barbershop for a shave. Pickard had gentle hands and he worked carefully and swiftly. He was shaving Utah's throat when Utah said, from under Pickard's left hand, "Goin' to be a break soon. I've got a lead on the man who's been doin' the killing around here."

For only a second the razor stopped moving, and then it continued more slowly. "I thought," Pickard said, "it was the work of casual drifters, or maybe a gang."

"No," Blaine said decidedly, "it's been one man. One mighty shrewd man. He's done it all, and he's been smart enough to protect himself. But every man has to have help, an' I've got a lead on that."

Pickard started to strop his razor, and then the door opened, and closed. "How are you, Mr. Church? Blaine tells me he has a lead on those murders we used to have before he came."

"That right, Utah?"

The razor smoothed a patch on his chin. "Yeah. Fact is, I've had a lead ever since I came to town. From the very hour I got in, you might say."

Pickard finished his job and dusted Blaine's face with powder. Utah sat up in the chair and felt his face. "You sure do give a fine shave, Pickard. . . . Close," he said, looking at the barber, "but not too close."

When they had gone, Blaine and Church walking

together, Pickard stared after them. A lead since the very moment . . . he might have seen Hibbs!

Yet, what could he have seen? And suppose he had seen Hibbs come to him? It would prove nothing, and Hibbs could not talk. He would not dare to talk. So there was nothing to worry about. Nevertheless, he did worry.

He had not been fooled by Blaine. The tall gunfighter was too friendly, too casual. His manner did not go with his cold, watchful eyes and the strong-boned face. Alone in the apartment back of his shop, Pickard paced the floor and thought.

It was time to go, but he must be careful. Suppose Blaine was only waiting for him to uncover his loot and so be caught with the goods? Or suppose he frightened Hibbs in some way and forced him to talk? The more he considered, the more he worried. He had been a fool to wait so long. He could have gone long ago. Why, he had over sixty thousand dollars!

Slowly, he went over the problem again. Hibbs might talk, of course, but he had already made plans for Hibbs and it was time he put them into operation. Pickard was a coolheaded man and utterly cold-blooded. He had long known that before he left, Hibbs must die. Aside from the knowledge of Hibbs's past, the one thing he knew was that Hibbs would wait for him to recover the hidden loot, and then Hibbs would try to murder him for it. Pickard knew that idea lay in Hibbs's mind as if he himself had written it there. And to an extent, he had.

If Hibbs betrayed him, he'd never get a chance at the money. It also allowed him the chance to trap Hibbs. So now to prepare that trap, he had to lead Hibbs out of town into the hills, and then kill him.

.   .   .

Blaine had formed the habit of riding out of town at least once each day. He varied the times of these rides so as to allow for no easy planning of future crimes or observation of his moves.

First, he rode to the scenes of the crimes and studied the terrain and approaches. There were, of course, no tracks. There had been rain and wind since, but they were not what he was searching for. Nor was he looking for any clue that might have been dropped. He was trying to imagine how the killer would have concealed his loot, for he would not have dared to risk being seen carrying it back into town.

The other rides were short, and they ended in a small clump of juniper atop a ridge outside of Squaw Creek. There, with a pair of field glasses, Utah Blaine watched the town.

The break came suddenly. On one bright and sunny Sunday morning he saw Hibbs come from the hotel and walk across the street. Going down the alley between the buildings, Hibbs turned suddenly into the old, abandoned store building on his right. Not two minutes later he stepped out, only now he had a rifle and a canteen.

Utah Blaine settled himself firmly and watched with care. Hibbs went down into an arroyo and out of town, working his way up the hill right toward Blaine's position! Just when he was sure he must move or be seen, Hibbs stopped and, settling down, began to wait.

Almost an hour passed and then Pickard came from the back door of the barbershop and slid down into the creek bed. Watching, Blaine saw the man working his way downstream, then saw him come out among some boulders. Hibbs got up and began to work his way along the flank of the mountain, keeping Pickard in view. Keeping higher and staying among the junipers, Blaine kept pace with Hibbs. Then the junipers grew more sparse and scattered out. Reluctantly, Blaine swung over the crest and kept the ridge between himself and the two men. From time to time he climbed higher and let his eyes seek out the clerk, then suddenly the man was gone.

Blaine swore bitterly. To cross the ridge within view of either Hibbs or Pickard would ruin the whole plan, and his only chance lay in riding ahead to intercept their trail as it left the ridge, which ended a few miles farther along. So swinging his horse, he rode down into the wash and followed it out until the ridge ended. It was only then that he realized how that ridge had betrayed him.

Some distance back the ridge divided into a rough Y, and he had been following the southernmost of the two arms, while Hibbs had obviously followed along the northern. It was at least two miles across the bottom to the other ridge and it was very hot now, and close to noon.

Before crossing the gap, he studied it with care, but there was no sign of either man. He crossed as quickly as he could, then climbed the far ridge and, taking a chance, mounted the crest. As far as the eye could reach, there was no living thing.

Irritated, he rode down the far side, scouting for tracks. He found none. The two men, and both on foot, had lost him completely. How long since he had lost Hibbs? He checked the sun and his memory. It must have been almost an hour, as best he could figure. Turning back, he rode toward town. He had gone no more than two hundred yards when he drew up sharply.

Before him on the trail lay the sprawled figure of a man, half-covered with the rocky debris of a landslide. Blaine dropped from his horse. It was Hibbs, and he was quite dead. Climbing the hillside, Blaine found scuff marks in the dirt where someone, almost certainly Pickard, had sat, bracing himself while he forced a large boulder from its socket of earth with his heels.

Pickard must have known Hibbs would follow, or had seen him, and had pushed down these boulders, probably coming by later to make sure there was no doubt. Yet allowing for the time it took Hibbs to get to this point on foot, it could have been no more than twenty to thirty minutes ago that he had been killed!

If he rode swiftly now, he might overtake Pickard before he could get back to Squaw Creek!

Yet his ride was in vain. All was quiet when he rode into town and stabled his horse. Pickard was quietly shaving Tom Church and had the job half-done. He glanced up at Blaine and nodded. "Hot day for riding, I guess," he said conversationally. "You can have it. I'd rather stay in my barbershop."

Baffled and irritated, Utah did not trust himself to speak. There was no way the man could have gotten back here that fast. It must be someone else whom he had seen, it must— He stopped. Suppose Pickard had a horse waiting for him out there on the ridge somewhere? And had raced back, changed shirts quickly, and returned to his work as he did each day? But where was the horse? And where had he been concealed?

.   .   .

Utah Blaine dropped in at the saloon for a drink and the first man he saw was Red Williams. The latter grinned, "Howdy, Marshal! No hard feelin's?"

Blaine chuckled. "Why should there be? What are you doin' in town in the middle of the week?"

"Come in after some horses. The boss keeps a half-dozen head of good saddle stock down at his creek barn in case any of the boys need a change of horse."

"Creek barn? Where's that?"

"Just outside of town a ways. We got two outfits, one west of town, an' the other seventeen miles northeast. We switch horses at the creek barn every now and again. It's a line shack right out of town."

"You taking all the horses?"

"Nope. Just four head. We're mighty short of saddle stock right now, the boys haven't rounded up the bunch off the west range yet. Funny thing," he said, "durned kids been ridin' 'em, I guess. One of Tom's best horses is stove up."

Utah Blaine turned his glass in his fingers. "Red, you want to do me a favor?"

"Sure. What is it?"

"Take all those horses with you and keep 'em away from that line shack for a week. If the boss says anything, I'll explain it."

Red shrugged. "Sure, I'll do it." He looked curiously at Utah. "Wish you'd let me in on it, though."

"Later. But don't even whisper it to anybody, you hear? And don't let anybody see you if you can help it. I've got a feelin' we're goin' to make a murderin' skunk mighty unhappy!"

. . .

The death of Hibbs was amazing to Squaw Creek only because the hotel clerk had been out of town. The curiosity of the loafers at the barbershop was aroused and they speculated at random on what he had been doing in that dusty wash when he was usually at work on the hotel books.

Blaine listened thoughtfully. Then he got up and settled his hat on his head. Inside the barbershop, Pickard was stropping a razor. "I figure he was hunting the loot from those robberies," he said, "and he had some idea where it was ... only he was too late."

"Too late?" Childress looked up. "You mean somebody found it?" The razor stropping had stopped abruptly.

"Uh-huh," Utah said, weighting his words carefully. "That's just what I mean. ... Well"—he stepped down off the walk—"be seein' you."

He walked away, feeling their stares on his back. It was rather obvious bait, but would Pickard really have the choice not to bite on it? Could he coolly ignore the possibility that all he had planned so carefully for ... killed for, might be gone?

Pickard stared out the window after Blaine. What did he mean by that? He was sure that nobody could find the money. It was still there where he'd hidden it, it had to be. ... He returned to his stropping of the razor, but his mind was not on his work. He scowled. How had Blaine found Hibbs's body so soon? He must have been out in the hills ... he might even have followed Hibbs.

Yet that could not be, for if he had, he would have been close by when Hibbs was killed ... or *had* he been close by? Suppose Blaine was less interested in finding the killer than in finding the loot ... and keeping it for himself?

Worried now, Pickard grew irritable and restless. If Blaine found that loot, then all his time here was wasted. Pickard would be chained to this barber chair! He would have killed and robbed and risked his life, for nothing!

Yet suppose it was only a trap? That might be Blaine's idea, but it would not work. He knew how . . . he glanced at the building's shadow. Two hours yet to sundown.

Alone in his shop, Pickard worked swiftly. There was no time to lose. Trap or not, he must know whether his loot had been found, and if it was a trap . . . well, they'd find out that their quiet town barber had teeth. He thrust a pistol into his waistband and picked up a shotgun.

When it was dark he slipped from the back of the shop and ducked quickly into the bed of the stream. Hurrying along it, he came out near the TC line shack and crossed quickly to the stable. Quickly, he struck a match and picked up the lantern . . . and then he stopped. The horses were gone!

Pickard froze where he was and the match burned down to his fingers before he dropped it. He had seen Red Williams in town, but he had no idea . . . now there was no other way. He must go on foot.

Suppose somebody came for him while he was gone? He would have to chance that. The shop was closed and he had left everything locked tight. He started down the draw, moving swiftly. At night and without a horse, it seemed much farther than the three miles he had to go, yet despite his hurry, he took his time when reaching the area where the loot was concealed. He waited, listened, then went forward.

Quickly, he moved a rock and reached into the cavity beneath. Instantly, his heart gave a bound. The loot was there! Blaine had been talking through his hat! It was safe! He struck a match, shielding it with his cupped hands. All there . . . should he take it with him now, or should he wait and pick it up, as he had planned, after leaving town?

Much of it was gold, but there was a good bit of paper money, too. It would be a load, almost a hundred pounds of it, but he could get it back. No, he changed his mind swiftly. He would take one sack of gold, just in case. He could always come back after the rest.

Taking the sack out, he carefully replaced the stone, then lit a match and had a careful look around to make sure the stone was in place and no damp earth was showing. As the match went out his eyes caught a flicker of white on the ground and he guardedly struck another. He stooped . . . merely some whitish-gray mud or damp earth. He dropped the match and, picking up his bag, started back.

Pickard hurried, desperately worried for fear of discovery, and his breath was coming hoarsely when he reached the back door of his shop. He opened the door, stepped in, and turning, he struck a match and lighted the lamp. Just as he replaced the chimney a shock of fear went through him . . . he had left the door *locked*!

Pickard turned sharply, half-crouched like an animal at bay, a sickness turning him faint with shock. Facing him from chairs ranged around the room were Tom Church, Childress, Hunt, and Red Williams!

Clutched in his hand was the sack of stolen gold, and then Utah Blaine spoke. "Drop your guns, Pickard! You are under arrest!"

His years of planning, working, scheming, his murders and robberies, the hot, stifling nights when he waited, when he struck with the knife or club, or tossed the noose over a neck, and strangled . . . all gone! All for nothing! All because . . . !

Like a cat he wheeled and plunged for the door. The move was so swift that Blaine swung, not daring to shoot toward the other men, knelt, and thrust out his foot.

Pickard tripped and sprawled through the door onto the step. Springing to his feet, his hands lacerated from the silvery-gray wood, he grabbed for his gun.

"Hold it!" Blaine yelled.

Pickard's gun swung up . . . and he felt his finger close, and then somebody smashed him a blow in the chest. He staggered, trying to bring his gun to bear, and another blow hit him, half turning him around.

What . . . what th—! His eyes blurred and the gun would not seem to come up and then something struck him on the back of the head and he was on the ground and he was staring up at the stars and then the stars faded and he realized . . . nothing more.

Tom Church stared at the fallen man, white-faced. "Dead center, Utah," he said quietly, "but you had to do it."

"Yeah."

"That's only part of the stolen money," Childress said. "You reckon he spent the rest of it?"

Utah Blaine indicated the dead man's boots, their soles stained with a muddy whitish substance. "I figure it's cached. He left the rest of it, but those white boots will lead us right to it."

"What is that stuff?" Church asked. "Never saw any clay like that around here."

"It's white paint," Blaine replied, "I spilled plenty of it inside the door of the TC barn and corral. I knew he'd come there, and that white paint would leave his marks to trail him by."

Hunt and Williams carefully picked up the body and carried it off down the street. Blaine stood in the alley while Tom Church locked up Pickard's shop. After a moment Childress swore softly. "What's worryin' me now," he said, "is what are we goin' to do for a barber!"

BATTLE AT
BURNT CAMP

The he Cactus Kid had crossed the Terlingua and was bearing right toward Black Ridge, when he saw the girl.

She was young and she was made up and she was pretty as a bay pony with three white stockings. She was standing beside the dim trail with her hands on her hips and her nose red from the sun.

The Kid drew up. "Howdy," he said gravely, "goin' far?"

"Without a horse?" Her eyes flashed. "Where could anybody go in this country without a horse? Where, I ask you?"

"Well," the Kid said seriously, "it depends on what you're lookin' for an' how far you need to go. Would you mind tellin' a feller what you're doin' out here afoot?"

"That's none of your business!" she flared. "Are you going to give me a ride, or not?"

The Kid looked at her sadly. "Ma'am, for one who's askin' favors you sure aren't very polite. Where were you raised, anyway?"

Her eyes narrowed. "Why, you—!" She stopped, flashing a sudden smile. "I'm sorry. It wasn't your fault at all. Please, would you give me a ride?"

"Get up behind," he said. "I'd sure not want to leave a lady out here in the desert with nobody to fuss at but rattlers. It wouldn't be civilized!"

Putting her foot in his stirrup, she swung up behind him, and then before he could even speak she shucked one of his guns from its holster and shoved the muzzle into his spine. "Get off," she said coldly. "Get off, an' see how it feels to be afoot!"

"Now, look—!" The Kid started to protest, but the gun peeled hide from his spine and he heard the hammer click back as she cocked it. "Get off!" she ordered. "One yelp out of you and I'll shoot your ears off!"

Carefully, the Kid swung down, and without a word she slapped spurs to his horse and started off. His lips parted in a smile, the Cactus Kid let her go, then suddenly he pinned his lips over his teeth and whistled shrilly. The horse stopped so sharply that the girl had no chance. She went right off over his head and fell hard. The horse trotted back toward him.

The Kid came up on the run, and before she could retrieve his gun, he grabbed it up. Then he caught her by the hands and twisted them behind her. With a piggin string from his belt he tied her wrists despite her struggles. He got to his feet and wiped the dust from his face and stared down at her. "There, now. That should hold you. Now, what's the idea?"

She glared furiously. "I'll kill you for this! I'll kill you!"

"No reason to get so wrought up." The Cactus Kid coolly began to build a smoke. "What's all the fuss? No need to steal my horse an' set me afoot just because you're mad at somebody. Tell me where you want to go an' I'll take you there."

"Untie my hands!" she demanded.

"Not a chance. You might try to steal my horse again."

"That was a nasty, vile trick!" she declared. "I skinned my nose!"

"That," he said, studying her nose critically, "won't do it any harm. I figure maybe it's a mite too long anyway."

She glared at him. "Let me up!" she demanded. "Turn my hands loose!"

"It's up to you. Be good and you get a ride to wherever you're goin'. Keep on fussin' an' I'll leave you right here to cook."

She stopped, still angry, but aware that he meant what he said. "All right," she said, "but you just wait!"

This time he took her on the saddle in front of him and that made it necessary for his arm to be around her waist, which was, he realized appreciatively, a small, firm, and very nice waist. Her reddish hair came against his cheek and her body pressed closely to him. This, too, he found agreeable.

She said nothing, but sat quietly. Finally, he asked, "Where do you want to go? Where's home?"

"I want to go to Burnt Camp, in the Solitario."

Now, the Cactus Kid, whose birth certificate might have said he was Nesselrode Clay, knew but little of the Big Bend of Texas. What he did know was that Burnt Camp in the Solitario was no place for a beautiful girl of eighteen or so. In fact, it was to just that place that the Kid himself was going, but for no friendly purpose. "That's no place for a girl," he said. "I'll take you to another place."

"You'll take me there, and when they find me with my

hands tied, it will be a sad time for you! Just wait until I tell Kit Branch about this!"

"He your sweetheart?" The Kid wanted to know.

"Branch?" she scoffed. "He'd like to be, but he's not! I'm Kirby Brock!"

"Bully Brock's daughter?" The Kid was aghast. "Don't tell me that old blister sired a sweet little filly like you!"

"He's my uncle! And he's not an old blister! Although I'll tell him you said that and he'll wipe the floor with you, that's what he'll do!"

The Cactus Kid chuckled. He felt good this morning. He wore his tailored gray trousers, a bright red shirt, and a black handkerchief tight about his throat. His hat was black with a snake-hide band, and his boots hand-tooled. The Kid was five feet nine and weighed exactly one hundred and fifty pounds soaking wet. He consulted a large railroad watch that he kept in the pocket of his pants; it was ten forty-five in the morning.

Black Ridge was north of them now and they cut the trail leading to the Black Tinaja. Although the Cactus Kid had never visited the wild and lonely region called the Solitario, he knew well the route that led to it. Leaving the tinaja, they would turn due west and hit the canyon of the Left-hand Shutup, which would take them right into the region.

As they rode he puzzled over the situation. What had Kirby Brock been doing out in the desert without a horse? And how could such a girl be the niece of Bully Brock? For years now Bully had ranched in the wild region around the canyon west of Burnt Camp. It was an area frequented by smugglers from over the border and by rustlers. And that was why he was coming here now. He was looking for some men.

Several days before, in San Antonio, he had left the Variety Theatre one night, and had seen a man behind him. Later he had seen the same man, and knew he was being followed. And then there had been three men.

He had turned the corner near his hotel when they closed in on him, one coming toward him, one crossing the street, and the third had come from nowhere to grab his arms. He had been slugged, robbed, and left lying in the street.

After he recovered he devoted two days to making inquiries, only to discover finally that the men had left town. The three were known as Farbeson, Breeden, and Jewell. They were known thieves and rustlers, and they ran with Kit Branch.

At Del Rio, he heard about Branch and that he could be found in the Solitario, but that a man would be some kind of a fool to try to go in after him. The Cactus Kid was that kind of a fool. They had slugged him, which was bad enough, but they had taken seven hundred dollars from him. It was more money than he had ever had all at one time.

"How's it happen you're afoot?" he asked suddenly.

"My horse threw me," she replied sullenly.

At the Black Tinaja they stopped, watered the horse, and drank. The dun was feeling the double burden, so the Kid put him on some grass and sat down in the shade. He glanced at Kirby and smiled. "Might as well sit down," he said. "We'll have to let that horse rest a mite."

She was looking at the ground nearby. Glancing over curiously, he saw she was intently studying some tracks. Suddenly she looked around at him. "Let me use that gun. I can get some horses for us." She spoke in a near whisper and appeared to tense.

"Nothing doing. You'd run off and leave me high and dry." He had untied her hands.

"Suit yourself," she said.

"So, Kit's bad medicine, is he? What about Jewell?"

She stiffened with surprise. "What do you know about him?"

"Not much. Not any more than I know about Breeden or Farbeson."

A slight sound made him turn, but there was no chance to draw. The man holding the shotgun was Jewell and he was no more than fifteen feet away. At that distance he would tear the Kid apart. His eyes widened when he saw the Kid. "You, is it? I figured you'd still be lyin' in the street. What you doin' here?"

"Huntin' you." The Kid spoke quietly. "Huntin' you an' those louse-bound partners of yours. I want my money."

The man laughed coarsely. "You'll git something, but it ain't gonna be what you're lookin' for!" he promised. Then: "Where'd you meet *her*?"

"Down the road a piece. Do you want to hand me over that money now or do I take it out of your hide?"

"My hide?" Jewell stared. "Who's holdin' this shotgun, anyway?" He did not move his eyes, but said, "Pick up his guns, Kirby. Go behind him."

He felt the girl move up behind him and felt his guns leave his holsters. His eyes narrowed slightly as he saw the evident relief in Jewell's eyes. Slowly, the shotgun lifted and he realized with a shock that the man was going to murder him.

"I wouldn't if I were you." Kirby Brock had the guns in her hands and was watching Jewell. "Bring up the horses and we'll ride in. Bully will want to see this gent."

Reluctantly, Jewell lowered the gun. When he led up the horses, the Cactus Kid was surprised to see that one of them was obviously the girl's horse. It carried a side-saddle and the stirrup was just right for her. The Kid was ordered to mount and they turned west.

It was late afternoon when they reached the houses and old stone corral at Burnt Camp. The smoke from several fires was rising, and the Kid saw a man come out and shade his eyes at them. They rode on into the camp and the Kid watched the big man coming toward them. He was almost twice the size of the Kid, towering several inches above six feet and weighing well over two hundred pounds. He had a thick black beard.

He looked at the Kid, then turned his eyes to the girl. The Cactus Kid frowned uncertainly, for the big man seemed almost frightened when he recognized her.

Other men came forward. Farbeson was one of them. He was almost as large as Bully Brock and he grinned when he saw the Cactus Kid. Breeden, who was standing nearby said, "What do you think, Farb? This kid came up here to git his money?"

The others all laughed and then the crowd parted for a slender, whiplash of a man with a narrow face and wide gash for a mouth. He came down the path and stood staring at Kirby with a slight smile. "Didn't get far, did you?" he said. "I told you we were meant for each other."

Breeden laughed and Farb joined in. The younger man made an inquiry about the Cactus Kid and was told the story of what had happened both in San Antonio and here. He listened, nodding slightly. "All right," he said, "we'll get this over with all at once."

He turned on Brock. "Bully," he said, "you're through here. We're taking over your ranch and all that goes with it. I"—he smiled unpleasantly—"will personally take over Kirby. We're going to show this country what we can do."

Brock stared back at him. "You're a fool, Kit. The Rangers never bothered us here because this was my place and they knew me. You know they can get in here an' they will, sure as you start anything."

"The Rangers ain't comin' now that we got Kirby back. Sendin' her was a dumb idea, Bully. You tipped your hand an' now we won't be needin' you any longer." Kit Branch turned his hand on a gun.

The Cactus Kid was still sitting his horse, as was Jewell. Now, suddenly, he slapped the spurs into the dun, and as the startled animal leaped, the Kid grabbed the shotgun from Jewell's hands as the dun lunged by. Straight into the center of the crowd he went, low over the horse's neck. Behind him a shot rang out, then another. The dun faltered, stumbled, and then fell all sprawled out. The Kid hit the ground rolling and came up with the shotgun at his shoulder. The first person he saw across the sights was Breeden. He squeezed the trigger and saw the big outlaw take the full charge in the stomach. The man gave a grunt and sat down hard and rolled over to his face.

The Kid lunged to his feet in a spatter of bullets and ran into the rocks. He made them, felt the tug at his shirt, and hit the ground sliding. Almost as soon as he hit it, he was up and ducking into a thick stand of greasewood. He froze in place. Behind him were shouts and yells, so he moved on quietly, circling toward the corral. The men had fanned out and were working toward him. Studying the terrain, he felt himself grow sick. No alternative awaited him. The basin was rockbound and to climb that wall would mean that he would be picked off before he had gone a dozen steps. Nor could he remain where he was, for they were moving in.

The shotgun was a single-barreled gun, a breechloader. And he had no more shells.

The outlaws searching for him were not fooling. Obviously, they had decided to organize, take over Brock's ranch and saloon as a hangout, and raid the country. Kirby Brock seemed to have slipped away for help but then had lost her horse. She had probably taken him for another outlaw.

Still clutching the shotgun, the Kid rolled behind some rocks and wormed his way right back toward the stone corral and the houses. Several times he had to lie still to allow men to pass within a few feet of him. When he reached a nest of rocks to one side of the corral, he peered out.

Three men remained in the yard with Brock and the girl. Bully Brock had blood running down his face where he had been struck with a gun barrel, and his hands were tied behind him. The girl's hands were also tied, and Kit Branch stood nearby, with Farb and Jewell. The body of Breeden was nowhere to be seen.

Other men were scattered out, and from time to time he could hear shouts from them. He had succeeded in getting back through their line, but they would be doubling back at any time and he must at all costs find a place to hole up. As he had crawled an idea had come to him. There might yet be a chance to use the shotgun.

Beyond the stone corral, back from the scattered area of campfires and shelters, was an ancient stone wall that appeared to be the face of a dugout. Obviously unused, it was the place most likely to be overlooked in any search for him. Using the corral as shelter, the Kid worked his way along the far side, then ducked into the open door of the dugout.

It was about twenty feet long and the roof sagged dangerously. The remains of some crude bunks and a few pieces of broken bench were mingled with the litter on the floor. Working his way back into the dugout, the Cactus Kid found it was L-shaped, and around the bend of the L the roof was intact except at the very back, where a hole about three feet across opened into a pile of brush, boulders and cacti.

Crouching in the half-dark of the dugout, the Kid opened the breech of the shotgun. There had been no chance to dispense with the brass shell, for he had been moving too fast and had nothing to replace it, anyway. Now he got out his pocketknife and went to work. Taking several bullets from his cartridge belt, he opened them and extracted the powder. Outside, the search continued, but in the dugout sweat poured down the Kid's body as he worked. Several times he stopped to wipe his hands dry and then went on with his work. He cut several of the pistol bullets into three pieces and with a rock pounded off the rough edges of the lead and shaped the pieces into fairly round slugs. With utmost care he pried a primer out of one of the shells and fit it into the back of the shotgun cartridge. It was a bit loose but seemed like it would stay centered. He now had a heavy charge of powder and twelve slugs; using some bits of paper from an old letter in his pocket as wadding, he soon had a charge for his shotgun. When it was reloaded he felt much better. If they got him now, he was at least taking one man with him. At close range his contrived shotgun shell would tear a man wide open.

As he waited, his eyes accustomed to the dim light, he looked around the interior of the ruined dugout. The floor was a litter of old paper, sacks, bits of rawhide, old clothes, and odds and ends of broken bottles. Suddenly he had an unaccountable fit of depression. Unaccountable for him, for the Cactus Kid was wont to look upon life as his particular bailiwick, and he had spent most of his time trying to find the bright side of every situation.

This, he decided, was the limit of something or other. That he, the Cactus Kid, whose cheerful grin and ready sense of humor had carried him through the worst of times, should be hiding here in a ruined dugout in the last hours of a hot Texas day was absolutely unacceptable. The Cactus Kid made up his mind. Come what may, he was going out and he was going to leave his mark on this outfit—but good.

Dusk came at last and the fires were built up and soon he could smell coffee. With nothing to eat since daybreak, that added to the Kid's disgust. In all this time he had not dared look out, yet now, with the darkness bringing deep shadows around the dugout, he moved to the back and thrust his head and shoulders through the hole. He found himself looking out through a curtain of brush over the whole area of the hideout. To his left was the stone corral, part of it almost in front of him, and in the corral were the horses. Beyond it, on the slope and almost facing him, was the main house. There was an old stable, open-faced and now used by some of the outlaws, and there were four fires going. In all, he surmised there must be sixteen to twenty men at the hideout.

Slipping out of the hole, he crawled down to the corral wall. Flipping a loop over a horse's neck, he drew the animal to the wall and saddled it. A second horse snorted and leaped when the rope touched it and one of the men at the fires got up. "Somethin' botherin' the horses," he said.

"Aw! They're just fightin'!"

The outlaw stood looking toward the corral, but as all was quiet he soon subsided and returned to his seat.

Swiftly, the Kid saddled the second horse and another. Then he tied the three horses and circled the corral.

Lying flat on his stomach, he looked past the corner at the group of outlaws. If he only had his guns! The one shot in his shotgun meant little; he could only take one man, two at best, and then they would have him.

Suddenly the girl and her uncle were led from the house and brought down to the nearest fire. With them was Kit Branch and Farbeson. Jewell was at the fire and he got up as they approached, grinning at Bully Brock. "Does me good to see this!" He sneered. "You been struttin' high-an'-mighty for a long time!"

Brock straightened his shoulders. "Branch, give Kirby a horse an' let her go. She's done nothin' to you. Let her go back home to San Antone."

"Not a chance! We've got her an' we'll keep her. We'll keep you, too, Brock, as long as you behave. We've got an idea that maybe you can keep the Rangers off us."

"Don't be a fool!" Brock retorted. "The only reason the Rangers stayed away was because nobody from around here did anything but rustle a few head of cows once in a while. They knew I was mostly honest and they didn't want to come all the way out here for a few young fellers who they could never prove had done anything. You start somethin' an' they'll be down on you like a flock of wolves."

Branch smiled. "You expect me to believe that, Bully? You *know* folks. Come daylight we'll round up that kid. He won't get far without water or knowin' the country."

A big man sat with his back to the Kid and not over twenty yards away. The Kid could see the pistol in his belt. If he was going to start something, it would have to be soon. The horses might be discovered if he waited, and the sheer surprise might help, also; the girl and her uncle were close at hand now, but after they had eaten, they would probably be returned to the house.

They had just come to the fire. It would be twenty minutes, thirty at most, before they would be returned to the house. There was a chance. He drew back suddenly, straightened to his feet, and turned.

He stumbled straight into the very same outlaw who had been bothered by the horses acting up. The Kid's sudden rise from the ground had been a complete surprise and now he gaped foolishly at the Kid. Then his surprise faded and he began to grin. "Got you!" he said hoarsely. "I got you!"

"You got *me*?" The Kid jerked the shotgun. "What do you think this is?"

"You had one shell." The man was grinning, enjoying himself. "You killed Breeden with it . . . *uuhhh!*"

The Cactus Kid acted suddenly. He was gripping the shotgun with both hands and he simply jammed the end of the barrel in the man's solar plexus with wicked force. The outlaw grunted and hit the dirt on his knees. Instantly, the Kid smashed him on the back of the skull with the butt of the shotgun, then stripped the man's gun from his holster. Swinging the extra cartridge belt over his shoulder, the Kid quickly rounded the back corner of the corral toward the haystack. Dropping to his knees, he struck a match, then another and another.

Grabbing a pitchfork as the flames leaped up, he forked two quick bunches of flaming hay high into the greasewood surrounding the camp. Then he went over the corral rails with a leap, grabbed the bridle reins of the three horses, and swung into the saddle.

"*Fire!* The hay's afire!" Other voices took up the call and men charged toward the stack. The fire scattered in the greasewood, caught, and the resinous wood and leaves burst into a crackle of flame. Crouching low in the saddle, his shotgun ready, the Kid rode for the corral gate and kicked the latch open. The balanced gate swung and instantly he was through.

A man saw him coming and the Kid yelled, "Get the horses! Save 'em!" With a shrill whoop he rode down on the fire where Bully Brock stood beside the girl. Her hands were free, but his were still bound and they had been making the girl feed him, fearing what he might attempt if he wasn't restrained.

Men were racing toward the flames, and the Kid's call made them realize the danger of the horses without noticing who it was that yelled. Racing up to the fire, the Kid called to Kirby. "Hit the saddle! Hit the saddle! Let's *go*!"

After one startled instant of hesitation Brock raced for the nearest horse and, without even waiting to have his hands untied, jumped for the saddle and got a foot in the stirrup. With his left hand, the Kid pulled the big man into the saddle while Kirby swung up. Behind them there were yells and he could hear Kit Branch shouting angrily. Turning in the saddle, the Cactus Kid saw a big man take three running steps and stop, whipping a Winchester to his shoulder. The Kid pulled the trigger on his shotgun and the gun boomed and slammed his shoulder. The big man staggered and the Kid wheeled, jumping his horse away as he threw the shotgun into the face of another man. And then they were off and running.

Behind them men raced wildly about, grabbing at the thrashing horses, the whole scene lighted by the whipping flames. The breeze was stiff and the flames had leaped across the greasewood until the whole hillside was a roaring flame. Kirby was leading the way due west and the three rode desperately, crouching low in their saddles to escape the hail of bullets.

Weaving among the boulders, Bully led west, then south, then doubled back to the north. At a stop to let the horses breathe, the Kid leaned over and cut Brock's hands free of the top loop of rope, and Brock did the rest himself. Slowing down, the Cactus Kid looked around and could see the loom of Solitario Peak off to the north and a little east. Kirby was riding west, following some vague sort of trail, weaving through some rough country. Dropping into Fresno Canyon, they turned north and kept a good pace until the peak of Solitario was behind them to the east. Then she led them out, going northeast. They stopped briefly at a tinaja; nearby was the dark outline of what had once been a frame of a mine scaffold and prospector's shack, now partially collapsed.

Bully chafed his wrists and grinned at the Cactus Kid. "You sure are hellfire when you cut loose, mister! We'd better hightail it northwest. Maybe we can make a settlement before they catch up to us. I'd at least like to have a gun!"

"You ride on." The Cactus Kid shoved his hat back on his head and began to build a smoke. "I'm going back."

"Back?" Kirby cried. "Are you crazy? You want to go back there and get shot?"

"No, ma'am, I sure don't. On the other hand, those hombres took seven hundred dollars of money off me. I want it."

"Why are you so interested in getting—!" Kirby was breathless. The moon was rising and he could see her face in the light.

"Here, now!" Brock said mildly. "Let him alone. If he wants to go back, he wants to go back and that's his affair. Although," he added, "I do think it a foolish thing."

"Nevertheless," the Kid insisted stubbornly, "I am going back." He turned his horse. "You two ride on. I've got business to attend to!"

Kirby stared at him, her anger fading. "Don't go back!" she pleaded. "They'll kill you! They will! I know they will!"

Brock held up his hand. "You won't have to go back," he said gravely. "I can hear 'em coming."

"How far off?" The Kid strained his ears to listen.

"Down the canyon. It could be a mile or more."

"Hit the saddle, then," the Kid said quietly. "I'll wait for 'em. I've got a Colt and plenty of ammunition. I'll stand 'em off."

"We'll wait," Kirby said. "Maybe we can get hold of some guns once the fighting starts."

"Then get out of the way," the Kid agreed, ". . . back near that mine. I'm going to wait right here by the tinaja for them."

It was well after midnight, but how late he was not sure. The Kid waited, occasionally drying his palms on his jeans. The riders were taking their time, evidently searching the rocks as they came along. Probably they were not sure which way the Brocks had gone with the Kid. When at last he heard them close by, there was a faint gray in the east. The outlaws—and he decided there were at least four of them—drew up in the blackness near the cliffs.

His horse concealed among the rocks, the Cactus Kid settled down for a wait. He could hear voices arguing, and then a rider started forward. When he was still some thirty yards off, the Kid spoke. "Better stay where you are. I'm heeled for trouble."

"If you hadn't butted into this"—it was Branch speaking—"everything would be all right. Suppose you mount up an' light a shuck? We want the Brocks, not you."

"Sorry. It'll cost you to get 'em. I got a gun now."

"Don't be a fool!" Branch said angrily. "You won't have a chance!"

The Cactus Kid settled himself for a wait. Without doubt most of the outlaws were awaiting daylight to hunt up their horses, and he had a hunch that Branch would wait for day also. Well, that suited him.

An hour passed, and the gray grew stronger. Another hour, and although the sun was not up, it was light. Behind the Kid was the canyon mouth where Bully and Kirby Brock had taken shelter; beside the Kid was the tinaja with its store of water. Before him the slope fell away to the bottom of a shallow canyon and somewhere across it were Branch and the others.

Once, the Kid thought he heard a stone rattle, then a footstep. He got to his feet and peered around but could see nothing—and then he saw Kirby, motioning violently.

"Hey!" she called. She held up a brown stick in her hands. "Blasting powder!"

Scrambling back over the rocks, he stopped beside her. "Uncle found it in the prospector's shanty. There's almost half a box, and some caps and fuses."

The Cactus Kid grinned suddenly. "Bring 'em down! This'll be good!"

A half hour later Branch called out. He was not over thirty yards away, probably less. "You comin' out or are we comin' after you?"

"Come and get us," the Kid said hopefully. "Come right on up." As they hesitated he lighted a short fuse. The giant powder was tied to a rock for better throwing, and as the fuse spattered, the Kid drew back his hand and threw, and Bully Brock, nearby, did the same.

He never saw the dynamite. The stick hit somewhere in front of him and blew up with a terrific concussion, scattering rocks and gravel. Brock's throw had been the stronger and it lit between two head-sized rocks atop a boulder. It blasted with even greater force and scattered rock in every direction.

Jewell came out of the rocks, running, and Farb with him. Both men had their hands up.

"Come on, Branch!" Brock yelled. "The next one's right in your lap!"

Kit Branch came out of the rocks. He came walking toward them, his hands swinging, and the Cactus Kid stepped out in the open. Branch stared vindictively. "Nobody gets the best of me, boy. You're gonna get yours and I'm gonna be the one givin' it to you."

The Kid's eyes never left those of the gunman. "Well, I'll be—!"

Branch's hand swept down for his gun. Triumph was on his face as the gun lifted and then something struck him a wicked blow just below the breastbone. He staggered, seeing the smoking gun in the Kid's hand, then fell over on his face.

The Cactus Kid walked over to Jewell. "All I want from you is my money," he said. "Dish it out."

Reluctantly, the two outlaws dug out the money and handed it back. When he counted it, the sum came to two hundred dollars more than he had lost. "For my trouble," he said calmly, and pocketed it. "That's all I want with you fellows. You can beat it."

"Oh, no, they can't!" Kirby Brock walked up to Jewell and Farb. "Push me around, will you?" She kicked Jewell right on the shins.

Farbeson bellowed with laughter, and coolly, she turned and kicked him in the same place. With both men howling with pain, Kirby turned and gathered up the reins of her horse. "Maybe," she said, glaring at the Cactus Kid, "that wasn't ladylike, but it sure was satisfying!"

The Cactus Kid gathered up their weapons. Farbeson had been wearing the Kid's own guns. Gravely, he handed guns to both Brock and Kirby.

Mounting up, he studied Kirby. "You know, ma'am," he said, "if you get a husband who'll keep a tight rein on you, you'd make him a mighty good wife, but if you ever get the bit in your teeth, heaven help him!"

He turned his horse and headed off up the trail.

IRONWOOD STATION

T he riders met where the trails formed a Y with the main road. The man from the north was fat, with a narrow-brimmed hat and round cheeks. He raised a hand in greeting. "Mind if I ride along with you? Gets mighty lonesome, ridin' alone. I ain't seen even a jack-rabbit last ten miles, an' a man can say just so much to a horse.

"Figured to make Ironwood Station before sundown. They feed passengers, an' I'm mighty tired of my own cookin'." The fat man bit off a chunk of chewing tobacco and offered the plug to the other man, who shook his head. "Long empty stretch in here," the fat man continued. "Never see nobody 'ceptin' Utes, whom nobody wants to see." The fat man glanced at his companion. "Ain't much for talkin', are you?"

"Not much."

"Well, I'm ready for Dan Burnett's cookin'. That man can sure shake up a nice mess o' vittles. Makes a man's mouth water."

"Somebody north of us," the other rider said. "Somebody who doesn't want to follow a trail."

The fat man glanced at him. "You hear something?"

"I smell dust."

"Could be Utes. This here is Ute country." The fat man was worried. "The Utes have been killin' a lot of folks about here."

"There's three . . . maybe four of them."

"Now, how would you know that?"

"Dust from one horse wouldn't reach this far, but the dust from three or four would."

"My name is Jones," the fat man said. "What did you say your name was?"

"Talon . . . Shawn Talon."

"Odd name. Don't reckon I ever heard that one before."

"You would in County Wicklow. My father was Irish, with an after-coating of Texas."

They rode in silence until they dipped into a hollow, and Talon drew up briefly. "Three riders," Talon said, "on mighty fine horses. See the stride? A long stride and good action, although they've been riding a long time."

"You read a lot from a few tracks."

"Well, they've had to be riding a long time," Talon said, smiling. "This isn't camping country, and where would a man come from to get here?"

Sun glinted on the rifle barrel a split instant before the bullet whipped past his ear, but the brief warning was enough. Talon slapped the spurs to his horse and was off with a bound, the report of a rifle cutting a slash across the hot still afternoon.

Ahead of him there was a burst of firing, and as the two men, riding neck and neck, came over the rise, they saw three others in a hollow among the rocks defending themselves against an attack by Utes. Glancing back, Talon saw several Indians closing in from behind them. Jumping their horses into the circle of rocks, Talon rolled on his side and began feeding shells into the Winchester. Briefly, he glanced at the other men.

The three strangers were tough, competent-looking men. One, a slim, dark man, had his holster tied down. He was unshaven and he glanced at Talon and grinned. "You showed up on time, mister."

It was very hot. From time to time somebody thought they saw a target and fired, and from time to time the Utes fired back . . . but they were working closer. "Getting set for a rush," Talon said aloud.

"Let 'em come," the man with the tied-down gun said. "The quicker they try it, the quicker this will be over."

Neither of his companions had said anything. One was a short, dark man, the other a burly fellow, huge and bearded. All three looked dirty, and showed evidence of long days in the saddle. Talon noticed that his talkative friend was suddenly very silent.

The rush came suddenly. Talon got in a quick shot with his rifle, and then the man with the tied-down holster was on his feet, his six-gun rolling a cannonade of sound into the hot afternoon. He shot fast and accurately. With his own eyes Talon saw three Indians drop under the gunman's fire before the attack broke. With his rifle Talon nailed another, and saw the gunman bring down the last Indian with a fifty-yard pistol shot.

"That was some shooting," Talon commented.

The man glanced at him briefly. "It's my business," he said.

In the distance, beyond the trail, dust arose. "Thought so," the gunman said. "They're pullin' out."

Talon waited a moment, watching the trail, and then he turned and walked toward his horse, standing with the other horses in the low ground behind the rocks. "Let's ride, Jones."

They mounted up and the three men watched them in silence. The gunman stared at Talon as he swung his horse to ride out. "Something about you," he said. "I've seen you before, somewhere."

"No," Talon said distinctly, "I don't believe so."

"You ridin' west?"

"To Carson City, probably."

"Make it definitely . . . you take my advice and don't stop this side." The gunman grinned. "You might run into more Utes without me to protect you."

Talon said, "You know something? You're in the wrong business."

He loped his horse out of the basin without waiting for a reply, and Jones pulled in alongside him. Jones looked back over his shoulder. "You should be careful," he said. "That was Lute Robeck back there. He's a mighty dangerous man. You see the way he emptied that six-gun?"

"He didn't empty it," Talon said. "He had one shot left."

The desert lay empty and still under the hot morning sun. Heat waves shimmered over the red-brown, sun-baked rocks of the distant mountains, but there was no other movement until a lone dust devil danced out of the greasewood clumps and gained size in the flatland, then died away to nothing.

In the back room of the stage station at Ironwood, Dan Burnett lay on his back with a broken hip and three broken ribs. It was close and hot in the small bedroom and he gasped painfully with every breath.

Kate Breslin, in the big main room of the station, went

to the door for the fiftieth time and stared up the narrow, empty road that went down the flat and curved out of sight around the hill. The road was empty . . . in all that hot, vast, and brassy silence, nothing moved.

Kate Breslin was twice a widow, once by stampede and once by the gun, but at forty-five she was all Western, with no idea of ever going elsewhere. She had rolled into Ironwood on the stage bound for Carson and they had found Dan Burnett dragging himself toward the station door with a broken hip . . . he had been kicked by a mule and was in bad shape.

Immediately, she volunteered to remain until a relief man could come and somebody to care for Dan. On impulse, Ruth Starkey had stayed with her. Now, as Ruth could plainly see, Kate was worried, and she was worried about something other than the injured man in the back bedroom.

"Can you handle a gun?" Kate asked suddenly.

"I've shot a rifle, if that's what you mean."

"You may need to. . . ." Kate Breslin looked at her quickly. "You know what he told me? There's seventy thousand dollars in gold on that westbound stage . . . seventy thousand."

"Does anybody know?"

"You darned tootin', somebody knows. Trouble is, they don't know who. Feller worked for the mining company, he suddenly took off, didn't even pick up his wages . . . he lit right out of town. They thought about holding the gold, then decided they would be safer to ship it. That's why Dan is so worried."

"But don't they know about Dan?"

"West they do, but that gold's shipped from east of here . . . and back there they'll think Dan is on his toes. This is one place nobody will expect trouble."

Ruth was standing in the door. "Kate," she said, "two men are coming up the road . . . from the east."

Kate Breslin joined her in the door. Two men riding toward them, both on fine, blooded horses, definitely not the sort of horses ridden by cowhands. One man was short and thickset, the other was a tall man.

"Be careful what you say," Kate said. "You just be careful."

When they rode up it was the tall man who spoke. "Ma'am, we've heard they served the best food along the line at Ironwood, and we're hungry. Could you manage to serve a meal for two?"

"I reckon," Kate said. "Get down and come in."

When they had stabled their horses, the two men came in and the fat one walked to the bar. "I'd like a whiskey," he said, "I surely would."

"Pour one for him, Ruth." Kate was already rattling dishes in the kitchen. "I'll feed these men so they can get on their way. I expect they're in a hurry to get to Carson."

Talon glanced at her and then at Ruth, momentarily puzzled by the presence of the women. His eyes strayed toward the closed door of the bedroom, but what it was or who was there, Talon had no idea. He sensed that for some reason his presence was not wanted, and he wondered why this was so. He was a sensitive man, aware of changes in the atmosphere, and he was aware of a subtle coldness now.

He had not expected to find women here, and the younger one, the one called Ruth, was extremely pretty . . . but an Eastern girl or one who had lately been east. Disturbed, he walked outside and went to the stable, where the mules that pulled the stage over this rough stretch were kept. There were twelve of them, and walking past the stalls, he suddenly glimpsed a gun, half-concealed by the hay on the barn floor.

He picked it up, a worn Remington pistol, but well kept and oiled . . . the man who owned a gun so well kept would not be one to leave it lying carelessly on the dirt floor. Curious, aware of a mystery here, he looked slowly around the long building. The fallen gun was directly behind a stall, and at that point the dirt of the floor was stirred up by boot marks . . . he tried to work out the sign but could make nothing of it, although it looked like a scuffle had taken place. Whatever it was, it had made the owner forget his pistol.

Walking outside, he looked carefully around, and there was little to see. The mules, the barn, the corrals, and several haystacks aside from what hay was in the barn itself. A couple of poles leaned against the side of the house with two coats buttoned around them to make a crude stretcher. So that was it . . . somebody had been hurt.

Strolling across the yard, he stopped to light a cigarette and glanced out of the corner of his eyes at the stretcher. He was close to it now, but he could see no signs of blood, such as would be visible if the man had been shot or injured so that he would bleed.

Jones stepped outside. "Woman in there is Kate Breslin," he said. "Dan's off in the hills rounding up a beef."

"Dan a friend of yours?"

"Sure . . . that is, we talk friendly, and we feel friendly. I don't know Dan the best, but I've stopped by here six, eight times."

"Doesn't make much sense, rounding up a beef when they've plenty of supplies in the station . . . not with the Utes running wild over the country."

"Could be, though." Jones glanced at Talon. "What's wrong? You got something in mind?"

"They're hiding something." Talon jerked his head to indicate the women. "There's something wrong around here." He slid the Remington from his belt. "You ever see this before?"

"Sure. That's Dan's gun. I'd know it anywhere."

"Think he'd be apt to go into the mountains without it? I found it lying in the barn, half-covered with hay."

"Dan's hurt . . . got to be. He was a careful man with a gun, cared for 'em well, and he never left one lyin' around careless."

Kate Breslin appeared in the door, staring at them suspiciously. "You can eat," she said. "I don't want to hold you up any longer'n I have to."

The food was good, the usual beef, beans, and biscuits of the frontier, but potatoes had been added, and beside each plate was a healthy slab of apple pie. Dried apples, Talon reflected, but pie, anyway.

He glanced again at the carefully closed door. Ruth was pouring coffee, and he said, "Burnett should be getting back. What time's the stage due?"

The hands pouring the coffee trembled a little and the girl straightened. "There's plenty of time. Dan will be back, all right."

He took out the gun. "Better give this to him. I found it in the barn."

She picked up the gun quickly, almost snatched it from him, and Talon glimpsed Kate listening in the door to the kitchen. "It's all right . . . he has another."

Talon refilled his cup from the coffeepot and began to build a smoke. Were they worried because they were two women alone? It might be, but he doubted it. Maybe Ruth might worry, although she looked like a girl who could take care of herself, but Kate Breslin wouldn't. She had been in such positions too many times to be daunted by the presence of men, and she would know what to do. So what, then, was wrong?

His thoughts returned suddenly to the gunman on the trail behind them. Odd, when a man came to think of it. "I wonder what became of our friends?" he asked mildly.

Jones looked up from his pie. "On their way, prob'ly."

"They were riding west when we met them."

Jones tore off a slab of bread and began to butter it, ignoring the biscuits. He looked at Talon, his mouth full and chewing, then the chewing slowed and Jones looked thoughtful. "Maybe they turned off," he suggested lamely.

"To where? This is a big, empty country." Talon lit his cigarette. "Remember his advice? To keep riding for Carson? He sounded like he didn't want us to stop this side of there."

"So?"

"So we've stopped . . . and this might be the place he didn't want us to stop."

"I don't figure it . . . what you gettin' at?"

"These women are scared about something, and this is the loneliest stage stop in the country . . . and back along the trail we meet three very handy men riding horses no cowhand could afford, horses with speed and staying quality."

"You think they were outlaws? I noticed them horses."

"What else?"

Jones stared at him thoughtfully. "Talon," he said carefully, "you ride a mighty fine horse yourself. One with speed and staying quality."

Talon smiled. "That's right," he said quietly.

Ruth collected the dishes. "Do you plan to make Carson tonight? You can do it if you push right along."

"You wouldn't be trying to get rid of us, would you?" Talon smiled at her. "I don't think you women should be here alone with Dan Burnett laid up."

Ruth almost dropped the dishes. She turned sharply,

but Kate spoke from the kitchen. "Dan may be laid up, but I'm not. You ride out of here, both of you!"

Jones put his cup down hard and stared at her, his fat jowls quivering. "Now, looka here—!" he started to protest.

"Get! . . . Get goin'!"

Talon picked up the coffeepot and refilled his cup. "Like I said, you're going to need help. Especially with a gold shipment on that coach."

Jones turned to stare at him, astonished. But Kate Breslin walked on into the room, and she had Burnett's Remington in her fist. "You know about that, do you? That means you're what I figured you were. You get goin', mister."

"What else would keep you scared?" Talon asked mildly. "Only that you were afraid of something happening while Dan's laid up."

"We'll handle that. . . . *Ride!*"

Suddenly there was a rush of horses in the yard, and Talon said, "Now you'll really need me. Those riders are the worst kind of trouble."

"Don't give me that!" Kate said, but she hesitated, lowering the gun a little.

"There's three men, Kate," Ruth said.

The door opened and the three men from the Indian fight came into the room. The gunman leading them stopped and his expression hardened when he saw Talon and Jones. "You should have kept going," he said. "We told you."

"Tracey, isn't it?" Talon asked the bearded man. "And you," he said to the gunman, "are Lute Robeck."

"That's right." Robeck walked to the bar and picked up a bottle.

"That's two bits a shot," Kate said.

"Shut up." Robeck merely glanced at her.

Kate started to speak, then tightened her lips and was still; her eyes went from face to face and she walked back to the door of the bedroom and stood there, waiting. She knew all about Robeck . . . the man was known to be a gunman, a killer, a rustler, and occasional robber of payrolls at outlying mines. Tracey, too, was a known man. Her eyes went to Talon. Who was he? What was he?

"Well," Robeck said, "you're here, and the stage is due in a couple of hours, so you'll stay, right here, until we're ready for you."

"Lute," Jones said, "you'd better take Talon's gun. I don't know who he is, but he's too smart."

"Let him have it," Robeck said. "It may give me an excuse to kill him."

Talon glanced at Jones. "So you're one of them?"

"Sure." Jones smiled. "I worked for the mining company until they got a good shipment ready. No use pulling holdups when there's no cash coming; we just wait until we know they've got it. Like now."

The dark outlaw who had said nothing loitered in a corner of the room almost beyond Talon's view. There were four of them now, four to one. "Watch that Breslin woman," Jones said. "She's got Burnett's gun."

"Where's Burnett?" Robeck demanded.

"Back of that door. I figure he's hurt. Leastwise that's what Talon here figured out."

Robeck grinned at Talon. "I hope you try for that gun," he said. "I don't like you, much."

Talon lifted his cup and sipped coffee slowly, watching Robeck over the cup's rim.

The outlaw walked to the door, and when Ruth made as if to stop him, he shoved her roughly aside and opened it.

He strode to the bedside and looked down at the suffering man. "You lie quiet, Burnett," he said, "and maybe you won't be killed."

"You let me get my hands on a gun," Burnett said, "and I'll not make you any promises!"

Robeck chuckled. "Flat on his back and still full of fight." His eyes went to Ruth. "Food, liquor, a gold shipment, and a girl . . . what more can a man ask."

"You'd be wise to let her alone."

Robeck turned his head slowly to look at Talon, who had not moved. "Don't push your luck," he said.

Tracey got out a deck of cards and was joined by the dark man, whom he had called Pete. Tracey began to lay out a game of solitaire. Lute Robeck walked to the now open door and leaned against the doorjamb, watching the empty road.

Four to four, Talon thought, only there were two women on his side, and a sick man. And they were all around the room, and even when they did not appear to be, he knew they were watching him. He also knew that he, at least, was to be killed. That was why they had left him his gun . . . Robeck fancied himself with a gun. He wanted Talon to try it so he could test himself.

An hour went slowly by. Talon wanted to move, but hesitated to give Robeck the chance he might be wanting. The two women had gone quietly to work, cleaning up his table and, at Robeck's order, preparing food for the others. At least one of them watched the women at all times, without making an issue of it.

Talon got out the makings and rolled a smoke. He touched the cigarette paper to his lips and then put the cigarette in his mouth. Robeck watched him with bright interest, but there was a matchbox on the table and Talon took out the match and struck it on the table edge in plain sight.

Robeck chuckled. "Cagey, ain't you?" he said. "Where'd I ever see you before?"

"You never did," Talon said.

Robeck's eyes sharpened. "Maybe . . . You wanted by the law?"

"No." He turned his head. "Ruth, I'd like some more coffee, if you will."

It was very hot and still. Perspiration stood out on their faces. He had one gun against four, and they were not worried by him . . . Robeck was actually anticipating trouble. "If you're going to try for that gun," he said, "you'd better have at it. When the stage comes we're going to take it away from you."

"I can wait."

Robeck chuckled, watching Ruth carry the coffee to the table. He got to his feet and walked to the bar to pour a drink. Ruth gave Talon a look then slanted her eyes quickly away in the direction of Robeck. She looked back and gave him a slight little nod. She wanted him to go ahead, she was ready to take her chances.

Robeck's eyes followed the girl. "Now, there's a woman for you. Fire in her, I'll bet." He glanced at the clock on the shelf. "And we've got most of an hour yet. Maybe her and me—"

"Leave her alone."

Robeck turned, his smile gone. Before he could speak, Talon spoke again. "Leave her alone, Robeck. You'll get the gold if you're smart, but leave that girl alone or I'll kill you."

"*What?*" Robeck was on his feet facing Talon. "You'll kill *me*? Get on your feet, tall man, and I'll cut you down! Get up, you hear? *Get up!*"

Talon did not move. He looked at Robeck and smiled. "Don't be in a hurry," he said. "You have some time left."

The moment died. Pete walked to the door, then stepped outside and walked toward the barn. Ruth served the others and watched them eat. Kate Breslin had done nothing since the gun was taken from her but to cook and remain silent. It was very hot, and Talon loafed in his chair, waiting.

A fly buzzed on the window. Pete walked out to the road and looked off into the distance, shading his eyes against the glare. Jones got up and walked to the window and then turned back, and as he came back toward the table he was behind Talon. Suddenly his gun was thrust against Talon's spine. "You may want to play games," he said to Robeck, "I don't. That stage is due any minute." Jones reached down and took Talon's gun, then stepped back away from him, careful not to get within reach of Talon's hands.

"All right." Robeck shrugged. "I just figured maybe he'd like to try it with me." He grinned at Talon. "No guts."

Talon got slowly to his feet and stretched his long arms. Idly, he walked to the bar where Robeck was seated, and poured a drink. Robeck moved back a little, watching Talon cheerfully. "I'll still kill you if you start anything, Talon," Robeck warned. Ruth, tense only a moment before, relaxed, accepted her fate . . . she and Kate were one step further from safety.

In the kitchen, Kate Breslin had taken an old .31 Colt from her valise, and she slipped it into Ruth's hand. "Only if the chance is just right," she whispered. "Then give it to him."

Pete walked out to the road. "Not much more time, Lute."

"No." Lute glanced around the room. "They don't

know the women are here, anyway. They can't know, with the only stage since Burnett was hurt going out the other way. We'll hide them . . . put 'em in Burnett's room."

Tracey got up. "What about Talon?"

Ruth came into the room and crossed to the table where Talon sat. Lute watched her with bright interest, never missing a move. The butt of the little Colt was visible to Talon from under Ruth's apron, but he carefully ignored it. Ruth fussed with the dishes, waiting, and suddenly Robeck began to laugh.

"He's yellow! Yellow! Ruthie, you picked yourself the wrong man!"

Ruth turned away from the table and instantly Robeck motioned to Tracey, who grabbed the girl and shoved her across to Robeck, who jerked the apron from her, and the gun. "You little fool!" He slapped her wickedly across the mouth. "Who do you think you're fooling?" He shoved her back against the counter and slapped her again. Instantly, she lashed out and slapped him, then kicked him on the shins. There was a momentary struggle, and then he shoved the girl from him and slapped her again, thrusting the pistol into his waistband.

Talon stood flat-footed, watching, but making no move away from the table. His expression had not changed as he watched the brief struggle. When it was over he stepped over and helped the girl to her feet. Angrily, Ruth jerked away from him. "Don't touch me, you coward!" she flared.

Robeck laughed.

Pete ran in from the road. "Here she comes!" he said.

Tracey grabbed Ruth and shoved her toward the bedroom door. Robeck stood watching Talon and smiling. "No hurry," he said. "They're bringing it right to us."

Tracey ordered Kate from the kitchen and into the bedroom. "If they make a wrong move," Robeck ordered, "use your gun barrel. And I don't care how hard you hit."

Lute Robeck walked to the door and looked out. The stage was rolling into the yard. "All right." He gestured to Talon. "Walk out there ahead of us and don't say anything or make a wrong move."

Whatever happened now would depend on fast thinking and breaks, and the shotgun guard must do some fast thinking, too. He walked outside with Lute beside him; Jones and Pete moved up behind. Talon angled toward the stage, knowing the men behind him would spread out. If the shotgun guard started shooting, which Robeck well knew, Talon would be the first man killed.

The stage whirled into the yard and came to an abrupt stop in a cloud of dust. The shotgun guard was staring from the door to the waiting men, and as Talon slowly turned he saw a rifle barrel glinting from the bedroom window . . . Tracey was going to kill the guard.

"Holdup!" Talon yelled, and a Colt Lightning slid from under the arm of his coat.

Robeck swore and swung his gun, blasting fire. His first shot was too quick, Talon's was not. The bullet caught Robeck over the belt buckle and he started back. Talon fired again, then nailed Jones. Pete was already falling and suddenly there was silence broken only by the plunging of the horses and the rattle of harness. They quieted down and Talon got slowly to his feet.

Talon walked over to Robeck and kicked the gun from his hand, but the man was dead.

Tracey was standing in the door, his hands high. "Don't shoot!" he said. "I've quit!"

Ruth came from the door, but the shotgun guard reached Talon first. "Thanks," he said. "When I didn't see Dan I figured something was wrong."

"I'm sorry," Ruth said, "I just thought—"

"I always carry a spare," he said. "You know, any of us in there could have been killed. Sometimes it's better to reserve judgment . . . when a man's life is on the line, he naturally wants to wait until the time is right."

He walked to the stable for his horse. It was still a long way to Carson.

HERE ENDS
THE TRAIL

C old was the night and bitter the wind and brutal the
trail behind. Hunched in the saddle, I growled at
the dark and peered through the blinding rain. The
agony of my wound was a white-hot flame from the bullet
of Korry Gleason.

Dead in the corral at Seaton's he was, and a blessed
good thing for the country, too, although had I gone down
instead, the gain would have been as great and the loss no
greater. Wherever he went, in whatever afterlife there may
be for the Korry Gleasons of this world, he'll carry the
knowledge that he paid his score for the killing of old Bags
Robison that night in Animas.

He'd been so sure, Gleason had, that Race Mallin had
bucked it out in gun smoke down Big Band way. He'd
heard the rumor all right, so he thought it safe to kill old
Bags, and he'd nothing on his mind when he walked,
sloshing through the mud toward Seaton's—and then he
saw me.

He knew right off, no doubt about that. He knew before

he saw my face. He knew even before I spoke. "Good-bye, Korry," I said.

But the lightning flashed as I spoke and he saw me standing there, a big, lean-bodied man wearing no slicker and guns ready to hand. He saw me there with the scar on my jaw, put there by his own spur the night I whipped him in Mobeetie.

He swore and grabbed for his gun and I shot him through the belly, shot him low down, where they die hard, because he'd never given old Bags a chance, old Bags who had been like a father to me . . . who had no father and no mother, nor kith nor kin nor anything. I shot him low down and hard and he grabbed iron and his gun swung up and I cursed him like I've never cursed, then I sank three more shots into him, framing the ugly heart of him with lead and taking his bullet in the process.

Oh, he was game, all right! He came of a hard clan, did Korry Gleason, big, bloody, brutal men who killed and fought and drank and built ranches and roads and civilization and then died because the country they built was too big for them to hold down.

So now I'd trail before me and nothing behind me but the other members of the Gleason clan, who, even now, would be after me. The trail dipped down and the wind whipped at my face while the pain of my wound gnawed at my side. My thoughts spun and turned smoky and my brain struggled with the heat haze of delirium.

Gigantic thunder bottled itself up in the mighty canyons of cloud and then exploded in jagged streaks of lightning, cannon flashes of lightning that stabbed and glanced and shimmered among the rock-sided hills. Night and the iron rain and wet rock for a trail and the thunder of slides and the echoing canyons where they ended, the roaring streams below and the poised boulders, revealed starkly by some momentary flash, then concealed but waiting to go crashing down when the moment came. And through it I rode, more dead than alive, with a good seat in the saddle but a body that lolled and sagged. Under me there was a bronco that was surefooted on a trail that was a devil's nightmare.

Then there was a light.

Have you ever seen a lighted window flickering through the rain of a lonely land? Have you ever known that sudden gush of heart-glowing warmth at such a sight? There is no other such feeling, and so when I saw it, the weariness and pain seemed warranted and cheap at the price of that distant, promising window.

What lay beyond that light? Warmth and food? The guns of enemies old or new? It did not matter, for since time began, man has been drawn to the sight of human habitation, and I was in an unknown land, and far from anywhere so far as I knew. Then in a lightning flash I saw a house, a barn, and a corral, all black and wet in the whipping rain.

Inside the barn, there was the roar of rain on the roof and the good, friendly smells of horses and hay, of old leather and sacks, and all the smells that make barns what they are. So I slid from my horse and led him into the welcome stillness and closed the door behind us. There I stripped the saddle from him and wiped the rain from his body and shook it from his mane, and then I got fresh hay and stuffed the manger full. "Fill your belly," I told him. "Come dawn we'll be out of here."

Under my slicker, then, I slipped the riding thong from the butt of my Colt and slid my rifle from the saddle scabbard. The light in the window was welcoming me, but whether friend or enemy waited there, I did not know. A moment after I knocked on the door, it jerked open under my hand and I looked into the eyes of a woman.

Her eyes were magnificent and brown, and she was tall and with poise and her head carried like a princess crowned. She looked at me and she said, "Who are you?" Her voice was low, and when she spoke something within me quivered, and then she said, "What do you want here?"

"Shelter," I said, "a meal if you've got the food to spare. There's trouble following me, but I'll try to be gone before the storm clears. Will you help? Say the word, yes or no."

What she thought I'd no idea, for what could she think of me, big, unshaven, and scarred? And what could she think when my slicker was shed and she saw the two tied-down guns and the mark of blood on the side and the spot where my shirt was torn by the bullet.

"You've been shot," she said.

And then the room seemed to spin slowly in a most sickening fashion and I fell against the wall and grabbed a hook and clung to it, gripping hard, afraid to go down for fear I'd not again get to my feet.

She stepped in close and got her arm about my waist and helped me walk toward the chair, as I refused the bed. I sat while she brought hot water and stripped my shirt from me and looked down at the place where the bullet had come through, and a frightening mess it was, with blood caked to my hide and the wound an ugly sight.

She bathed the wound and she probed for the bullet and somehow she got it out. This was something she had done before, that I could see. She treated my side with something, or maybe it was only her lovely hands and their gentle touch, and as I watched her I knew that here was my woman, if such there was in the world, the woman to walk beside a man, and not behind him. Not one of those who try always to be pushing ahead and who are worth nothing at all as a woman and little as anything else.

She started coffee then and put broth on the fire to warm, and over her shoulder she looked at me. "Who are you, then? And where is it you come from?"

Who was I? Nobody. What was I? Less than nothing. "I'm a drifting man," I said simply enough, "and one too handy with a gun for the good of himself or anyone. I'm riding through. I've always been riding through."

"There's been a killing?"

"Of a man who deserved it. So now I'm running, for though he was a bad lot, there's good men in his line and they'll be after me."

She looked at me coolly, and she said, "You've run out of one fight and into another, unless you move quickly."

"Here?"

"Yes. We have moved in and planted crops and now a cattleman would be driving us out. There are eleven of us—eleven that can fight, and fourteen women, who can help. Some have been killed, my father for one. There are more than thirty tough hands riding with the cattleman, and one of them is Sad Priest."

There was no good in Priest. Him I knew well and nothing about him I liked. "Who is the cattleman?"

"Yanel Webb. It's a big outfit."

"I know them." By now I was eating the broth and drinking coffee and the chill was leaving my bones, but my lids were heavy and there was a weight of sleep on my eyes. She showed me to the bed where her father had slept and helped me off with my boots and guns, and then what happened I never knew, for sleep folded me away into soft darkness.

Though I remembered but fragments, there was a fever that took me and I tossed and turned on the bed for hours. A drink of water from a cup in her gentle hand exhausted me and the medicine in the dressings for my wound stained the sheets. At last I faded off into a dreamless sleep that seemed to go on forever. When next my eyes opened to awareness, there was daylight at the window and a clear sky beyond it and the girl was standing in the door. I had a vague memory of someone knocking on the door, voices, and the pound of hooves receding into the distance.

"You'd best get up. They're coming."

"The Gleasons?"

"Webb and Priest, and his lot. And we're not ready for them. We're all scattered." She dried her palms on her apron. "You'd best slip out. I've saddled your horse."

"And run?"

"It's no fight of yours."

"I'm not a running sort of man. And as to whether it's a fight of mine or not, time will be saying, for you've done me a turn and I pay my debts when I can . . . have you coffee on?"

"My father said there must always be hot coffee in a house."

"Your father was a knowing man."

When I had my boots on and my guns I felt better, favoring my side a bit. When they rode into the yard I was standing in the door with a cup of hot, black coffee in my left hand.

There were at least twenty of them, and armed for business. Tough men, these. Tough men and hard in the belly and eyes. The first of them was Webb, of whom I'd heard talk, and on his left, that lean rail of poison, Sad Priest.

"Morning," I said. "You're riding early."

"We've no talk with you, whoever you are. Where's Maggie Ryan?"

"This morning I'm speaking for her. Is it trouble you're after? If it is"—I smiled at them, feeling good inside and liking the look of them—"you've called at the right door. However, I'll be forgivin'.

"If you turn about now and ride off, I'll be letting you go without risk."

"Let *us* go?" Yanel Webb stared at me as if I was fair daft, and not a bad guess he'd made, for daft I am and always have been, for when there's a fight in the offing, something starts rolling around in me, something that's full of gladness and eagerness that will not go down until there's fists or clubs or guns and somebody's won or lost or got themselves a broken skull. "You'll let us go? Get out of here, man! Get out while we see fit to let you!"

That made me laugh. "Leave a scrap when the Priest is in it? That I'd never do, Webb." I stepped out onto the porch, moving toward them, knowing there's something about closeness to a gun that turns men's insides to water and weakness. "How are you, Sad? Forgotten me?"

He opened his scar of a mouth and said, "I've never seen you before—" His voice broke off and he stopped. "Race Mallin . . ."

That made me chuckle. There'd been a change in his eyes then, for he knew me, and I knew myself what was said about me, how I was a gun-crazy fool who had no brains or coolness or anything, a man who wouldn't scare and wouldn't bluff and who would walk down the avenues of hell with dynamite in his pockets and tinder in his hair. Now, no man wants to tackle a man like that, for you know when the chips are down and you've got to fight, he'll die hard and not alone.

Sad Priest was a fast hand with a gun, maybe faster than me, but there'd been other fast men who had died as easily as anyone.

"Right you are. And it looks like some of these boys here will be able to tell it around the bunkhouses next year, the story of how Sad Priest and Yanel Webb died with Race Mallin in an all-out gun battle! What a story that will make for those who yarn around the fires!

"Yanel Webb, all his cattle wasted, his ranch in other hands, his wife a widow, and his baby son an orphan, and Sad Priest, the fastest of them all, facedown in the dirt of a nester's yard with his belly shot full of lead bullets!"

Beyond them were the others and I grinned at them. "Oh, don't you lads worry. Some of you favored ones will go along. How many is a guess, but you'd best remember I've ten good bullets here, and while I've gone down three times in gunfights, it was every time with empty guns!

"Tell them, Sad! You were on the Neuces that time when the four Chambers boys jumped me. They put me down and filled me full of holes and I was six weeks before I could walk, but they buried three of the Chambers and the other one left the country when I left my bed."

"You talk a lot," Webb said sourly.

"It's a weakness of the Irish," I said.

They did not like it. None of them liked it. At such a time no man feels secure and each one is sure you're looking right at him.

"What are you doin' here?" Webb demanded. "This is no fight of yours."

"Why, any one-sided fight is my fight, Yanel," I explained. "I've a weakness for them. I could not stay out of it, and me with the Gleasons behind me."

That I said for the smartness of it. I'm not so crazy as I sound, and wild as I get in a scrap, I knew they'd salt me down if the guns opened here. But my deal was to bluff them, for no man wishes to die, and once the bluff started, to offer them an easy out, a reason for delay.

The Gleasons made a reason. I knew they would figure that if the Gleasons were after me, all they had to do was sit back and let the Gleasons kill me—and any gain in time was a gain for us.

Webb hesitated, soaking it up. He didn't like it, but it was smart, and Priest said something to him under his breath, and probably a warning to let the Gleasons come. Then Webb said, "Why are the Gleasons after you?"

"Korry," I explained, "shot down an old friend of mine when I was down Del Rio way. I hightailed it back and met him last night and he was a bit slow. He died back there and the Gleasons will be after me."

"That," Webb said, "I'd like to see. We'll camp out and see what happens."

Now, that I'd not expected. I'd believed they would ride out and leave us alone, but with them here . . . Maggie Ryan spoke beside me. "What will we do, Race? The others will be here soon, and they are not fighting men, they are quiet, sincere men with families and homes. If there is a fight here, some of them or all of them will die. Webb won't stop killing once he starts."

"It isn't Webb," I said. "It's that cold image of a buzzard beside him, it's Priest that worries me."

Strange is the world that men are born to, and strange the ways of men when trouble comes. Yanel Webb was not a bad man, only a hard man who thought cattle were the only way of life and would stop all others who came into the country. And those with him—they were hard, reckless men, but cowhands, not killers. Fight they would, if they must, but with a decent way out . . . and the Gleasons who were coming. Korry had been the only bad apple in that lot. They knew it as well as I, but they were honor bound to hunt me down, but I'd no stomach for killing honest men.

Across the hard-caked earth of the yard on that morning after the rain I looked at Sad Priest.

"Maggie," I said. "there's a chance that we can work it out, but only one chance. What stake has Priest in this?"

"Webb's given him land and a job. He's the worst of them, I think."

"How was Webb before he came?"

"Angry, and ordering us off, but he wasn't so strong for killing."

"Maybe," I said, "if Priest were out of it, we could talk."

Then we heard the rattle of hooves on the bridge and the sound of riders and I looked around over my shoulder and saw the Gleasons come into the yard.

There was the weakness from my wound, but no time for weakness now. There they were, the three of them, and they were looking around at what they had ridden into. And then I took my gamble as a man sometimes must. I'm not a talking man when the chips are down and the love of battle is strong within me, but there was more at stake now than me or my desires, for there was a handful of kindly folks and their farms and wishes.

There comes a time to every man when he must drop the old ways and look ahead, so here was I, a man who had ridden and roistered and rustled a few head, who had shot up the wrong side of town on a Saturday night. I'd killed a few hardcases and lived the life of a wild land growing, and now suddenly I could see a chance for my own life: a wife, my own home, my own green and growing land, my own children about the door—maybe all of it lay out there beyond that hot, sunbaking yard where my enemies stood. Twenty-odd men with reasons for killing me, and not one for helping me stay alive.

"Maggie," I said, "I'm a changed man. I'm going out there and talk. Pray if you can, for you're certain to have more of a voice with the Lord than I, for it's got to be blarney rather than bullets if we come out alive from this."

So I walked out there and faced the Gleasons, three hard, tough, honest men. Three men who had ridden here to kill me.

"Pat," I said, "we rode a roundup together. Mickey, you pulled me out from under a steer one time, down Sonora way, an' you, Dave, I've bought you drinks and you've bought them for me. That's why I ran after I'd shot Korry. He had it comin', an' deep in the heart of you, you all know it.

"Korry got what he asked for, and had it not been me, it would have been another, but I ran, for I'd no desire to kill any of you."

"Or to be killed, maybe."

Then I shrugged. "That's a gamble always, but the Chambers boys went down and a fool knows no lack of confidence. Surely, I'm a fool, and a great one."

"Why the palaver?" Pat demanded. "What trick is this?"

"No trick," I said. "Only I've no wish to kill any one of you, nor to kill anyone anymore but one man.

"These"—I gestured at the gathered riders—"are fine upstanding men who've come to rob a girl of her home! To take the roof from a girl who's but recently lost her father!

"They want to run out a lot of fine, homemaking men who are irrigating land and building the country. And they've brought a killer to do their dirty work, a buzzard named Sad Priest!

"I don't want to fight you. I've this fight to think of now. Never yet have I shot an honest man, and I've no wish to begin.

"Only one thing I want now," and when I spoke my eyes went to Sad Priest across the yard. "I want to kill the man who'd run a girl with no family from her house!"

Oh, I didn't wait for him! Nobody waits for Sad Priest! So when I spoke, I reached, but he drew so fast his gun was up and shooting before I'd more than cleared leather. But I'd known he'd shoot too fast and he did. His bullet tugged at my shirt and I triggered my six-gun, two quick, hammering shots, and then ran!

Right for him, his gun spitting lead and the blood of my bullets showing on his neck and shirtfront, but my running made him miss and only one of the bullets hit me, taking me through the thigh, and I went down and felt another bullet whip past my skull, and then I fired up at him and the bullet split his brisket and his knees let go and he started down just as I rolled on my side and fired into him again at eight feet of distance.

He hit ground then and lay there all sprawled out, and one of the Webb hands started for me and Pat Gleason levered a shell into the barrel of his Winchester. "Hold it, mister!" he said. "That was a fair fight!"

They stood there, all of them, nobody quite knowing what to do, and then Maggie Ryan ran to me and with her hands under my arms I got to my feet. I stepped away from her and pushed her back toward the house. This was not yet over. Blood was running from my side where the other wound had started to bleed.

"Got you twice," Dave Gleason said.

"No," I told him, "the one in my side was Korry's. Only he was a few inches too low."

"Korry got a bullet into you?" Mickey said. "If he did that he had a fair shake. He wasn't fast enough otherwise."

"It's his," I said. "You can see the wound's not fresh."

Yanel Webb stood there with his hands at his sides, not sure of what to say. And his hands waited for him, for he was their boss and they rode for the brand, but knowing their kind I knew their hearts weren't in it.

"Yanel," I said, "Priest was long overdue. Ride home. You've land enough, and when you want eggs and fresh vegetables, come down on the creek and trade with these people.

"You and me," I said, "we've got to grow with the times. The day of the gun and the free range is past. We've got to accept that or go like the buffalo went."

He was reluctant to leave, and he stood there, knowing the truth of what I'd said, and knowing that nothing now stood between him and my first bullet.

"He's calling them fair," Pat Gleason said. "I stand with him on that."

Webb turned to his hands. "Well, boys," he said, "we'd best take Sad along and plant him. I reckon we've played out our hand. These farmers best keep their crops fenced, though." It was his final chance to bluster. "If their fields are eaten or trampled, it's not my lookout!"

They went then, and we watched them ride, and then I faced around and looked at the Gleasons and they looked at me. Maggie Ryan had her arm around me and then she spoke up and said to them, "There's coffee on. Will you come in?"

So we went in and the coffee was hot and black, and there by the table there was warm and pleasant talk of cattle and grass and what a man could do in a green growing valley, with time on his hands.

LAST DAY
IN TOWN

The riders moved forward in a body, then halted.
"Strike a match, Reb!" Nathan Embree's voice trembled with triumph. "We finally got one, I heard him fall."

Reb Farrell slid from the saddle. "I see him! He's right over here!" A match whispered on his jeans and the light flared.

All necks craned forward. The man on the ground had a bullet through his head, but the face of the man was placid. It was a quiet face, seamed with care and years that had not been kind. The face of a man tired of the endless struggle of living. It was the face of Reb Farrell's father.

Numb with horror, Reb stared down at the man they had killed, the man who had fought to give him some little education and a sense of honor, who had fought so hard and lost, and who now was dead, killed, possibly by a bullet from the gun of the son he loved.

"My God!" Dave Barbot's exclamation was low. "Not Jim Farrell! It can't be!"

Nathan Embree's own shock changed to sudden, bitter

fury. "So that was it? That was why you couldn't find any rustlers for me, Reb? Maybe this explains how they always knew when an' where to strike! Maybe this explains why they were always one jump ahead of us!"

Reb Farrell stared unbelievingly at the body of his father, shocked as much by his father's presence here as by the feeling that he had himself shot him. He did not hear the words of Nathan Embree. He did not hear Dave Barbot's refusal to agree.

"You don't believe that, Nathan!" Dave's voice was sharp. "Reb's fought them harder than anybody! He's recovered two herds for you!"

"Uh-huh." There was cold certainty in Nathan Embree's voice. "Why did he find 'em when nobody else could? Maybe it was because he was the only one who knew where to look? When did this rustling start? Right after I made him foreman, wasn't it?"

Reb Farrell looked up. "What was that? What did you say, Nathan?"

Nathan Embree was a wealthy man and he was a driver. He was also a just man, but hard and merciless. The moon had emerged from under a cloud and showed him the face of his young foreman.

"You're fired, Reb! Get your gear an' get off the place! I can't prove anything against you, but if you're still in the country within twenty-four hours, we'll hunt you down an' you'll hang!"

Astonishment held Reb speechless for a full minute, and then as the riders began to turn their horses to ride away, he found his voice. "You accusin' me of rustlin', Nathan?" His eyes seemed to flare. "I won't take that from no man! Don't call me a rustler unless you're willing to grab iron!"

Embree turned on him. "Yes," he said contemptuously,

"you would try something like that! Oh, we all know you're a gunfighter, Reb, but now that your own father's dead, you should have some sense in that head of yours!"

Reb Farrell stared, unable to believe what he heard. Embree had shouted at them to fire as they heard the rush of hooves, and he had fired at the silhouette of a man in the saddle.

"By rights you should be hangin', an' it's only because of my daughter that you ain't! But get out, an' don't ever show your face around my place or my daughter!"

Wheeling his horse, he led the group away, and only Dave Barbot lingered. "Sorry, Reb," he said softly. "I'm really sorry."

Alone in the darkness, Reb Farrell stood beside the body of his father and the ashes of all that had mattered to him, and listened to the sound of their retreating hooves.

Like a man walking in his sleep, Reb caught up his own horse and then his father's. He loaded the body across the saddle and started for home. He rode slowly, his head hanging, devoid of thought. It was the end of everything for him. The job on the ranch he loved, Laura, everything.

The old cabin where he had spent his boyhood was dark and silent. Dismounting, he went inside and lighted a lamp. Without waiting for day to come, he got some loose boards and knocked together a crude coffin, lining it with an old poncho. Sodden with grief, he went to the place under the trees and there beside the grave of his mother, who died when he was a child, he buried his father.

Although he had eaten nothing since morning, he had no thought of food. Slowly, he looked around the cabin that had been his home until he moved out to the ranch. What should he take with him? What was there to take? Though men may die, the living must continue to live, and he must think of food, bedding, guns.

Guns . . . his father's fine old Sharps .50, the new Winchester .44 which his father had . . .

The Winchester was gone!

Reb felt a queer tingle of excitement go through him. The Sharps was in its place on the rack, but the new Winchester was gone? And there had been no saddle scabbard on the saddle of his father's horse. Knowing his father, Reb knew he would never have gone out at night without taking a rifle, and that meant the Sharps. Despite the fact that Reb had made him a present of the Winchester, his father had kept it on the rack and held to his familiar old buffalo gun.

Aware of something wrong, Reb stood stock-still in the middle of the cabin and looked around. Suddenly he thought of the carefully hoarded cache of money his father had. A few hundred dollars only, it was his insurance against illness or old age. Reb dropped on his knees and slid the board from its grooves in the floor. The money was gone!

Slowly Reb got to his feet. No money had been in his father's pockets. Something was wrong, but what could it all mean?

Looking around the cabin, Reb was suddenly struck by the coffeepot on the stove, and going to it, he lifted the lid. There were still grounds in the pot. Either somebody else had made that coffee and left the pot or Jim Farrell had been drawn from his fire while making coffee, for Jim had habits of neatness acquired from years of living with his wife. He never left a pot on the stove and never left a dish unwashed.

As he packed the remaining food Reb Farrell considered all the possibilities, and slowly the conviction gathered in his mind that either his father had been somehow alarmed and left the cabin or he had been taken from it by force.

It was daylight when Reb Farrell finally left the cabin. He took with him two packhorses and four head of saddle stock aside from the horse he himself rode. There were Rocking F cattle around that belonged to him, but they would have to wait.

Reb struck for the hills above Indian Creek. He was not leaving the country, not until he knew exactly what had happened. Of one thing he was sure. His father had never done anything dishonest. There had been too many times in the past when he might have profited without anyone the wiser, but Jim Farrell had not taken one single thing that did not belong to him. Not even when, as had happened, he had a shadow of a claim.

As Reb rode up the narrowing canyon he thought the matter over. His father had no enemies. A kindly man, he never had trouble with anyone, working at whatever he could to eke out his existence, and selling off little by little the once fair-sized herd he had owned. Therefore, if his cabin had been looted, it had been by chance thieves. Or . . . the thought came to him suddenly . . . enemies of Reb's!

But who were Reb's enemies? Aside from a few fist-fights at dances, none of which led to enmity, Reb had no enemies.

Except . . . except the rustlers themselves. Reb had found and recovered two herds of stolen cattle, and he had upon several occasions trailed the rustlers for miles. In fact, he had been the only man they had reason to fear. Suppose they had chosen this way to strike at him?

Skirting South Peak, Reb Farrell rode into a narrow canyon where he had once trailed a wounded elk, and circling into the back of the canyon, he dismounted and opened an old corral and turned in his horses. Then he switched saddles from the animal he had been riding to a long-legged zebra dun. There was plenty of grass in the corral, growing rich and green, and a small stream flowed through one corner of it. Several years ago he had built that corral himself, but had never expected to use it as he was now.

There was no cabin, but the deep overhang of a cliff provided all the shelter he needed, and the firs growing before it would keep his fire from reflecting by night and would dissipate his smoke by day, for Reb had no intention of leaving the country.

The dun was a fast and tough horse, one whose staying power and heart he had tested before this. In the saddle, he headed for town. First, he had to see Laura Embree.

The town of Palo Seco was resting when he rode in. There were lights in the two saloons and in a few scattered houses. One of these was Nathan Embree's town house. Knowing well the hardheadedness of his former boss, Reb dismounted in the cottonwoods some fifty yards from the house and walked up along the rail fence surrounding the Embree garden. Easing into the yard, he glanced through the window.

Laura was at the piano and there was no one else in the room. Swiftly, he mounted the porch and tapped gently on the door. A second time he tapped, and then the music stopped. He heard the sound of steps and the door opened.

"Reb!" Laura's hand went to her lips and her eyes widened. "If Father finds you here, you'll be killed!"

"Maybe. But I had to see you." His eyes searched her face. "Where do you stand, Laura? Do you believe I am a rustler?"

"I don't know, Reb," she said cautiously. "But I don't know if I can take a chance on you either."

"You can trust me! You just watch, I'm gonna—" She

closed the door in his face and he stood staring at it, his world collapsing around him.

Laura, too! Stunned, he turned away and walked back to the dun. Somehow, even when he tried to convince himself that she would think as her father did, he had not believed it. But tonight she had looked at him as though at a stranger!

One hand on the pommel, Reb Farrell hesitated, scowling. All right, he had to begin somewhere. He knew his father was not a rustler. He knew his father had not been out there willingly. As long as he knew those things there was a chance to prove himself right.

One other person, perhaps several others, knew the truth also; the rustlers knew he or his father had been framed.

But who would be doing the rustling? The most likely person was, he knew, Lon Melchor over on Tank Mesa. Melchor had rustled cattle before, but had always been too quick to be caught at it. But somehow he could not believe that Lon would kill his father. They had been on opposite sides of the fence but they had always been friendly. Regardless, it was a place to start.

Hard riding put him at Lon's place shortly after midnight. All was dark and still. Swinging down from the dun's saddle, Reb moved swiftly along the side hill toward the cabin where Lon Melchor lived. All was still, but there was something about the feel of the night that he did not like. Hesitating, he tried to resolve the feeling into something concrete and definite.

He moved up to the corner of the house. The door was standing open, which was unusual, for the night was cool. Straining his ears, he could hear hoarse breathing but no other sound. He spoke softly. "Lon!"

All was still. He stepped into the door of the cabin and

pushed the door shut, listening. Again he spoke the old rustler's name, but again there was no sound. Then he took a chance and struck a match.

Lon Melchor was sprawled on the floor, lying in a stupor, his shirt stained with blood!

Forgetting his mission, Reb dropped to his knees and made a quick examination of the old man, and then he began to work swiftly. He got a fire going and put water on the stove, and then he put a pillow under the old man's head and stretched him out easier, rolling him over onto a blanket which he placed on the floor. When the water was hot he bathed the wound, which was a nasty bullet burn along his left side, and only when he had the wound bandaged did he turn to look around.

Lon's gun lay on the floor, and picking it up, Reb saw it had been fired three times. His rifle was nowhere about, and was probably on his horse. Slipping out of the door, Reb looked about until he found the horse. The saddle was wet where the old man had bled, and Reb stripped the saddle from the horse and turned him into the corral. There was water in the trough and he forked down some hay, then returned to the cabin.

Lon's eyes were open. "Reb!" he gasped. "You seen 'em? Them rustlers, I mean?"

"Who were they, Lon? Did they shoot you?"

"Yep." He stared up at the younger man, his misery showing in his face. "They got your dad and it's my fault, too. I knowed Joe Banta was a bad—"

"My dad?" Reb Farrell leaned over the bunk. "What do you know about him?"

"He's dead. Banta come in here wantin' a hideout, maybe three weeks ago. I knowed he was a plumb bad hombre, but I let him stay on. Fact is, I couldn't have drove him away. Then he did leave, only to come back with a bunch of hardcases. They were rustlin' cattle an' slippin' them out of here at night . . . you know that."

"You're durned right I do. What about my father?"

"They were talkin' about what to do about you." The old man coughed, and then grimaced with the pain. "They wanted to warn you off.

"I waited until they left, then I took off, tried to beat 'em by going across the mountains. I got there too late! They killed him! Dragged him right out in the yard and shot him! I opened up at them with my Winchester and one of 'em shot me. I got back on my horse and rode right out of there. . . . I guess none of them followed."

"They thought he was doing it, Lon." Briefly, Reb explained all that had taken place. The old man was angry.

"Nathan Embree was always a pigheaded fool!" he snorted. He grabbed Reb's hand. "Get you some men, son! I know where he'll go! He'll head for the old hideout at Burro Springs! You got to follow Dark Canyon to get there. Right up the canyon through all them boulders! From there he can sell that herd to the minin' camps easy as pie!"

Reb hesitated, but the old man waved him on. "What're you going to do for me, boy! I lost a sight of blood, but you ain't no doctor. You get some men and go after those coyotes. I'll get along."

Reb wheeled and ran to the door. His horse was excited, seeming to realize what was at stake. There was no time to go for help, and there was a chance he might get shot on sight if he went back for it.

Day was just breaking in the east when he first found the opening into Dark Canyon and rode down from the lip of the mesa into the deep, shadowy green recesses of this oasis in the desert.

Long suspected as a possible hangout for rustlers, the

canyon had been searched several times in the past year, but Lon's remark about the boulders explained why they had found nothing. Searchers had always been stopped by the seemingly impassable jumble of boulders, some of them so close together there seemed no way through. Moreover, the place was exceedingly dangerous. If caught in the canyon bottom during a heavy rain, there would be small chance of escaping the roaring flood which came down the canyon, fifteen, sixteen, sometimes twenty feet or more high.

Now Reb knew there was a way through those boulders, if the cattle had been taken through, then he could go through. He rode now with extreme caution, pausing to study the canyon ahead of him, and then pushing on. Soon the huge boulders that had hitherto blocked all progress in the ancient riverbed were before him. Long before this point they had always lost all tracks, a matter the occasional rains would attend to or a few hands dragging brush behind their horses. The boulders seemed to block all advance. Riding up to them, he searched for a way between, but try as he might, he could find none that would allow the passage of a horse or cow. Yet with Lon Melchor's statement to urge him on, he persisted, and it was finally a mark on the canyon wall that tipped him off. It was such a mark as might have been made by the brushing of a stirrup or stirrups. Riding close to the wall, ducking his head because of the overhang, he suddenly saw the opening, only wide enough to allow for passage. He rode through, then paused in the shadow of the cliff.

The canyon continued a jumble of boulders, and nothing could be seen for some distance ahead. After a careful study of the rocks and earth, he rode on, then turned up a narrow path that showed at one side of the canyon. It was a little-used trail that looked like it was probably made by

wild horses. It led him into the broken rock of the shattered canyon wall, and then on to a green-topped mesa.
Crossing this, he paused under some trees and looked
down. Below him, the canyon widened out into a long,
green, and well-watered valley of some five hundred
acres. Two huts and a long bunkhouse or boardinghouse
were against the wall of the canyon below him. There was
a stable and some corrals, and scattered over the canyon
several hundred head of cattle were feeding.

As he watched, two men came from the long building
and strolled toward the corrals. They walked as men do
who have enjoyed a good meal and are in no hurry to go
to work. One of them was Joe Banta.

Banta had never been known to operate in this part of
the country, and Nathan Embree would have been the first
to scoff at such an idea, yet here he was, and in plain sight.
He was a stocky man of considerable breadth and little
height, a swarthy fellow with a battered gray hat. Even at
this distance Reb could recognize him without trouble.
When they turned around, Reb recognized the man with
him as Ike Goodrich, a small-time outlaw and occasional
hand who had once worked for Embree.

Two hours of waiting and watching while his horse
cropped grass contentedly gave Reb Farrell the idea that
at least four men were below. Aside from Banta and Ike,
there was the cook, whom Reb had seen come to the door
to throw out some water, and a thin, redheaded fellow
who walked with a slight limp and appeared to favor one
leg considerably, as though it had been injured at some
time not long since. This man went to the corral and saddled four horses.

There was no time to go for help. It would take hours to
get out and hours to get back, even if he could convince
somebody of the truth of his story. Barbot might believe

him. Embree never would, but by the time they returned, the cattle might be gone, for it was likely there was another way out of the canyon, probably the route that led over to the mining camps.

Leading his horse, Reb left the mesa top and made his way slowly down a back trail into a deep draw that opened on the valley where the rustlers were holed. Leaving his horse in the brush, Reb walked down the canyon, rifle in hand. From the mouth he looked out over the valley. The nearest corral was not twenty yards away, the back of the nearest shack about the same distance. The redhead was standing in front of the stable, tightening a saddle girth.

Reb walked out of the canyon mouth and strolled along the corral bars until he was facing the man in front of the stable. Nobody else was in sight.

"All right, Red." His voice was low but strong enough. "Unloose your gun belts and turn around. One wrong move and you die!"

Red turned slowly, his hands wide. His face was tight with surprise. "Where'd you come from?" he demanded.

"Unloose that belt!"

Red's hands went to the buckle, then he hurled himself to one side and grabbed his gun. Reb's Winchester barked and Red kept falling, the gun slipping from his fingers and sliding along the earth a foot from the outstretched hand.

A chair slammed over inside the house and Goodrich jumped into the door. Reb was waiting for him and he fired. The shot burned Ike on the neck, cutting along that side nearest the cabin. Goodrich jerked away and fell out the door.

From the window a bullet slammed near Reb, and Reb charged. Goodrich grabbed his gun and rolled over. Reb chanced a running shot and saw the bullet kick dirt in

Ike's face. While the gunman swore and grabbed at his eyes, Reb dropped his rifle, grabbed a pistol, and lunged through the door. He took a chance, gambling that Joe Banta would be expecting nothing of the kind. Banta wheeled as Reb came on and both men fired at once and both missed. Reb grabbed the edge of the table to stop his forward movement and fired again. Banta jerked hard and his shot went wild. Then Reb jumped at him, clubbing with his six-gun barrel. Banta went down to his hands and knees, and started to get up when Reb hit him a second time.

Wheeling, he sprang to the door. Goodrich was crawling for the rifle Reb had dropped and Reb put a bullet in the ground before him. Goodrich stopped, and glared at the doorway. "You'll suffer for this! If I live a thousand years, I'll never forget it!"

A board creaked and Reb looked up. The cook was facing him across a double-barreled shotgun. "Drop it or I'll cut you in two!"

Reb Farrell's gun was level and he did not hesitate. "You fire," he said, "and I'll kill you. You'll get me, but I'll take you with me. Now go ahead and shoot, because I'll not miss at this range!"

"Go ahead!" Ike shouted. "Shoot, you greasy fool!"

The cook stared, gulped, and his eyes shifted. He didn't like the situation even a little. That Reb would not surrender in the face of the scattergun was something of which he had never dreamed. Now it was quite obvious that while he would kill Reb, the bullet from the pistol would unquestionably kill him. And he was not ready to die. Moreover, Reb Farrell's very heedlessness in attacking four men when alone was enough to prove that he just didn't care. The cook hesitated.

"Shoot," Reb said, "or drop it! I'm tired of waiting."

The cook's eyes wavered to the man on the ground. "Yeah"—he sneered—"a lot you care what happens to me." His eyes swung back to Reb and the six-gun was unwavering. "Never was much of a poker player. I reckon you got me. I'd rather be alive an' in jail than dead on the ground." He bent over and placed the shotgun carefully on the ground and took a step back. "Hope you'll recall that when the trial comes."

Quickly, Reb gathered up the loose weapons, including the rifle he had given his father, found inside the cabin. He tied the hands of Ike and the cook, then bandaged Banta's wounds. The redhead was dead.

It was noon on the following day when Reb Farrell rode down the street of Palo Seco. Doors began to open and people stepped out to look at the procession. Joe Banta, the cook, and Ike Goodrich followed by the horse carrying the body of Red, and behind them all, his rifle across his saddle, was Reb Farrell.

Nathan Embree stepped from the saloon and stopped. Laura was standing at the door of the post office, her face suddenly white.

"Embree." Reb's voice rang loud in the street. "Here's your rustlers. You'll find your cattle in Dark Canyon. This here, in case you don't know him, is Joe Banta. They carried my dad's body out here as a warning, but when we shot they dropped the body an' ran."

Embree's face was red. "I guess I owe you an apology," he said stiffly, "but you'll admit that I had reasons. . . ."

Reb Farrell looked at him. "Reason to doubt a man who had worked hard for you, for years? Reason to suspect an old man who had harmed nobody? Embree, I'm ridin' out of this country, but I'll be back for the trial. *And* the hanging." He shot a cool look at Banta. "Nathan, I hope this teaches you a lesson. Next time don't be so quick to judge."

Laura stood beside her father, her face white, her teeth touching her lip. Suddenly Reb felt sorry for her.

"Reb!" She put up a hand as if to hold him back.

He drew up. "I'm not blamin' you, nor anybody. I figure you never knew me real well or you'd not have been so quick to doubt. Next time I'll think twice before I figure someone's my gal."

Reb moved on; Dave Barbot was standing on the walk. "Dave, you were the only one who gave me a kind word. Understand you're in the market for some cows? Well, between Dad an' me we had maybe four hundred head."

"I'd say a few more," Dave said. "You aim to sell?"

"To you, and the price is one thousand dollars and the care of my dad's grave so long as you live."

"A thousand, Reb?" Barbot was incredulous. "They're worth twice that!"

"That's my price. How about it?"

"Sure," Dave said, "I'd be a fool to pass it up."

Reb told him about the horses in the corral at the lone cabin. "Pick 'em up, Dave. They are yours."

"We'll trade, Reb. Down in the livery-barn corral there's a horse you'll know. My 'paloose stallion. You always fancied that horse. Well, he's yours. Throw your saddle over him an' take this one for a packhorse. This deal you're giving me isn't fair to you, so let me throw this in."

"All right, then. Have the money when I come back from the jail."

On his way back down the street, Reb saw an old man standing on the edge of the porch, leaning against the awning post. It was Lon Melchor.

"Well, all right. I ain't so strong right now, son, but I

aim to be. I'd have to ride a mite easy the first few days, because this side pains me some, but if you'll have me, I'll trail along."

He waved a hand at the town. "Folks here don't cotton to me and I want to see some new country."

Reb Farrell's heart warmed to the old rustler. "Get up in your saddle, Lon. We're headin' up to Denver to see us some of these electric lights and telephones and such."

The old man crawled painfully into the saddle and faced around. His face was strained, but his lips smiled and there was even humor in his eyes. "Let's go! Denver it is!"

The sun was high and the mountains in the distance were a far purple. The air was fresh and there was the 'paloose stepping out, tugging the bit.

STRAWHOUSE TRAIL

He looked through his field glasses into the eyes of a dying man.

A trembling hand lifted, the fingers stirred, and the dying lips attempted to form words, trying desperately to tell him something across the void, to deliver a final message.

Chick Bowdrie stared, struggling to interpret the words, but even as he stared he saw the lips cease their movements and the man was no longer alive.

Lowering his glasses, Chick studied the wide sweep of the country. Without the glasses he could see only the standing horse that had first attracted his attention. The canyon between them was deep, but the dead man lay not more than one hundred yards away.

Mounting his hammer-headed roan, Chick Bowdrie swung to the trail again and started down the steep path into the canyon. By this route the man must have come. Had he been dying then? Or had he been shot as he reached the other side? There had been a dark blotch on the man's side that must be blood.

Twenty minutes later he stood beside the dead man. No tracks but the man's own. Falling from his horse, the fellow had tried to rise, had finally made it, struggled a few steps, and then fallen, to rise no more.

Chick knelt beside the dead man. About fifty-five, one hundred and thirty pounds, and very light-skinned for a Western man, which he obviously was. He had been shot low down on the left side.

No . . . that was where the bullet had come *out*. The bullet had entered in the man's back near the spine.

Nothing in the pockets, no letters, no identification of any kind . . . and only a little money.

The jeans and shirt were new. The boots also. Only the gun belts, holster, and gun were worn. They showed much use, and much knowing care. The trigger was tied back . . . the man had been a slip-shot.

The dead man's hands were white and smooth. Not the hands of a cowhand, yet neither was the man a gambler. Getting to his feet, Chick walked to the horse. A steel-dust and a fine animal, selected by a man who knew horseflesh. The saddle was of the "center-fire" California style, of hand-worked leather and with some fine leather work on the tapaderos. The rope was an easy eighty feet long, and new.

No food, which indicated the man expected to reach his goal before night. He had been shot not more than two hours before dusk, which implied his destination could not be far off. Surely not more than fifteen miles or so.

A new Winchester rifle with a hundred rounds of ammunition. An equal amount for a pistol, and then, curiously enough, a box of .32-caliber pistol ammunition. Returning it all to the saddlebags and a pack under the slicker, Bowdrie slung the body over the dead man's saddle, then mounted his own horse.

Four miles from where the body had been found, the tracks of a shod horse turned into the trail. Chick swung down and studied them. The shoes were not new and were curiously worn on the outside. Stepping back into the leather, Chick rode on.

Valverde came to life when Chick rode down the street. A man got up from a chair in front of the livery stable, another put down his hammer in the blacksmith shop. A girl came from the general store. As one person, they began to move toward the front of the Border Saloon, where Chick Bowdrie had stopped.

"Deputy sheriff here? Or marshal?"

A bulky man with a star came from the saloon. "I'm Houdon, I'm the marshal."

"Found him on the trail." Bowdrie explained as the marshal examined the body, yet as he talked Chick's eyes strayed to the faces of the crowd. They revealed nothing. Behind him, there was a click of heels on the boardwalk, a faint perfume, then a gentle breathing at his shoulder.

The girl who had come from the store looked past him at the body. There was a quick intake of breath and she turned at once and walked away. Because she had seen a body? Or because she knew the man?

After answering questions, Bowdrie walked into the saloon. The bartender shoved the bottle to him and commented, "Eastern man?"

"California," Bowdrie replied. "Notice his rig?"

The bartender shrugged, making no reply. Chick downed his drink, filled his glass again, and waited, listening to the discussion in the bar.

There was, he learned, no trouble in the vicinity, and jobs were scarce. Occasionally he helped the conversation along with a comment or a question. Most local cowhands worked years for the same outfit, and most of them were

Mexicans. The Bar W had let two hands go, but that was an exception. The Bar W was in old Robber's Roost country, over against the Chisos Mountains.

"That trail I was followin'," he commented idly, "wasn't used much."

"It's the old Strawhouse Trail. Smugglers used it, a long time back. Only the old-timers know it."

But the dead man had been riding it. Was he an old-timer returning? Chick threw down his cigarette and crossed to the restaurant.

Pedro opened one eye and looked at Bowdrie. A fat, jolly Mexican woman came from the kitchen. She jerked her head at the man. "He is the sleepy one! Good for nothing!"

Pedro opened the eye again. "Juana have nice restaurant, six leetle ones. Good for nothing! Hah! What can we get you, señor?"

"How about *arroz con pollo*?"

Chick Bowdrie dropped to a bench beside the table, considering the situation. A man had bought an outfit, then loaded for bear, he had come to the border, a man who knew the old trails and who probably had been here long before. From his age, however, the sort of man who would not lightly return to the saddle.

He was eating when the girl came in and stopped near his table. She hesitated, then abruptly, she sat down. She put her hands on the table before her and he glanced at them, carefully kept hands, yet Western hands.

"That man . . . did he say anything? I mean, was he still living when you found him?" She was very lovely, tall, with blond hair bleached by the sunlight.

"He was alive when I first saw him through my field glasses, but by the time I had crossed the canyon, he was dead." He tasted his coffee. It was cowpuncher coffee, black and strong. "Did you know him?"

"No." The suit she wore was not new. Excellent material and beautifully tailored, but growing shabby now. "I . . . I thought he might be coming to see me. I'm Rose Murray."

The RM. He knew the ranch; from what he had heard earlier, he had ridden over part of it on his way into town. He waited for her to continue, and after a minute she said, "I'd never seen him. He . . . he knew where something was, something that belongs to my family. He was coming to get it for us."

Gradually, she told him the story. Her ranch had steadily lost money after the death of her father. Rustlers, drought, and the usual cattle losses had depleted her stock. With only a few hands left and badly in debt, a letter came from out of nowhere.

Long ago an outlaw band had roamed the area and they had raided the hacienda, stealing several sacks of gold coins, a dozen gold candlesticks, a gold altar service from the chapel, and a set of heavy table silver by a master craftsman. Owing to the weight of the treasure and the close pursuit, the thieves had been compelled to bury the loot. Taking only what gold coins they could safely carry, they had scattered.

Two of the six had been slain in a gun battle with the posse and another had been shot down on a dark El Paso street a few weeks later. The writer of the letter, who had not given his name, had gone west. He had fallen in love, married, and gone straight.

Hearing of the collapse of the once great fortune and the dire straits of the girl, his conscience troubled him. His own wife had died and he was once more alone. Some word had come to him from Texas that worried him, so he had written the girl that he was coming to her.

"He mentioned no children?"

"There was a son."

When Rose had gone, Chick crossed to the stable for his horse. The hostler walked back with him. "Ain't you that Castroville Ranger? Name of Bowdrie?"

Bowdrie nodded, waiting.

The old man nodded widely. "Figured so. Gent comes in askin' who your hoss belonged to. Seemed mighty interested. I told him I didn't know."

"What did this fellow look like?"

"Oldish feller, shabby kind of. Thin hair, gray eyes. No color to him but his guns. They seen plenty of use."

The hostler pointed out the inquirer's horse. Chick looked it over thoughtfully. Dusty and tired. He put a hand on the horse. "So, boy," he said gently, "so . . ." The horse was too tired to resent his hand as he picked up the hoof. Holding it an instant to let the horse get used to it, he turned it up and examined the shoe. It was badly worn on the outside. So were the others.

Bowdrie straightened. "Thanks. Do you a favor some time."

At daylight he was out of town and riding for the border. Crossing the river, he pulled up at the house of an old Mexican he knew in Boquillas.

Miguel watched Bowdrie as he came up the walk from the gate where he had tied his horse. He started to rise, but Chick put a hand on his shoulder. "Don't get up, my friend. I have come to talk to the one who remembers all."

"You flatter an old man, señor. What is it you wish to know?"

When he explained the old man nodded. "Sí, I have not forgotten, but it was long ago." He leaned forward. "It was the Chilton gang, amigo. There were six, I was among those who fought the two who were killed. Before one died he told us one of the others was Bill Radcliff."

"The Chilton gang . . ."

Bowdrie remembered them from the files of the Rangers. Dan Chilton, Bill Radcliff, and Andy Short had been the core of the group. Robbing payrolls had been their game, at ranches, mines, and the railroad. "One was killed in El Paso," he said.

"Radcliff." Miguel lighted a fresh cigarette. "The killer was never known. Some thought John Selman. He was marshal then. I do not think so."

"Chilton?"

Miguel shrugged. "Who knows? He was the best of them. Wild, but a good man. My brother knew him. Short was the worst. A killer."

They talked into the hot afternoon about the border and bad men and Indians and wars. It was only with great reluctance that Bowdrie got up to leave.

"Vaya con Dios."

"Adios, amigo. Till next time . . ."

Bowdrie rode toward Glen Springs Draw. He thought again of Andy Short . . . it could have been the name the dead man had been saying, shaping the name with his lips as he died.

Sunlight flashed on a distant hillside, and instantly Chick Bowdrie reined the roan over and slapped spurs to his ribs. The horse jumped just as the bullet whiffed past Bowdrie's head, but the roan was startled and the second bullet missed by yards. Only the sunlight on a rifle barrel had saved his life.

The shot had come from the slopes of Talley Mountain, and Chick kept the roan running, dodging from arroyo to arroyo and swinging back toward the mountain whence the bullet had come. Suddenly he eased to a canter, then a walk.

Dust in his nostrils, a settling of dust in the road, and the tracks of a horse . . . with shoes worn on the outside!

Making no attempt to follow, he turned his horse into the trail that led to the Bar W and the RM. Both outfits had headquarters beyond the ridge, and the trail swung suddenly left into a narrow cut. Hesitating only briefly, Bowdrie started into the opening. The sheer walls offered no place for a sniper, and the low rocks within the cut gave no shelter. He rode slowly, however, his six-gun in hand, and suddenly drew up, aware of a clicking. The sound stopped, and he started on. It began again. Suddenly he smiled ruefully. His horse's hooves were scraping against the eroded stones that lined the base of each wall. . . .

Shortly before sundown he walked the roan into the yard of the Bar W. The old adobe house, the pole corrals, the sagging roof of the barn gave no evidence of life. Then a rusty hinge creaked and Bowdrie saw a man step from the barn.

He saw Bowdrie in the same instant, and for a moment he hesitated, as if half-inclined to drop the bucket he was carrying and grab for a gun.

Unshaven, big and rough, his shirt was dirty and he had a narrow-eyed look like a surly hound.

There were, Bowdrie noted, six mules in the corral, and several fine horses . . . he took out the makings. "Howdy"—his voice matter-of-fact—"takin' on any hands?"

"No." He jerked his head. "Go try the RM."

Bowdrie continued working with his smoke, taking his time. "Old place," he commented, "could stand some work. Figured there might be a job."

"You figured wrong."

"Don't rush me, amigo. I'm interested in old places. Why, I'd bet this one was here in the days o' the Chilton gang."

The name brought no reaction. "Never heard of 'em."

"Some years back. Nobody ever did find all that loot."

The big man was interested now. He walked toward Chick. "What loot?"

It was possible, Bowdrie decided, to drop a pebble in this pool and see what happened to the widening ripples. It might cause dissension in the ranks of the enemy. Or create a diversion. "A quarter of a million in gold and jewels," he said carefully. "It was cached. Somebody right close about knows where it is."

"You don't say!" The man was interested now. "So, what's the yarn?"

Bowdrie explained, then added, "Ticklish business, huntin' for it. Two of the outlaws must be still alive."

The man was greedy and interested, but obviously a hired hand who knew nothing. Chick reined his horse around. "Your boss prob'ly knows the story. Oldish man, isn't he?"

"Not more'n twenty-six or seven." The big man grinned maliciously. "An' pure D poison with a six-gun. You maybe heard of Rad Yates."

Bowdrie had . . . no definite record. Bought and sold cattle, gambled a good bit, usually consorting with outlaws and men along the fringe. He had killed, according to report, nine men. All had been in what were apparently fair fights.

Yates was not old enough to have been one of the Chilton gang, but the Strawhouse Trail pointed right at the Bar W . . . or the RM. Scowling, Bowdrie considered that as he headed off, down the trail.

Somebody had attempted to dry-gulch him, and that

somebody rode a horse with worn shoes, as had the killer of the man in Venado Canyon. That somebody had come from this direction.

Tracks in the dust stopped him. Again the worn shoes . . . and the tracks were fresh!

He skirted wide around a clump of mesquite, then spotted the rider ahead of him, just disappearing down a slight declivity. Swinging wide again, he took the roan at a run toward the wash. Sliding into it, he put the horse up the far side along a trail cattle had taken. Dust hung in the air, and it followed the rider he was seeking. He swung around and drew up at the trailside. There were no tracks . . . and then he heard the hoofbeats of a cantering horse.

The rider rounded a low knoll, and Bowdrie stepped his horse forward, gun in hand. "All right. Get your hands up!"

He stared into the astonished eyes of Rose Murray.

His astonishment matched hers, but he was quick to note the rifle in her scabbard. After all, what did he know about her? She had been curious about the dead man, and a woman can squeeze off a shot as well as a man. He lowered his gun.

"Can I lower my hands?" Bowdrie nodded. "Who did you expect to see?"

"Not you . . ." He hesitated only briefly. "Riding home?"

As they rode he explained about the mysterious rifle shots and his visit to the Bar W.

"Rad Yates seems very nice," Rose said. "He's called at the ranch."

They rode into the yard and swung down. Bowdrie caught a vague movement up the mountainside. There was a man there, his clothing blending perfectly with the background. Only his movement had betrayed him. Rose had just stepped inside, so he followed, getting a corner of the barn between the hill and the door as he reached it.

A Mexican woman brought coffee, and after a few minutes Bowdrie asked, casually, "Had that horse long? The one you were riding?"

"He was born from one of my mares. Nobody has ever ridden him but me."

There had been her chance and she had passed it up. She seemed to have no suspicion of his reason for asking the question. In fact, she was not suspicious as a guilty person should be.

A drum of hooves and a hail. The Mexican woman answered the door and a moment later a big young man walked in. He had brown hair and a bold, handsome face. He walked with a casual swagger and his guns were tied down.

This would be Rad Yates. He was not the man on the hill; his clothing was bright and colorful. He grinned when he saw Bowdrie. "Heard you were out at the place," he said. He turned and spoke to Rose, and Chick moved where he could see Yates's horse. It was a flashy paint.

Rose came over to him, followed by Yates. "We're going towards Rad's place to start a tally on the cattle in those canyons," she said. "I'm sorry I can't stay to entertain you. Would you like to come along with us?"

Chick Bowdrie looked thoughtfully from one to the other. His dark eyes showed one of their rare flashes of amusement. The pieces were beginning to fall into place now. "Maybe," he said. Then he shifted to the attack. "Sure he's got himself in place yet, Yates?"

Rad Yates tightened and his head lowered a little. His smile remained, but became set and hard. "What're you talkin' about?"

"That gent up on the mountain with the rifle."

Yates was caught flat-footed. "What gent? I don't know what you're talking about."

Bowdrie's hands were on his hips, only inches from his guns. "Your first name is Radcliff, isn't it? Maybe the son of Bill Radcliff? Or his nephew?"

"And if it is?"

"Well, it's an interesting point, Yates. But even more interesting if you and the gent up the hill get what you're lookin' for. Then what happens? You shoot it out?"

Rose was looking from one to the other, frankly puzzled. "What are you two talking about?"

Bowdrie smiled. "Why, Rose, we're talkin' about the loot from this ranch stolen and buried by the Chilton gang. Andy Short was one of them and Bill Radcliff another. Unless I miss my guess, that's Andy up there on the mountain right now, waitin' for me with a rifle."

Yates had recovered himself. "Rose, I reckon these Rangers are suspicious of ever'body. We'd better forget the ride. All right if I come over tomorrow?"

"Of course, Rad." Her voice chilled. "But I expect that Mr. Bowdrie will be leaving now."

She turned on him when they were alone. "You've no right to accuse on so little evidence. Rad is one of my best friends."

"Yes, ma'am," Bowdrie said. "But I would bear in mind that a man's been murdered for coming to help you. You should be careful."

Rad Yates was frankly stumped. When they learned a Ranger had come upon the body of the dead man, they were worried. For the first time an unforeseen element had intruded upon what seemed a perfect plan.

Almost a year before, Andy Short, only recently released from prison, had come upon Yates in an El Paso saloon. A casual word had told Yates who Short was, and he was disappointed to discover that Short did not know the whereabouts of the loot. Only Dan Chilton actually knew . . . and nobody knew where Dan Chilton was.

Yet Andy Short had an idea. Using Yates's place as a base, he had searched the hills to no avail. He could not locate the hidden loot. But on a casual visit to the RM, Rad Yates had seen the letter from the mysterious man in California and had gone at once to Short.

Short, a slender man, gray of face and cold of eye, had been immediately excited. "Chilton!" He slammed his fist on the table. "He's comin' to give that loot back! He was always a namby-pamby!"

Chilton had had a map. Short took it from the body after the shooting, mounted his horse, and rode off. From the side of a distant hill he glanced back and suddenly he was frightened.

Dan Chilton's body was gone!

Swinging back, he had seen the bloodstains and the tracks of a staggering man. Somehow, Chilton was still alive, and he had gotten into the saddle again.

Short had gone after him, but Chilton had disappeared. When he saw him again it was in the streets of Valverde and Chick Bowdrie was explaining to Houdon.

Had Chilton lived to talk?

Carefully, they remained away from the location of the loot, waiting to let the Ranger move first. He would show his hand if he knew anything. If he came after the loot, they could kill him. They watched and waited, and then, on Bowdrie's return from Mexico, they had tried and failed.

Now he was here. And he had known, somehow, about Andy Short being on the mountain.

The plan had been simple enough. Yates would get him out on the mountainside, Short would do the shooting, then Rad would make a show of chasing the killer. He'd impress Rose and then he and Andy Short would go dig up the loot. But the Ranger was onto them, somehow, and he had posed a disturbing question. What would happen when they got the money? Was he ready to kill to get it all? Was he ready to kill simply to keep his part of it?

When Chick Bowdrie had scouted the area to be sure he was not to be the target of a hidden marksman, he rode away and took back trails for town. His warnings to Rose Murray had gone unheeded. That she liked Rad Yates was obvious, that she did not appreciate Bowdrie's seemingly unfounded suggestions was equally obvious.

The existence of at least two sets of shoes worn in an identical manner damaged what little case he had and left him without evidence. For a supposedly abandoned route, the section of the Strawhouse Trail through the sandstone bottoms got more use than he would have expected. The horse Rose Murray had ridden was not the horse he had seen in town. Neither was the horse ridden by Yates.

Valverde was somber with darkness when he dismounted at the stable. The hostler took his horse. "I'll give him a bait of oats," he offered. Pausing, he added, "Stranger in town. Tall young feller. Askin' about the dead man."

Over a late supper, Chick pondered his problems. He had stumbled upon the body of a murdered man, yet he was no further along than in the beginning. Andy Short could be the killer. If he was actually around. On the other hand, so could Rad Yates. And Rose? That was still an open question. There might be more to this than appeared on the surface.

A quicker solution might be reached if he found the loot. The outlaws had been hotly pursued. Implying little time to conceal the treasure. No time to dig a deep hole. If it had not been recovered by the surviving members of the gang—and he was positive it had not—then that implied a place not too easy of access or too easy to guess.

The outlaws' line of flight had been from the hacienda through the Chisos Mountains, but by the time they reached Rough Run the loot had already been cached. That left many miles of country to be searched. Yet, there could not be too many possible hideaways on that route.

The door opened and he looked up. A tall young man had entered the room. He was blond and deeply tanned. "You're Mr. Bowdrie?"

"And you'll be Dan Chilton's son."

The blond young man was surprised. "Why, yes. As a matter of fact, that's my name, too. I didn't expect you to know me."

Chick Bowdrie was thinking swiftly. Chilton was an attractive young man, and more attractive, if he was any judge, than Rad Yates. He grinned suddenly. "Look," he said, "your father was trying to do a good deed out here, that's what got him killed. . . ." Bowdrie carefully explained to the young man what he knew and what he suspected. He ended by asking for young Dan Chilton's help. "Rad Yates is involved somehow, and he's currying favor with Rose Murray. You go down there, and no matter what happens, stick close to her. I don't know what his scheme is, but you'll be in his way."

Chilton nodded. "And what excuse will I give? The son of the man who robbed her family?"

"Just that. You want to atone for what your father did. He was returning to help her; you want to carry on. She'll listen."

He hesitated, trying his coffee. "Can you use a gun?"

"I have one. A thirty-two Smith & Wesson."

That explained the ammunition. Bowdrie nodded. "It's small, but it will have to do. Don't use it unless you have to." He explained about Yates, who and what he was. Chilton nodded, offering no comment.

In their conversation Chilton had been able to tell him very little, but Bowdrie sat alone over his coffee in the now silent town and pieced that little together with what he knew.

The searchers, old Dan had told his son, had all looked in the Chisos Mountains, and that was the wrong place. This narrowed the distance by more than half. The old trail led from Oak Spring at the foot of the mountains to the Rock Hut at the base of Burro Mesa. I'll lay two to one it wasn't cached far from that Rock Hut, he told himself.

One thing he decided. If, as he believed, the presence of Chilton at the RM would keep Rad Yates around Rose's ranch, it would leave him free to hunt down Andy Short. For he no longer had any idea of waiting to be shot at. Now he was going to hunt the hunter.

Finishing his coffee, he got up and walked to the door. Pedro and his spouse had long since retired, so he merely blew out the light and turned the knob. For several minutes he waited, listening to the night sounds in the empty street of Valverde.

A sign creaked rustily in the vague wind. A paper brushed along the street. All was still.

Suddenly a horseman appeared at the end of the street and started forward, coming along toward the saloon. Bowdrie stepped through the door and eased it shut behind him. Then he shifted away from the door and stood flat against the building.

The rider reached the marshal's office near the saloon and drew up. His saddle creaked as he swung down. Chick strained his eyes in the dim light and could see only that this was a big man, vaguely familiar.

Taking a careful look around, the man eased his gun in his holster and moved forward, and suddenly Chick knew him. It was the big cowhand from the Bar W!

Frowning, Chick waited. This . . . it simply did not fit. Unless the man had discovered something.

Opposite the door of the marshal's office, the big man paused. The man was in the darker shadow now, away from the gray of the street, and Chick only knew he was there, he could see nothing.

A flicker of movement drew Bowdrie's eyes and suddenly he realized there was another person—man or woman—in the space between the saloon and the office. Chick Bowdrie, suddenly comprehending, stepped out of the shadow and started forward.

Even as he moved he saw the big man, warned by some vague sound, grab frantically for his gun. Another gun boomed heavily between the buildings and the big man staggered, then fell back off the boardwalk. He tried to get up, and a shot nailed him to the spot. Chick tried a fast shot at the darkness whence the gun flashes had come, and a return shot whipped past his face.

Running, he dashed forward, hearing a door slam open and a shouted question. He reached the alleyway and plunged recklessly into it. At the far end of the dark alley a horse and rider lunged suddenly, running away behind the buildings. When Chick reached the spot, the rider was gone . . . out of sight. Only a drum of running hooves fading in the night.

Breathing hard, he walked back. It was utterly impossible, yet the gunman had somehow outdistanced him. He turned again, looking down the long alley.

Rad Yates?

It simply could not have been Andy Short. No man of the age he had to be could sprint sixty feet while Chick Bowdrie was covering less than thirty. And yet the man was gone.

Several men were gathered around the body and one had lighted a match to examine him. Pedro came from the back door of the restaurant, stuffing his shirt into too tight jeans. Closer by, Houdon came from his office, buckling his belt.

Without doubt the big cowhand had learned something, and he had come to town with it. Someone had followed him, not wanting him alive to repeat what he knew.

Easing away from the circle of talkers around the body, Chick walked back through the alley to where he had seen the horse. Distance was hard to estimate, and the horse might have been right behind the saloon. Yet when he reached the spot, two struck matches revealed nothing.

Not far away was a huge cottonwood, and near it, several smaller trees. It was the logical place. Here Chick found more hoof tracks than he had expected. He also found five cigarette butts. Here a man had waited, at least an hour . . . for what?

This man was here *before* the big cowhand arrived in town. He must have been here most of the time Chick was in the restaurant. Could he have followed him there? But that did not make sense, because from under the trees the watcher could not have seen the café.

What, then, had he waited for? And the tracks were those of a horse with shoes worn on the outside.

Houdon was waiting for him when he walked back to

the street. The body of the man had been moved. The marshal jerked his head toward the street. "What did Jake want at this time of night?"

Houdon was unshaven and he looked tired and irritable. He stared at Chick and absently scratched his stomach. Briefly, Bowdrie outlined the situation, identifying himself to the marshal for the first time. Nothing seemed to arouse the marshal until Bowdrie mentioned the man who had lurked under the cottonwoods.

"Somebody else," he said, nodding his big head ponderously. "After me, I betcha. Man makes enemies in this here job." He looked shrewdly at Bowdrie. "Folks sometimes don't take kindly to the law."

"I think," Chick suggested, "it was Andy Short."

The scratching fingers paused momentarily. Other than this there was no reaction. Houdon shrugged. "Ain't from around here, I reckon. You see him, you let me know."

At daylight Bowdrie was getting a quick cup of coffee and some breakfast at Pedro's. The fat Mexican leaned his big elbows on the oilcloth-covered table. "You savvy Burro Mesa?" he asked suddenly.

Startled, Bowdrie looked up. Pedro glanced around, yawned widely, and put a stubby finger on a spot on the oilcloth. "Here," he said, "is the Rock Hut. And here is the trail across the mesa. On the west side is another spring. My compadre, he ride in last night. He say a man camps in the brush near that spring."

It was high noon when Bowdrie rode the hammer-headed roan into the scrub near Oak Spring. Burro Mesa loomed on the skyline only a short distance ahead. The morning ride had been a long one and both horse and man were tired.

Well back in the brush, Bowdrie made a fire of dry sticks that gave off no smoke, and prepared a meal of coffee, bacon, and sourdough flapjacks. He stretched out after eating and lighted a smoke. Above him a pin oak was shelter from the blazing sun.

Half-asleep and completely relaxed, some half hour later, he heard a horse approaching. Instantly he was alert. His hand touched the roan and the horse relaxed slowly. He waited, listening. The horse was coming through the pass from the Chisos.

It slowed . . . a saddle creaked . . . with a warning signal to the roan, Chick eased himself forward on cat feet.

The horse was drinking at the spring, and as he watched, the rider got up from the ground. It was Rose Murray. She wiped the water from her mouth and looked carefully around.

What was *she* doing here? And where were Yates and Chilton?

He watched her step into the leather and turn west, then mounted his own horse. Was she involved in the plotting? Or had she come upon some clue?

Holding a course that kept him inside the brush, he worked his way along the mountainside in the direction Rose had chosen. Suddenly he drew up.

A horse with shoes badly worn on the outside had come off the mesa from the west. A blade of grass in one of the hoofprints was just springing into place. This could be the mysterious camper in the brush of whom Pedro had told him.

Chick Bowdrie followed on, but slowly. He had good reason to know the skill and trickiness of Andy Short. The quiet, gray-faced man in the nondescript clothes, described to him by the hostler, but whom he had never seen. That the man was a gunman, Bowdrie knew from the Rangers' Bible—his agency's file of outlaws.

At the edge of the pin oaks he drew up, scanned the empty country before him, then moved ahead, alert for trouble. His eyes roved, and suddenly held.

The Rock Hut.

And two horses standing near a mesquite tree. One was the horse Rose had ridden. The other was the horse he had seen once before, the horse of the mysterious rider.

He waited, studying the lay of the land. There was a door, obviously, from the path, leading from the front of the building toward where the horses stood. There was no window on this side, but there was a window behind. A small window.

Swinging down, he moved carefully, closing in. From the window came half-heard voices.

"So, you trailed young Radcliff. What a joke! He's back at your place taking care of Chilton's greenhorn son."

The girl spoke, too softly.

"You just sit there, Missy. We'll figure out . . ." The man's voice dissolved into a murmur.

Chick started to move closer, then he dropped to his haunches behind a boulder and some brush. A hard-ridden horse was coming down the trail. It was Rad Yates.

Chick moved away then stepped out from the brush as Yates slid his horse to a stop. His face was a study in cold fury. Bowdrie knew how tricky the situation was. "Rad." He spoke quietly, striving to keep his voice casual and calm on the other man. "Whatever you're figurin' on, don't do it." Yates's head snapped around.

Before Rad could speak, he continued, "Think now! You're clean. Nobody has anything on you. We have plenty on Short. Why butt into something where you're not wanted? Turn around and ride out of here a free man. Stay, and you become an outlaw."

The view was so eminently reasonable that Rad Yates hesitated. What Bowdrie said was true. He was still on the right side of the law. If he went ahead, there would be no return trail.

But the lure of the gold was strong. "No." He spoke slowly. "I've come too far—waited too long." He swung to the ground. As he turned he drew.

Whatever he planned failed to materialize. In the instant he swung down, Bowdrie had closed in. As Rad turned, his gun coming up, Bowdrie slapped the gun aside and down and hit him on the chin.

It was a short, wicked blow. Yates tottered and stumbled against his horse, the startled bronc moved, and Yates lost his balance and fell. As he hit ground, Bowdrie kicked the gun from his hand.

Yates came up fast and Bowdrie was too close to chance a draw. But Yates's rising lunge met the battering ram of Bowdrie's rock-hard fist and the bone in Yates's nose crushed under the impact, showering him with blood. The man was game, and shaking his head, he got up. Bowdrie let him rise, taking time for one quick glance toward the Rock Hut. No sign of life there at all.

The idea of Short discovering them frightened him and he stepped in quickly. For all his size, Rad was no fistfighter. He threw a long swing and Bowdrie went inside with a wicked right to the chin that dropped Yates. Grabbing the man's gun and taking his rifle, he threw them, whirling, high over the brush. Then he ran for the Hut.

He was running on soft ground and he heard voices, then stopped. "How come you knowed about this place?"

"I heard you tell Rad you'd meet him here today. Then I realized this *might* be the place."

Chick heard the chink of metal on metal. "You're hard luck, kid, you shouldn't have come here."

Andy Short came through the door, his hands and pant legs dusted with dirt, dragging a sack. His eyes went wide and he swung up the gun he carried in his right hand, and fired. The shot was too quick, a startled response to the unexpected sight of the Ranger. It missed.

Chick Bowdrie palmed his Colt and fired, but Short had dropped low and the bullet took him through the shoulder. It knocked him around and his second shot missed, and then Bowdrie put two fast bullets into him.

Bowdrie stepped back, his dark, Apache-like face grim and lonely. He began to shove out the shells for reloading when from behind him he heard Yates's voice. But it was a warning, not a threat.

"Bowdrie! Look out!"

Chick turned . . . another rider sat his horse, and he held a four-shot Roper revolving shotgun in his hands. It was Houdon, the marshal.

Bowdrie could see Yates, blood still streaming from his nose, and Yates had another cut now—on his skull. But he was not out.

Houdon's face was grizzled and old, his jowls heavy, his small eyes no longer looked dopey or sullen. Now they held amusement, and cunning.

"Killed Andy, did you? Can't say I'm sorry. Andy there could be right slick with a gun."

Bowdrie watched the man carefully. Slowly, things began to fit together.

"You're the sixth man," he said suddenly. "You're the last survivor of the Chilton gang."

Houdon did not change expression for a moment, then he chuckled. It was a slow, fat, easy chuckle. "Yep, an' I'm the one killed Dan. It wasn't Andy, like you prob'ly figured. I took Andy's horse from the livery, knowin' a body could track them shoes. I think that might've turned him against me, what d'you think?"

"You were all trying to find the treasure?"

"We were gonna be partners. But now . . . well, the deal's off. Knowed I had to move quick when you told me Andy had been layin' for me back o' the saloon.

"I killed that cowpoke, too. Heard he was huntin' around up here."

Bowdrie was thinking. He held his six-shooter and it was still partly loaded. Did Houdon know that? Or did he think because he had pushed out two shells that the gun was empty? But where were the loads? For the life of him, he could not recall. There should be one empty under the hammer, but was it there, or just above the loading gate?

"How'd you get away? I ran right into that alley," he asked.

Houdon chuckled. "The office is raised up, maybe two feet off the ground. I went under it, up into the trapdoor. I made that so's I could sweep right out and not have to use no dustpan. Pays to be a lazy bachelor, sometimes."

He nodded at the gold. "Old Dan never guessed when we made that strike at the RM that I'd wind up with it all. He sure didn't."

This was the last of the outlaws—what had his name been? Hopper? He had murdered Chilton in cold blood. Had killed two in gunfights, but he was a sure-thing killer, the kind who never gave anyone a break.

Chick Bowdrie smiled suddenly. He was a Ranger and this was his job. He felt the skin drawing tight over his wide cheekbones. He lifted his left hand and moved his hat back on his head. "You know, Hop, I think—" He threw himself in a wild lunge, low down and straight at the horse!

The startled bronc gave a leap, snorting. The shotgun blasted and dust kicked into Chick's face. Then he came up to his knees as Houdon fought the frightened horse and swung up his gun.

Houdon saw it coming, and left the saddle in a leap of agility surprising in a man of his years. He hit the ground in a crouch and triggered the shotgun, but the muzzle was high and the charge of shot blasted by, high and to the right.

Bowdrie's gun clicked on an empty chamber, then fired, then he threw himself into a roll, came up, and fired again.

Houdon took the shot right along the top of the shotgun. Smashing into his chest. He tried to come up, gasping, and Bowdrie shot into him again.

He fell, staring for one awful instant into Bowdrie's face, and then lay stretched out, choking horribly, his fingers working.

Chick Bowdrie turned away and walked to Rose. She stood in the Rock Hut door, her face in her hands.

He looked over his shoulder at Rad Yates. "Can you ride?"

Yates got slowly to his feet. His nose was smashed, and the cut on his head still bled.

"I can ride."

"Then get on your horse and get out of here. Don't stop until you're somewhere else."

Rad Yates wiped blood from his face. He started for his horse, then halted. "That Chilton kid . . . you'll find him in the smokehouse with a headache. He wasn't man enough for the job."

"Beat it," Bowdrie said.

Rad Yates walked his horse away, and after a minute Chick told Rose, "Get your horse. I'll load up the gold, then follow."

"There's blood on it," she said, dazed.

"Yeah"—Bowdrie's voice was dry—"but it'll buy cows."

THE MAN FROM THE DEAD HILLS

The sagebrush flats shimmered in the white heat of a
late-summer sun, and a gray powder of dust lay
thick upon the trail. Far away the hills loomed purple against the horizon, but the miles between were endless flats dancing with heat waves.

Leosa Barron stood in the door, shaded her eyes against
the glare, and searched once more, as she had so often of
late, for a figure upon the road. There was nothing. The
road was empty of life, vanishing in the far hills where lay
a little cow town known as Joe Billy.

She looked away. She must not expect him yet. Even if
Tom Andrews received her letter and was able to come, he
could not arrive so quickly.

When her housework was finished, during which time
she resolutely refused to look at the trail, she walked again
to the door. Yet there was nothing but the white dust and
the heat. Then her eyes turned back up the even lonelier
trail to the badlands, the trail to the dead and empty hills
where nothing lived. Her lips parted suddenly, and she

stared, refusing at first to believe what she saw between her back fence and the dark cliffs.

Someone was coming. Someone was coming from the direction of the Dead Hills.

Unable to return to the shaded coolness, she waited in the door watching. She was a slender girl, taller than most, and graceful in her movements. She had a friendly mouth, eyes that smiled easily, and lips that could laugh with her eyes. The few freckles scattered over her nose only added a piquant touch to an already charming face.

Much later she was still standing in the doorway when the solitary figure had shaped itself into a man, a man walking.

His hat was gray and battered, his plain wool shirt had a dark spot on the shoulder and was gray with dust. The man was unshaven, and the eyes under the dark brows flashed with a quick, stabbing glance that made her start with something that was almost fear.

The jeans he wore were roughened by wear, and his boots were run-down at the heel. His belt was wide leather, and curiously handworked. Leosa thought she had never seen a man in whom strength was so apparent, strength and ruthlessness.

Yet he wore no gun.

She had been watching him for two miles when he reached the gate. Now he fumbled with the latch and swung it open. He did not speak, but turned back, closing the gate carefully.

As he faced her she knew she was looking at a man exhausted but not beaten, a man whose lips were cracked with thirst, whose flanks were lean with starvation, but a man in whom there burned an indomitable fire, a fire of whose source she knew nothing, and could sense nothing.

Several times she had seen him stagger upon the road,

and now as he faced her, his feet wide apart, it suddenly occurred to her that she should be frightened. She was alone here, and this man was from the Dead Hills. Her eyes went to that dark spot on the shoulder, a spot that could be only blood. His face was haggard, a gray mask of dust and weariness from which only the eyes stared, hard and clear.

He walked toward her, and his eyes did not leave hers, fastening to them and clinging as though only their clear beauty kept him alive and on his feet. As in a trance, she saw him stop at the well coping and lift the rope. He staggered, almost losing balance, then she heard the bucket slap on the water.

Quickly she was beside him. "Let me do it— You're nearly dead!"

He smiled then, although the movement of his lips started a tiny trickle of blood from the heat cracks. "Not by a durned sight, ma'am."

But he let her help him. Together they drew up the bucket, then he lifted it and drank, the water slopping over his chin and down his shirtfront. After a minute he put the bucket down and stared at her, then around the place. His eyes returned to her. "You alone here?"

She hesitated. "Yes."

He held the bucket in his hands, and waited. She knew how the body yearns for water and more water when one has been long without it, but this man waited. He impressed her then as a man who could do anything with himself, a man who knew his strength and his weaknesses. His eyes glinted at her, then he lifted the bucket, drank a little more, and put it down.

Turning away from her, he picked up the washbasin and sloshed water into it. Stripping off his shirt, he began to bathe his body. Standing behind him, she could see that there was an ugly wound near the top of his shoulder and a dark stain of dried blood below and around it. Hurrying inside, she secured medicine and clean linen and returned to him.

He accepted her ministrations without comment, only watching her with curious eyes as she cleansed the wound and bandaged his shoulder.

As she worked she was wondering about him. Long ago she had taken a ride into that remote desert country around the Dead Hills. Outlaws had lived there before the gangs were wiped out, but nobody else. There were hideouts near some of the water holes, but those water holes were hard to find unless one knew the country.

To a stranger the region was a waterless horror, a nightmare of grotesque stones and gnarled and blasted cacti, a place where only buzzards and an occasional rattler could be seen.

How far had this man come? What had happened to his horse, and where and how had he been shot?

When she had finished with his wound, she stood back from him and looked up into his eyes. He was smiling, and the expression in his eyes startled her, for it was so different from the lightning of that first glance from the gate. His eyes were warm and friendly, even affectionate. Yet he stepped by her and into the coolness of the room beyond. Without a word he lay down on the divan and was at once asleep.

Returning to the door, she looked down the road again. If Tom Andrews were to arrive in time, there was need that it be soon. If she lost possession of the ranch before he arrived, she had been told there was small chance they would ever recover the property.

Then, almost at sundown, she saw them coming. Not Andrews, but Rorick and Wilson, the men she feared.

They came into the yard riding fast, drawing up without dismounting. "Well"—Van Rorick's voice was cool but triumphant—"are you ready to leave? All packed?"

"I'm not leaving."

Leosa Barron stood straight and still. She knew these men, and for all Rorick's pretended interest in her, she knew there was nothing he would not stoop to do if it obtained results. Lute Wilson was just a tool for Van, and a dangerous man to cross. Yet it was Rorick she feared the most, for she knew the depths of malice in the man, and she had once seen him vent his hatred on a trapped wildcat.

"Then you leave us no choice, Leosa," Rorick replied. "We'll have to move you. If we do that, we might have to handle you rather roughly. You've had plenty of time to leave without trouble."

"I told you I was not going." Leosa stood even straighter. "You will leave this ranch at once!"

Rorick's eyes narrowed a little, but he laughed. It was not a pleasant sound. "If you want to come to my place, I could make you comfortable. If you don't come with me, there will be no place in Joe Billy where they will have you."

Leosa knew the truth of this. Van Rorick was known and feared in the cow town, but more than that, she was herself a stranger, and unkind rumors had been set afloat because of her living alone. She had no doubt that those rumors had been originated by Rorick himself. He knew so well the prejudices of a small town.

"I told you I was staying."

Yet there was no chance of winning. Had Tom Andrews made it, she might have stood them off. She could rely on Tom. Alone against them, she was helpless. And where could she go? She had neither money nor friends. Only Andrews, who had failed her.

"All right, Lute. I guess we move her."

Lute was the first to reach the ground. He turned to face the porch, then stopped, his face stupid with shock.

Surprised, Leosa turned, and found the unshaven stranger at her side. He had belted on her uncle's guns.

"You heard the lady. Get goin'! Get out of here!"

There was a low, ugly sound in the man's voice that frightened her and apparently had something of the same effect upon Lute Wilson, for he froze where he stood, uncertain how to move.

"Leosa," Rorick demanded, "who is this man? What is he doing here?"

The stranger stepped down to the ground, his movements swift and catlike. "Shut up," he said, and his voice was not hard, only somehow more deadly for it. "Shut up an' get out!"

"My friend"—Rorick's face was a study in controlled fury—"you don't know what you're buttin' into!"

"I can tell a coyote when I see one," the stranger said coolly.

Wilson reached for him. But the stranger sidestepped and smashed him in the stomach with a lifting uppercut that stood Wilson on his toes. Before Rorick could think to move, the stranger smashed a right and left to Wilson's face, and the rider went down in the dust, his face smeared and bloody.

Rorick reached for his gun, reached . . . then stopped, for he was looking into the muzzle of a pistol in the stranger's hand. "Get off your horse," the stranger said quietly, and when Van Rorick, still amazed by the speed of that draw, had dismounted, the stranger said, "Now turn around, take your friend, and start walkin'. When you're out of sight I'll turn your horses loose."

The two men turned, and with Rorick half supporting

Wilson, they lurched out of the yard. Together, the new-comer and Leosa stood watching them go, and when they were out of gunshot, the stranger stooped and, lifting the bucket, drank for a long time. It was only when he re-placed the bucket that he turned the horses loose, each with a ringing slap on the haunches.

"Those horses will run all the way home, so I figure we've nothin' to bother us for a bit. Meanwhile, you can give me the hang of this so I'll know what's goin' on."

"Your shoulder," she said suddenly. "It's bleeding again!"

"Yeah." He grinned sheepishly. "I reckon I forgot all about it until I began throwing punches. Man, but it hurts!"

"You've had a hard time." She hesitated, wanting to know what had happened to him, but not liking to ask.

Then she hurried about, getting food on the table and making coffee. He sat in a chair near the door and dozed; as she looked at him she marveled at the strength of the man. Nowhere was he bulky, yet his shoulders were com-pact and hard looking under the faded color of his shirt.

"Do you have a home?" she asked suddenly. "Or are you just drifting?"

His eyes opened sleepily, and he shrugged. "Home?" He shook his head. "I've no home. I always"—his eyes showed a strange wistfulness—"always sort of wanted one."

"I see," she said softly, and she did.

"Who was that man?" he asked suddenly. "What's he want?"

She frowned. "Van was born around here, has lived here most of his life but for some six years. He went away and joined the army, and when he came back, he seems to have become a changed man. Or so they tell me. I've been here but a short time. I guess war does change some men," she added.

He shrugged, watching her. "Maybe. It may, like anything, bring out what's in him. I don't know if it would put anything there that wasn't there before."

"Well, when he came back he moved onto a small spread and began expanding his herd. He prospered, with Lute Wilson to help him. He gets along with some people, rides roughshod over the others. He didn't get along with my uncle, who owned this place. About a year ago my uncle was thrown by a bad horse, just after he had invited me to come here to live with him.

"He died a few days later, and it seems he left some debts. Rorick heard of them, and he bought up the notes and got a lien against this place. He offered to pay me two hundred dollars and give me the notes if I would leave, and I would not.

"You see, there's a valley back of the house that is well watered and every year my uncle got two good cuttings of hay off that piece, and a good deal of grazing after the hay was cut. He also has an orchard and a good-sized garden plot. However, that is only a part of it, for there are some five hundred acres that could be developed into good hay land by putting in a dam on Placer Creek."

"No wonder he wants to get you off," he said dryly. "You could get rich with that amount of hay, and this land." He looked up suddenly. "You haven't even asked who I am."

"Well, I thought you'd tell me if you wanted to. We don't ask many questions around here. Especially," she added, "from men who come out of the Dead Hills."

"I know." He said nothing for a minute, staring out the window. "Better call me Rock," he said. "It's a good name around here."

She laughed. "There's plenty of it, certainly!"

The way he looked at her made her wonder if she'd missed something. "You've no friends to help you?" he said.

"There's one man. His name is Tom Andrews, and he used to ride for my uncle, and he knew my father. I've written to him and he's on his way."

Rock nodded, then he said quietly, "You'd better stop waitin' for him." He drew a wallet from his pocket. "Did you ever see this before?"

She took it in her fingers, and her lips trembled. She had seen it, many times. "Where . . . where did you get this?"

"I found him back in the hills. He'd been wounded, and was in mighty bad shape. I tried to help him, and got shot for my pains. They killed both our horses."

"Who was it?" Leosa asked quickly.

"That"—his eyes were suddenly hard—"is what I'd like to know!" He got to his feet. "About that dam now. How much money would it take?"

"Whiting, he's my lawyer, he said it could be done for a couple of thousand dollars for wages if one used native rock and earth. He said a better dam could be built later, if necessary."

"That makes sense. I'll look the spot over." He touched the guns on his hips. "I'll need these. Is it all right?"

"Of course! Do you . . . does that mean you intend to stay?"

He smiled. "If you'd like me to. I think you need me right now, and I've some resting up to do. I want to get the lay of the land around here."

She nodded. "Please stay on. I don't know what I'd have done today without you. See this through with me and I'll give you a share in the place."

"Now, that there's an interesting idea."

"Good!" Leosa said quickly. "Fifty percent. It won't be worth anything if I lose."

"I'll settle for that." His eyes were thoughtful. "This Rorick got any property around other than his spread?"

"Yes, he owns the Longhorn Hotel and Saloon, and I hear he has an interest in another saloon. There are," she added, "nine saloons in Joe Billy. Nine saloons, four stores, one hotel, one church, and a few other businesses, including a livery stable."

She watched him as he walked toward the empty bunkhouse. Her brow furrowed a little. Was she wrong in accepting the help of a total stranger? In taking as a partner a man she had known but a couple of hours? Who did not even volunteer his full name?

On the other hand, had she a choice? He had at least come to her aid in an hour of need. He had brought Andrews's wallet to her and he seemed ready to accept the task Andrews had been unable to attempt.

Leosa opened the wallet thoughtfully. There was money in it, almost a hundred dollars, and a few papers. One of them was a scrawled signature on a piece of torn envelope.

Last Will: All my belongings to Leosa Barron, friend and daughter of a friend.

Tom Andrews

The signature was merely a scrawl, and her eyes filled with tears at the thought of Tom, his last thoughts for her, a girl he had known only as a skinny child with freckles and braids. And from him had come this stranger. With a shock of something that was half excitement and half fear, she remembered the sheer brutality of his attack on Wilson, the flashing speed with which the gun had leaped to his hand. Who was he? What was he?

. . .

In the bunkhouse there was an empty bed with folded blankets, and several with no bedding beyond mattresses. Obviously, this was the bunk awaiting Tom Andrews. Rock sat down and studied the room. It was strongly built, as everything seemed to be on this ranch. No effort had been spared to make it strong or comfortable.

He walked to the door and stared toward town. Joe Billy . . . *his town!*

There would be trouble when they knew, and plenty of it. They did not know him now, yet already he had met Rorick and faced him down. His advantage had been surprise, and next time they would be prepared for him. How soon, he wondered, would they realize who he was and why he had come back? All hell would break loose then and Van Rorick would be the one who led it.

In a way, Leosa's fight was his fight. His thoughts went back to the tall, rather shy girl, who had accepted him so readily. He pulled off his shirt and hunted the cabin for shaving gear. He found an old razor, and after a healthy stropping, he shaved. It was dark when he had finished cleaning up, and he walked outside.

Whiting, that was the name of the lawyer that Leosa had mentioned. He would go to him. He walked outside and roped and saddled a horse, then he mounted and rode to the door. "Ridin' to Joe Billy," he said quietly. "You better stay in an' keep a rifle handy."

She watched him ride away, liking the set of his shoulders and the way he rode. Queerly disturbed, she returned inside, pausing to look into the fire. It was strange, having this man here, yet somehow he did not seem strange, and she felt oddly happy. . . . Security, that was it. What else could it be?

. . .

Rance Whiting had an office over the squat gray bank building. Rock glanced at the tall man who rose to greet him, and instantly liked the man. He had a thin face, high cheekbones, and an aquiline nose. His eyes were gray, and friendly. An open volume of Horace sat on the nearby table.

Rock glanced at the title, then at the lawyer. " 'We are dust and shadow,' " he quoted.

Whiting was surprised, and he measured the rider again. The cold green eyes, the shock of dark curly hair, the bronzed features, blunt and strong, the wool shirt under which muscles bulged. "You know Horace?" he asked.

Rock laughed. "Only that. Read it once, an' liked it. I used to read a good deal. Hombre left a flock of books behind an' I was snowed in for the winter. Mostly Shakespeare an' Plato."

"You were looking for an attorney?"

Rock drew several papers from a homemade buckskin wallet, a large wallet he took from the inside of his shirt. It was bloodstained. Without further comment, he handed it to Whiting.

The lawyer opened the papers curiously, then started and glanced up at Rock, then back at the papers. His face was curiously white. He skimmed over the others swiftly, then sat back in his chair, looking up at the man before him. "You know what these will mean, if you produce them? If you even hint they exist?"

Rock nodded.

"It means they'll kill you."

"They can try."

"Who sent you to me?" Whiting was measuring Rock with quick, curious eyes.

"Leosa Barron. I made a deal to help her out for a while."

"Then you're already in trouble! You can't stay there, you know, they'll run you off."

"You mean Rorick and Wilson? They had a pass at runnin' her off today. They didn't get far."

"You stopped them? Alone?"

He shrugged and changed the subject. "I'm going to build that dam for her."

"You are biting off a chunk."

"We'll see."

"What do you want me to call you, young man?"

"My name is Rock."

"Yes . . . yes, I see. Who have you told? Anyone beside Miss Barron?"

"I only told her the last name. Figured it was enough for now."

Whiting lifted the papers, then got to his feet. "When do you want to use these?"

Rock shrugged. "I came to ask your advice, but my idea would be now, down in the Longhorn."

"Now?" Whiting's exclamation faded into a smile. "Yes, it would be amusing. Can you shoot, friend? This is going to blow the top off the town. It might even blow our tops off."

Rock nodded. "It might. Let's do it this way. You put these in a safe place. Then you make out bills to all the folks who owe me money. Make them out particularly to Van Rorick. Then you go down to the Longhorn, and I'll drift in, too. Spring it on him and let's see what happens."

"Not tell them who you are?"

"Not right now. I'm not duckin' a fight, but what I want is to get the picture of things. Also, I'd like to have a showdown with Rorick on Leosa Barron. Because before he gets through, I'm goin' to give him so much trouble he'll forget her."

The lawyer considered. It was not a bad approach, and whatever was done had better be done at once if they were going to block Van Rorick in his attempt to dispossess Leosa Barron. He got to his feet. "You go first," he said, "then I'll drift in. This should be fun."

The Longhorn was ablaze with light when Rock pushed through the door and walked to the bar. Rorick was there, and he was seated at a table with Lute Wilson, whose face was puffed and swollen out of shape, and another man. Rorick looked up, and Rock felt the shock of his eyes, of the hatred in them.

The bartender served him without comment, and Rock scanned the room. He had never seen it before, but he knew it from the countless tales he had heard. He was barely tasting his drink when the door opened again and Rance Whiting walked in. Without seeming to notice Rock, he went to the bar and ordered a drink, then he glanced around at Rorick. "Van," he said, "I've news for you. News, and a bill."

"A bill?" Rorick was puzzled but wary. "What do I owe you for?"

"Not me. A client. The owner of this property, in fact. You owe him rent for four years on the Longhorn, and on the Placer Saloon, down the street. The total, according to my figures, comes to nine thousand three hundred and seventy dollars."

Rorick's face was ashen, then blood turned it crimson

and he started to his feet. "What's this you're givin' me?" he demanded. "I bought this place from Jody Thompson!"

"That was unfortunate," Whiting replied calmly. "You should have investigated his title. He owned neither the buildings nor the land on which they stand. Actually, he was a squatter here, and had no legal rights. This is not, as he supposed, government land. It belongs to my client, and has been in his family for forty years!"

Van Rorick was livid; also, he was frightened. He had built up his influence locally partly on wealth, but mostly on strength. He had little cash, certainly nowhere in the neighborhood of nine thousand dollars. If he were compelled to pay up, he could do so only by selling off all his stock; furthermore, he could be dispossessed here.

His eyes searched Whiting's face. "This is some trick," he protested. "You and that girl have rigged this on me. You won't get away with it!"

Rance shrugged. Glancing toward the far wall of the saloon, he caught the eye of an old man, bearded and gray, who sat there. "Mawson," he asked, "how did this town get its name?"

"Joe Billy?" Mawson got to his feet, enjoying the limelight. "Why, she was named for the son of the man that located the first claims hereabouts. He inherited this chunk of land, something like forty thousand acres, from his father, who got it through marriage to a Valdez gal."

Rorick walked to the bar. He was trapped, but he was thinking swiftly. He should be able to make a deal with Whiting. Certainly, the man had no money. He owed a bar bill, and he owed for supplies down the street. There was sure to be a way to swing it.

Yet even deeper within him, there was a feverish desperation, anger at Whiting for bringing this up, in public, and anger at it coming now when it might frustrate all his plans. His eyes were calm, but inwardly he was seething. There had to be a way . . . and maybe Lute could handle it. Lute, or—his mind returned to the slim and silent man who waited at the table with Wilson—or him.

"Your unsupported statement means nothing," Rorick said, fighting for calmness. "You have some papers? Deeds?"

"I have everything that's necessary," Whiting replied. "When the time comes I'll produce them. Not until then. I intend"—he smiled at Rorick—"to protect my client's interests so they will not disappear until we meet, if must be, in court. That," he added, "would be in Santa Fe."

Van Rorick winced. He dared not show himself in Santa Fe. Did Whiting realize that? But here . . . ? Anything might happen.

"We can make a deal, Rance," he said quietly. "I can't pay that money now, and I'm sure you don't want to hurry me. I can pay a part of it, and make a deal for the rest."

Whiting shook his head. "No, the saloon is doing business," he said. "Some of that profit can go to my client as well as to you. All he wants from you is the arrears in rent."

He paused, his eyes studying Rorick. "That, or you leave the country."

"What!" Rorick's lips thinned down. "So that's it? I'll see you in hell first! And whoever your client is!"

"You have five days. No more." Whiting finished his drink and placed the glass on the bar.

After Whiting had gone, Van Rorick stood at the bar for a few minutes, and for the first time recalled that the stranger from Leosa Barron's ranch was in the room, and that he had entered just before Whiting! Was there a tie-up there? No sooner had the thought entered his mind than he was sure such was the case. That this had come up when the stranger arrived was too much for a coincidence.

Whiting, and this man. Who was he, then? Rorick was thinking swiftly. Somehow, he must get rid of both. After all, hadn't he managed to rid himself of Tom Andrews? With Whiting out of it and whatever papers he had in his possession, he would be even more secure.

Thanks to his carefully planted rumors, Leosa Barron was disliked by all the women of the town, and suspected by most of the men. The presence of Rock on her ranch would make those suspicions seem fact. Moreover, his mysterious arrival would help . . . but whatever was done must be done carefully to avert all suspicion from himself. And there was a way . . . with them gone, he could always claim Whiting had tried to defraud him.

Rock left the saloon and, without returning to see Whiting, headed for the ranch. He had anticipated trouble, and knew that Rorick would not take this lying down. The man's sudden quiet disturbed him more than he cared to admit.

At daybreak Rock was riding, and by noon he had made a careful survey of the site chosen for the dam. It was a good spot, no doubt about it, and looking at the massive stone walls above, he had an idea how it could be done.

He said nothing to Leosa, but after a quick lunch, took some giant powder from a cache near the house and returned to the mountain. By nightfall he had his first set of holes in, and had them charged.

Leosa, a new warmth in her eyes, reported no sign of Wilson or Rorick. A passing neighbor, one of the few who condescended to speak, had told her there was a rumor that Art Beal and Milt Blue, the outlaws, were in the vicinity, that Blue had been seen riding near Joe Billy.

Leosa said this last with averted eyes. She was remembering that flashing draw, and the fact that Rock had come out of the Dead Hills. Milt Blue was a known killer, and a deadly man with a gun. She had never seen him nor heard a description, but she was afraid now. Afraid for Rock. Was he . . . could he be Milt Blue?

Yet if the rumors meant anything to him, he said nothing. "Art Beal hasn't been around much," he commented. "Disappeared a while back. Blue killed another man down to El Paso, only a month ago."

The following day, Rock returned and put in his second round of holes. When he had them charged, he studied the situation below. If the rock broke right, he would have a fairly good dam across the canyon. Then another charge, to help things along, and in no time the creek itself would finish the dam by piling up silt, brush and weeds to fill up the holes and gaps in the rocks.

Rock carefully lighted his fuses, then descended the rock face to the bottom of the draw. The fuses were long, for he had wanted to get both shots off approximately together. The climb to the opposite side took him little time, and in a matter of a minute he had spit those fuses and then slid rapidly down the steep declivity to the bottom. He turned and started up the draw, then glanced back.

Light glinted high on the rock, and instinctively, he hurled himself to the right. A rifle spoke, its distant bark swallowed by the huge, all-engulfing roar as the first set of powder-charged holes let go. It was an enormous sound, magnified and echoed again and again by the walls of the canyon, but Rock did not hear it. He was going over headfirst into the rocks. He landed facedown, slid a short distance, then his body ceased to slide and he lay sprawled out and unconscious among the greasewood and boulders at one side of the draw.

Beyond him rocks fell, then ceased to fall, and dust rose slowly, in a great cloud. When it stopped rising, there was a wall across the canyon, low in the middle, but high enough. The mountain stream, trickling down its normal bed, found the way blocked, it turned right, searching for a way under or through, but discovered no way to accommodate the swelling strength of water behind it. Spreading left, it found no way out, and so began to back up in a slowly widening and deepening pool.

It was dark when the lapping water reached the nest of rocks where the fallen man lay. Cold fingers encircled his outflung hand, crept up his arm with exploring tentacles, and flattened out, creeping along his side and toward his face.

A coyote, prowling nearby and sniffing blood, paused to stare at the man's dark body. Curious, he came near, stepping daintily to keep his feet from the water. When the man moved, drawing back a hand, the coyote drew back and trotted swiftly off.

It was the cold touch of the water that roused Joe Billy Rock. Water against his face and water along his ribs. For an instant he lay still, and then the meaning of the creeping coldness came to him with a rush, and he jerked back and lunged to his feet. The startled reaction that brought him up also brought a rush of pain to his head. His fingers lifted and explored. The bullet had caused chips of rock to pepper his face and arm, but there was at least one other cut caused by his fall, and his whole body was stiff and numb.

He staggered, splashing, toward higher ground. There

he looked back, and saw that almost an acre of water had already gathered behind his crude dam. A little work would make it more effective.

Memory returned, and he realized he had been shot at. Shot at the instant before the explosion by someone perched on the very rocks he was blasting! Whoever that unknown marksman had been, he was dead now. Survival, where he had been perched, was out of the question.

A half hour of staggering and falling brought him to his horse, which looked up quickly at the sight of him, tossing his head at the smell of blood. It was no more than fifteen minutes of riding to the house. All was dark and still.

Carefully, Rock considered this. Had Leosa been at home, she would certainly have a light. Moreover, she would be awaiting supper. The time he roughly estimated to be nine or past, but she knew he was working and would have heard the explosion. Had she gone out looking for him? Stealthily, he rode nearer, then dismounted. Ten minutes of careful searching proved the house, barn, and the whole ranch was empty. The stove was cold, no dishes on the table. No evidence that a meal had been prepared.

Squinting against the stinging pain in his cheek and forehead, he tried to assemble his thoughts. Somehow they must have gotten her out of here; believing him dead. Van Rorick had acted to seize the ranch.

The gray he was riding had a liking for the trail and he let him take it. He ran like a scared rabbit until the town lights were plain, then Rock slowed him to a canter and then a walk. He swung down from the horse near the livery barn, loosened his guns in his holsters, and started up the street. Voices made him draw back into the shadows. Between two buildings he waited while two men drew near.

"Hear about that gal out to the old Barron place? One said she was Barron's niece? She skipped out with that tough-lookin' hand who's been hanging around there. Somebody said they was seen on the road to Cimarron, ridin' out of the country."

"Good riddance, I'd say. I hear she carried on plenty!"

Rock stared after them. Rorick was shrewd. His story was already going the rounds, and it was a plausible yarn. But what had happened to Leosa?

He started up the street, moving more cautiously now. First, he must see Whiting. The lawyer would know what to do, and would start a search here. Then he would head for Rorick's own ranch.

It was possible that Rorick had killed the girl at once, or that Lute Wilson had. But the man on the rock before the explosion was probably Lute. Rorick was too smart to take such chances himself. It had been only bad luck that got Lute, however, for the man could not have known of the loaded holes and spitted fuses.

Rock climbed the stairs, then pushed open the lawyer's door. Rance Whiting's office was dark and still. Fumbling in his pocket, he got a match and lighted it. Whiting was sprawled on the floor, his shirt bloody, his face white as death.

Dropping to his knees, Rock found the lawyer had been stabbed twice, once in the back, once in the chest. The room was in wild disorder.

Working swiftly, Rock got water and bathed the wounds, then bandaged them. The lawyer was still alive, and the first thing was to get the bleeding stopped. When he had him resting easily on the bed, Rock turned to the door. He was opening it when he heard the lawyer's hoarse cry.

Instantly, he turned back. "The papers," Whiting whispered, "they . . ." His voice trailed feebly away. He had fainted.

Leaving the light burning, Rock ran down the outside stairs to the street, glanced once at the saloon, and then ran up the street to old Doc Spencer's home. In a few minutes he had the old man started toward Whiting's office.

Joe Rock stared at the Longhorn. This was his town. He owned the whole townsite by inheritance, and he intended to keep it, especially that part usurped by Van Rorick. He walked swiftly to the saloon and, from a position near the window, studied the interior. Rorick was there but he didn't appear happy. The same slight-figured man who had been with him before was with him now. Lute was not, which was all the assurance Rock needed that the man was dead. It was undoubtedly his failure to return that worried Rorick.

Circling swiftly, he came to the rear door, but reached it only to hear the front door open and close. When he looked in, Rorick and his friend had gone.

From the street came a sound of horses' hooves and then two men rode down the street and out of town. Hurrying to his own horse, Rock swung into the saddle and, kicking his feet into the stirrups, started in pursuit.

Rorick set a fast pace. Rock let his mind leap ahead, trying to get the drift of the other man's thinking. Wilson had not returned, and that could mean he had failed. It could also mean Wilson and Rock had killed each other. Rorick swung toward the Barron homestead, and drew up, staring toward it. Rock was no more than a hundred yards away and could see the men outlined against the sky.

Seeing the house dark, they evidently decided that Rock had not returned there. They pushed on. When they reached the now dry creek, Rock heard a startled exclamation, and then the riders turned toward the dam. He saw them ride up to it and look around, heard a low-voiced conversation of which he could guess the sense but understand no word. Then they mounted and rode on.

The course they followed now led deeper and deeper

into the rocky canyons to the north. This was lonely country, and was not, Rock was aware, toward Rorick's ranch. Suddenly the two men rode down into a hollow and disappeared.

Rock drew up, straining his eyes into the night, holding his breath for any sound. There was none. He walked his horse a short way, and was about to go farther when his eyes caught a vague suggestion of light. Turning, he worked his way through some willows and saw among some boulders the darker blotch of a cabin from which gleamed two lighted windows!

Swinging down, Rock stole toward the house, ghostlike in the night. She had to be here! His heart pounding, his mouth dry, all the fear he had been feeling all evening now tight and cold within him. What if something had happened to her? What if she had been killed?

A door opened and a man stepped out. He was a stranger. "I'll put the horses up," he said over his shoulder, "an' grub's ready."

The fellow carried a lantern and he walked toward a rock barn that stood close under a cliff. Joe Rock followed, and moved in behind him. The man placed the lantern on the ground and reached for a bridle.

In that instant Rock's forearm went across his throat and jammed a knee into the startled man's back, jerking him off balance. Then Rock turned him loose, but before he could get breath to yell a warning, Rock slugged him in the wind. He doubled up, and Rock struck him again. Then he grabbed him by the throat and shoved him against the wall. He was trembling with fury. "Is that girl in there? Is she safe?"

The fellow gasped and choked. "She . . . she's all right! Don't kill me! For Lord's sake, man!"

"Who's in there?" Rock demanded in a hoarse whisper.

"Just them two. Beal 'n Milt Blue."

Joe Rock froze. Then he said carefully, "Who did you say? Art Beal and Milt Blue? The outlaws?"

"They ain't sky pilots," the man said, growling.

"You mean Beal is the hombre known in town as Rorick?"

"Yeah, maybe." The man was talking freely now. "He said there'd be no trouble. I ain't no outlaw! I just needed a few dollars."

Roughly, Rock bound and gagged the man. He was aware now of his real danger, and of Leosa's danger. If Rorick was Art Beal, that accounted for some of the six years he had been away from Joe Billy, and also let Rock know just what sort of a man Rorick was. Yet for all of that, the real risk lay in facing Milt Blue, the gunslinger.

He left the man bound on the dirt floor of the barn, loosened his guns in their holsters, and started for the house. He carried the lantern with him, wanting them to believe he was their helper. As he neared the door he shifted the lantern to his left hand and drew his gun. Then he opened the door and stepped in.

Only Leosa was looking toward the door, and her eyes widened. Her expression must have warned them, for as one man they turned, and Blue went for his gun. Instantly, as though it had been rehearsed, Leosa threw her body against Rorick, knocking him off balance.

Rock had his feet spread and his gun ready. "Drop it, Blue!" he yelled.

The gunman grabbed iron. His gun leaped free with amazing speed, and as the muzzle cleared the holster Rock shot him in the stomach. He was slammed back by the force of the bullet, but fought doggedly and bitterly to get his gun up. Despite the fierce struggle against the wall, where Leosa fought desperately with Rorick, Rock took his time. He fired again. Blue's eyes glazed and the gun slid from his hand.

Rock turned and instantly Leosa let go and stepped back. Van Rorick stared across the room. "You think you've won!" he cried. "Well, you haven't! I got the papers! I burned them! Burned every last one of them! You've lost everything! And I sold my claim on her place, so you'll lose that, too! And now I'm going to kill you, gun or no gun."

His right hand had dangled behind him, and now it swung up, clutching a gun. Rock's pistol leaped in his hand, and the room thundered with a shot. Rorick's face twisted and he stepped back, shocked with realization. Awareness of death hit him, and his eyes widened, then his mouth dropped open and he crumpled to the floor.

Rock caught Leosa in his arms and hurried her to the door.

Doc Spencer met them when they reached the top of the office stairs. "He's in bad shape, but he'll pull through," he told them. "Few minutes ago he was conscious, an' he said to tell you the papers are stuck behind his volume of Horace. Those he left for Rorick to find were fakes he fixed up. He figured on somethin' like this."

They walked back down the steps to the silent street. Almost unconsciously, they were holding hands.

"Rock," Leosa asked gently, "what will you do now? You own the town? I heard you did."

"I'm goin' to give all these folks who shape up right deeds to their property. It ain't worth so much, anyway. The Longhorn I'll sell."

"What about you?" she asked, looking up at him.

"Me? . . . why, I was thinkin' of ranchin' an' watchin' hay crops grow out on the Barron place . . . with my wife."

MONUMENT ROCK

CHAPTER I

Lona was afraid of him. She was afraid of Frank Mailer, the man whom she was to marry. She realized that it was not size alone that made her afraid of him, but something else, something she saw in his blue, slightly glassy eyes, and the harshness of his thin-lipped mouth.

He was big, the biggest man she had ever seen, and she knew his contempt for smaller men, men of lesser strength and lesser will. He was five inches over six feet and weighed two hundred and fifty pounds. Whenever he stood near her, the sheer mass of him frightened her and the way he looked at her made her uneasy.

Her father looked up at him as he came in. "Did you get that north herd moved before the rain set in?"

"Yeah." Mailer did not look up, helping himself to two huge slabs of beef, a mound of mashed potatoes, and liberal helpings of everything else. He commenced his supper by slapping butter on a thick slice of homemade bread and taking an enormous bite, then holding the rest of it in his left hand, he began to shovel food into his mouth with his right.

Between bites he looked up at Poke Markham. "I saw the Black Rider."

"On our range?"

"Uh-huh. Just like they were sayin' in town, he was ridin' the high country, alone. Over toward Chimney Rock."

"Did you get close to him? See what he looks like?"

"Not a chance. Just caught a glimpse of him over against the rocks, and then he was gone, like a shadow. That horse of his is fast." Mailer looked up and Lona was puzzled by the slyness in his eyes as he looked at her father. "You know what the Mexican boys say? That he's the ghost of a murdered man?"

The comment angered Markham. "That's foolishness! He's real enough, all right! What I want to know is who he is and what he thinks he's doin'."

"Maybe the Mex boys are right. You ever see any tracks? I never did, an' nobody else that I ever heard of. Nobody ever sees him unless it is almost dark or rainin', an' then never more than a glimpse."

"He's real enough!" Markham glared from under his shaggy brows, his craggy face set in angry lines. "Some outlaw on the dodge, that's who he is, hangin' out in the high peaks so he won't be seen. Who's he ever bothered?"

Mailer shrugged. "That's the point. He ain't bothered anybody yet, but maybe he wants one certain man." Mailer looked up at Poke, in his malicious way. "Maybe he's the ghost of a murdered man, like they say, an' maybe he's tryin' to lure his murderer back into the hills."

"That's nonsense!" Markham repeated irritably. "You'll have Lona scared out of her wits, ridin' all over like she does."

Frank Mailer looked at her, his eyes meeting hers, then running down over her breast. He always made her uncomfortable. How had she ever agreed to marry him? She knew that when he drank he became fiercely belligerent. Nobody wanted to cross him when he was drinking. Only one man ever had tried to stop him when he was like that. Bert Hayek had tried it, and Bert had died for his pains.

His fighting had wrecked several of the saloons in town. All, in fact, except for the Fandango. Was it true, what they said? That Frank was interested in that Spanish woman who ran the place? Nita Howard was her name. Lona Markham had seen her once, a tall young woman with a voluptuous figure and beautiful eyes. She had thought her one of the most beautiful women she had ever seen. Lona's intended was often seen visiting with a beautiful woman who ran a saloon and gambling hall and Lona found she didn't care . . . not at all.

When supper was over Lona left hurriedly. More and more she was avoiding Frank. She did not like to have him near her, did not want to talk to him. He frightened her, but he puzzled her, too. For more and more he seemed to be exerting authority here on the Blue Hill ranch, and more and more her father was fading into the background. People said that Poke Markham was afraid of no man, but of late she'd begun to wonder, for several times he had allowed Mailer to overrule him.

She crossed the patio through a light spatter of rain to her own quarters in the far wing of the rambling old house. Once there, she hung up her coat and crossed to the window, looking off over the magnificent sweep of land that carried her eyes away to the distant wall of the mountains in the southwest. It was over there the strange rider had been seen.

Suddenly, as if in response to her thoughts, a horseman

materialized from the rain. He was out there, no more than a hundred yards from the back of the house, and scarcely visible through the now driving rain. As she looked she saw him draw up, and sitting tall in the saddle, he surveyed the ranch. Under his black flat-brimmed hat nothing of his face was visible and at that distance she could not make out his features. He was only a tall horseman, sitting in the rain, staring at the ranch house.

Why she did it, she never knew, but suddenly she caught up her coat, and running out into the rain, she lifted her hand.

For a moment they stared at each other and then suddenly the horse started to walk, but as he moved, the Black Rider raised a hand and waved!

Then he was gone. One instant he was there, and then he had vanished like a puff of smoke . . . but he had waved to her! Recalling the stories, she knew it was something that had never happened before. She returned to her room, her heart pounding with excitement. She must tell Gordon about that. He would be as surprised as she was. In fact, she paused, staring out at the knoll where the Rider had stopped, Gordon Flynn was the only one who seemed to care much what she thought or how she felt. Gordon, and of course, Dave Betts, the broken-down cowhand who was their cook.

Mailer dropped into a big chair made of cowhide. He rolled a smoke and looked across at Markham. The old man was nodding a little, and it made Frank smile. Markham, if that's what he wanted to be called, had changed. He had aged.

To think how they all had feared him! All but he himself. All but Frank Mailer. Markham had been boss here for a long time, and to be the boss of men like Kane Geslin and Sam Starr was something, you had to admit. Moreover, he had kept them safe, kept them away from the law, and if he had taken his share for all that, at least he'd held up his end of the bargain. He was getting older now, and he had relinquished more and more of the hard work to Mailer. Frank was tired of the work without the big rewards; he was ambitious. Sure, they had a good thing going, but if one knew the trails, there were easy ways out to the towns and ranches, and a man could do a good job on a few banks, along about roundup time. It beat working for money, and this ranch was as good as his, anyway, when he married Lona.

Looking over at the old man, he began to think of that. Why wait for it? He could shoot the old man right now and take over. Still, it would be better to marry the girl first, but he was not ready for that. Not yet. He wanted to move in on that Spanish woman at the Fandango, first.

There was that bodyguard of hers to be taken care of. He did not like the big, dark man who wore two guns and always sat near her door, faithful as a watchdog. Yet it would pay to be careful. Webb Case had been a fairly handy man with a gun, and he had tried to push this Brigo into a gunfight, planning to kill him. From all accounts, it had taken mightily little of a push, but Webb's plans backfired and he took a couple of slugs and got planted out on Boot Hill.

He began to think of that bank at the Crossing. Four . . . no, five men. Geslin and Starr, of course, among them. Geslin was a lean, wiry man with a pale, hatchet face and white eyes. There was no doubt that he ranked among the fastest gunmen of them all, with Wes Hardin, Clay Allison, Bill Hickok, or Kilkenny.

The bank would keep the boys happy, for however

much Poke Markham was satisfied with the ranch, his
boys were not. Poke made money, but most of the men at
Blue Hill ranch were not punchers. They were wanted,
one place or another, and when they'd tired of cooling
their heels, they'd leave. Frank Mailer wanted to take advantage of the situation before that happened. The bank
should go for eight or nine thousand, and they could make
a nice split of that. Four men and himself. That would be
enough. Nobody would tackle a gang made up of Geslin,
Starr, and himself, let alone the other two he would pick.

Thoughtfully, Frank Mailer considered Geslin. How
would he stack up with Geslin? Or Starr? He considered it
a moment, then shrugged. It would never happen. They
were his men, and they had accepted him as boss. He
knew how to handle them, and he knew there was a ri-
valry between Starr and Geslin. If necessary, he could play
them off against one another. As for Poke, he intended to
kill Markham himself when the time came.

He heaved himself out of his chair and stretched, enjoying the feeling of his powerful muscles. He would ride
into town and have a talk with that Howard woman at
the Fandango. He thought again of Jaime Brigo, and the
thought bothered him. There was something about the
big, silent man that disturbed him. He did not think of
Lona. The girl was here when he wanted her, and he did
want her, but only casually. His desire for Nita Howard
was a sharp, burning thing.

The Fandango was easily the most impressive place in Salt
Creek, and finer than anything in Bloomington. In fact,
finer than anything this side of Santa Fe. Nita Howard
watched the crowd, well pleased. Her hazel eyes with tiny
flecks of darker color were large and her lashes were long.

Her skin was the color of old ivory, her hair a deep, beautiful black, gathered in a loose knot at the nape of her neck. Although her lips were full, slightly sensual, there was a certain wistful, elusive charm about them, and a quick, fleeting humor that made her doubly beautiful. She was a tall woman, somewhere just beyond thirty, but her body was strong, and graceful.

Standing in the door, she said, without looking down at the man in the tipped-back chair, "Any message, Jaime?"

The Yaqui gunman glanced up. "No, señorita, there is none. He has been seen this day near Monument Rock. You have seen the map."

Nita Howard relaxed. "Yes, I know. As long as he is well, we had best leave him alone."

"He is loyal. A long time ago Markham, he befriended the señor when he was wounded and in danger. The señor does not forget. So he comes here. And you come here; so this means I do, too." Brigo shrugged. "We are all loyal to one another, but for now you must trust that our friend knows what he is doing."

The door opened suddenly and Frank Mailer stepped into the room; behind him were Kane Geslin and Sam Starr with another man known as Socorro. Mailer's eyes brightened with satisfaction when he saw Nita and he turned abruptly and walked toward her.

How huge he was! Could anything ever stop this man if he became angered? Nita watched him come, her mind coolly accepting the danger but not disturbed by it. Her father had died long ago and left her the doubtful legacy of a tough saloon on the Rio Grande border. She had directed its fortunes herself, with Brigo at her side, he who loved her like his own sister, and all because of her father's friendship to him.

Mailer stopped before her, his hard eyes surveying Nita

with appreciation. "You're all woman, Nita!" he said. "All woman! Just the kind I've been lookin' for!"

She did not smile. "It is said around town that you are to marry Lona Markham."

Mailer was irritated; there was no reason to think of Lona now and he disliked the subject being brought up. "Come on!" he said impatiently. "I'll buy a drink!"

"Good!" she said smoothly. Lifting her eyes, she glanced over at the bartender. "Cain"—the big bartender glanced up sharply—"the gentleman is buying a drink." Her eyes turned to Mailer. "You meant you were buying for the house, did you not?"

Crimson started to go up Mailer's neck. He had meant nothing of the kind, yet he'd been neatly trapped and he had the feeling that he would appear cheap if he backed out. "Sure," he said grudgingly, "for the house! Now come on." He reached for her arm. "You drink with me."

"Sorry, I do not drink. Cain will serve you." She turned and stepped through the door, closing it behind her.

Frank Mailer's eyes grew ugly. He lunged toward the door at the end of the bar.

"Señor." Brigo was on his feet. "The señorita is ver' tired tonight. You understand?"

Mailer glared at Brigo, but the Yaqui's flat dark face was expressionless. Mailer turned on his heel and walked to the bar in baffled fury.

The big bartender finished pouring the drinks, then looked over at Mailer. "That'll be thirty bucks," he said flatly.

His jaws set, Mailer paid for the drinks. Geslin was in a game with several others. One of them was a red-haired puncher, stocky and tough looking. Mailer dropped into an empty chair and bought chips.

At the end of the third hand the redheaded puncher

looked up at him. "Mailer, don't you ramrod that Blue Hill spread? I'm huntin' for work."

Frank Mailer's eyes slanted to the redhead. He was a tough, capable-looking man with hard, steady eyes. He packed his gun low. "You been anywhere I might've heard about?"

"I rode for Pierce an' for Goodnight."

"Then I can use you, all right." With the riding he planned to do with Geslin and the others, he would need a few good hands. Also, unless his guess was altogether wrong, this man had ridden the owl hoot himself. "Texas man, hey?"

"Big Bend."

"Know Wes Hardin?" Mailer asked. "I hear he's fast."

"Plenty, an' with both hands. Maybe as fast as Kilkenny."

"Kilkenny?" Geslin turned his white eyes toward the redhead. "You say he's faster than Hardin? Did you ever see Hardin?"

"Uh-huh." Rusty Gates picked up his cards. "I seen Kilkenny, too."

All eyes were on him now. Men who had seen Kilkenny to know him were few and far between. The strange drifting gunfighter had a habit of appearing under various names and nobody ever really knew who he was until suddenly there was a blaze of guns and then he was riding out of town. "What's he like?" Mailer asked.

"Fast."

"I mean, what's he look like?"

"Tall, black hair, green eyes that look right through you when he's riled up. Quiet feller, friendly enough mostly."

"Is it true what they say? That he's killed forty or fifty men?"

Gates shrugged. "Doubt it. A friend of his told me

it was no more than eighteen. An' he might have been exaggeratin'."

Hours later, when the game had broken up, Rusty Gates crossed to the bar for one last drink. The others had started back to the ranch and he was to come out the following day. He accepted his drink, and Cain grinned at him and shoved his money back. "I got the job," Gates said.

"Good!" Cain nodded emphatically. "I'll tell the boss."

Bright sunlight lay across the Blue Hill when Lona left the house the following morning. Frank Mailer had gone out early, and her father was fussing over some accounts in his office. Yet the night had neither lessened her curiosity nor changed her mood, and she started for the corral to catch up a horse, believing the hands were all gone.

The ranch lay between two peaks with its back to the low bench where Lona had seen the Black Rider on the previous night. These peaks lifted five hundred feet or so above the ranch house, and it was from one of them that the ranch had taken its name. The ranch house faced northwest, and off to the right, also running toward the northwest, lay the Old Mormon Trail to Utah. Beyond the trail the cliffs lifted high, and at one point a crown of rock reached out to need no more than a half mile to join the twin peaks at Blue Hill.

She had reached the corral when she heard a boot scuff stones and turned to face a strange, redheaded puncher who grinned at her in a friendly fashion. "Can I help, ma'am? I'm Rusty Gates, a new hand."

"Oh, would you? I was going to saddle my horse. The black mare."

Gates nodded. "I been studyin' that mare, ma'am. She's sure all horse."

He shook out a loop and caught the black. As the rope settled, the mare stood still, and when she saw Lona she even walked toward the gate. Rusty led the horse outside and glanced at Lona. She was very young, very pretty, and had a trim, neat figure, auburn hair, and gray eyes. She caught his glance and he grinned. "Your hair's 'most as red as mine, ma'am," he said. "I reckon that makes us partners."

There was something so friendly in his manner that she warmed to him instantly. On impulse, she confided in him. "Rusty," she said, "don't you tell a soul what I'm going to tell you, but I'm going to see the Black Rider!"

Rusty gave her a sidelong, cautious glance. "To see him? How do you figure to do that?"

"I'm going to ride out and look along the ridges for him, then if I see him, I'll leave it up to Zusa to do the rest. She'll run him down if anything can."

Gates was silent. After a while he asked, "You ever see the Rider?"

"I saw him last night, right back on the bench in the rain. I waved to him, and he waved back! Isn't it exciting?"

She expected him to disapprove or to caution her, but strangely, he did not. He merely nodded, then said, "Ma'am, if I wanted to see that Black Rider, you know what I'd do? I'd head across the valley for Monument Rock, an' then if I saw him, I wouldn't take after him none at all. I'd just sit still an' wait."

"Wait?" Lona's eyes widened doubtfully. "You mean he might come up to me?"

Rusty chuckled. "Ma'am, they do say that the Rider's a ghost, but flesh and blood or ghost, if anything that *is* male or *was* male saw you settin' a horse waitin' for him, he'd sure come a-runnin'!"

She laughed. "Rusty, you're just like all the cowhands! Full of the old blarney!"

"Sure I am. But, ma'am"—his voice dropped a note lower and the look in his eyes was not a teasing look—"you do what I say an' see if it don't work. But," he added, "don't you ever tell anybody on this ranch I suggested it. Don't you tell."

"Thanks, Rusty. I won't." She turned to go and he caught her bridle rein.

"Ma'am," he said, "before you go . . . who's your best friend on this ranch? I mean, ma'am, somebody who really loves you."

Surprised, she looked down at him, but he was in dead earnest. The question brought her up short, too, for it made her wonder. Who were her friends? Did she have any?

Frank? She shuddered slightly. Her father? For a long time she hesitated. He had never been close to her, never since she returned from school. He had been strict and stern, had given her what she wanted, but allowed her little freedom. She realized suddenly that her father was almost a stranger to her.

"I . . . I guess I haven't many friends, Rusty," she said, in a small voice. "I guess . . . Dave, the cook, and Gordon."

Gates relaxed his grip. "Well, ma'am," he said, his voice thick, "I reckon you can count on another friend now. You can count on me. If ever you need a friend, I'd admire to have you call on me." He turned away, then stopped and turned, glancing up out of his bright blue eyes. "Maybe you've got more friends than you realize, ma'am."

Lona turned the mare up the trail to the bench, and drawing up, she looked carefully around. There were no tracks!

A curious little thrill of fear went through her. Was it possible the stories were true? Had it been a ghost who waved at her? The rain could have wiped them out, of course, and there was much rock. She rode on, cutting diagonally across toward the Old Mormon Trail, which would make for easier riding until she had to leave the trail and ride across the rough grass country toward the high cliffs at Monument Rock.

North and east of her, the cliffs made a solid barrier that seemed to cut off the world from this valley, cliffs from four hundred to nine hundred feet high, a dark barrier of dull red now, with the sun just showing above them. Yet that barrier was not as solid as it appeared, for there were a score of places where a horseman might find a way through, and there were, almost due east of the ranch, three canyons that branched like three spread fingers from a given point. The only one she knew was Salt Creek Wash, and only the first half mile of that. Her father had never liked her to ride up into those rugged mountains alone.

It was early spring, yet the air was warm and vibrant, clear as only desert air can be. The black mare felt good, and wanted to go, but Lona held her in, scanning the country ahead and around her, hoping to see the Black Rider.

She had been wrong to come in the morning, especially when it was clear, for he was never seen but at dusk or in the rain. Was there method in that? So that he would be impossible to follow for long? Dust arose from her horse's hooves and she rode on until the cliffs began to rise above her and the sun was not yet high enough to show above their serrated rim. She reined in and looked up at their high battlement crest, then let her eye travel along it, but she saw no horseman, nothing but the rock itself.

What she had expected, she did not know. If she had expected her presence to bring the Black Rider suddenly springing from the solid rock, she was mistaken. It was still here, and lonely. She had stopped with Zusa headed north, so she started on, walking her along the low slope that ended in the cliffs.

Ahead of her she knew the cliffs took a bend eastward and through the gap flowed the occasional waters of Salt Creek, but there was, she knew, another wash beside Monument Rock, so she followed along and entered a narrow opening that had rock walls lifting six hundred feet and more on either side of her. It was shadowy and cool and so still as to be almost unbelievable. She rode on, the canyon echoing to her horse's hooves.

She drew up in a sort of amphitheater, the dark piñons clustering against the wall, and climbing it wherever a faint ledge gave precarious root hold. It was still here, and she drew up, her eyes wide and every sense alert. Even Zusa was on edge, for the mare's sensitive nostrils expanded and her eyes were wide and curious.

No sound disturbed the still afternoon. From the stillness she might have been sitting in a mighty cathedral, yet there was no cathedral so splendid or so tall as this, no man-made temple as grand or magnificent. And then Zusa's muscles twitched, and turning her head, Lona Markham looked straight into the eyes of the Black Rider!

He was about fifty yards away, his horse standing on a tiny knoll, outlined sharply against the green of the piñons behind him. The horse was a buckskin, a long-legged, magnificent animal, and the rider was tall, broad in the shoulder, and clothed in black trousers, a dark gray shirt, and a black Mexican-style jacket.

For an instant she might have turned and fled, so frightened was she, so startled by the horseman's unexpected appearance, but she sat her mare, her eyes wide and expectant, and then the buckskin started to walk down the knoll toward her.

Under the low flat brim of his black hat, the Rider's face was scarcely visible, and as he drew near she noticed that he wore two guns, tied down. He drew up suddenly and, to her relief, lifted a gloved hand and brushed his hat back.

She saw first that he was handsome, with a strong, rugged face, brown from wind and sun, and green eyes that had the look of the desert at their corners. "You are Lona?" he asked.

His voice was strong, clear, friendly. "Yes," she said, "how did you know my name?"

"I have known it for a long time," he said. "Why did you come here today?"

"Why, I . . ." She hesitated. "I was curious!" she said. "Just plain curious."

He chuckled, and she liked the sound. There was droll humor in his eyes. "Don't blame you! From what I hear, a lot of folks are curious. How about Frank Mailer an' Poke Markham? Are they curious?"

"A little. I think Father is more curious than Frank."

At her use of the word *father*, he looked at her again. "You call him father?" he asked.

"Why, of course! He *is* my father. What else would I call him?"

"I could think of a number of things," he said grimly. "Want to talk awhile?" he suggested suddenly. "No use you coming clear out here to see the strange rider and not getting to talk with him."

She hesitated, but he swung down, and so she dismounted. He took the bridle of her horse and ground-hitched them both on a patch of grass in the lee of a cliff where subirrigation kept the grass green. Then he took off his hat and walked toward her. He had dark curly hair and a quizzical humor in his eyes.

"Don't worry about this," he said, smiling at her. "I know this is a mighty lonely place for a girl to be talkin' to a stranger, but later you'll understand."

"What will I understand?" she said evenly. She was frankly puzzled by him and by his attitude. He had known her name, and he seemed to know something about her, but certainly there was nothing in his manner that would in any way offer a cause for resentment.

"Lots of things." He dug out the makings and dropped to a rock facing her. He was, she noticed, also facing the opening up which she had ridden. "How'd you happen to come here?"

"I heard you had been seen on the rims, and that I should come here and wait. Rusty, he's our new hand, told me that. Very mysterious, if you ask me!"

He grinned. "He's quite a guy, Rusty is. You can trust him."

"Oh, you know him?" She was startled.

"Rusty? If you ever need a friend, he's your man."

He drew deep on the cigarette. "You were away to school quite awhile, weren't you? How old were you when you left?"

She looked at him seriously. "Oh, I was only five then. Father sent me away to the sisters' school, said a ranch was no place to raise a girl who had so far to go. I mean, so many years in which to grow up. I used to return for vacations after I was fifteen. Once in a while, that is."

"I don't remember a lot of things from when I was five," he said casually. "Do you? I mean, do you remember your father very well?"

"Some things about him, but it's all sort of funny and

mixed up. He was awfully good to me, I remember that. He was sort of sweet, too. I remember riding in a wagon for ever so long, and how he used to tell me stories about my mother—she died a year before we started west—and about the ranch that was waiting for us out here. The place where he had hoped to take my mother. He said he had taken it in my name, and it would always be mine."

"Has your dad changed much?"

She nodded. "Quite a lot. But he's had trouble, I guess. He never says much anymore, not to me, at least, and sometimes he acts sort of strange. But he's all right," she added hurriedly. "I love him."

He turned his green eyes full upon her and there was something so searching in those eyes that she was disturbed. "Is that wrong?" she asked indignantly. "To love your father?"

"No, it isn't." He threw down his cigarette and rubbed it out with his toe. "In fact, that's the way it should be. On the other hand, maybe this particular gent doesn't deserve loving." He looked over at her. "Lona, we've got to have more than one talk, I can see that. Some things I might want to tell you, you wouldn't want to believe now. Later you might.

"But first off, I want to ask you to mention meeting me to no one. Rusty would be all right, if you could do it where nobody could hear. Remember this: I'm your friend and you've got to trust me. You're in a position right now where you'll need friends, and badly!"

"Why do you say that?" she demanded.

"Haven't they talked to you about marryin' Frank Mailer?"

She nodded. "Yes, of course. Father wants me to marry him."

"You want to marry him?"

Lona hesitated. Why was this stranger asking all these questions? Who was he?

"No," she said honestly. "I don't."

"Then," he said, "you mustn't. No matter what they say or what they do," he insisted, "don't marry him! Don't refuse right out, just evade the issue. Find excuses . . . clothes you have to have, plans for the wedding, just anything. You won't have to delay it long, because I think there will be a lot happening and soon. If the worst comes to the worst, see Rusty. You can trust him, like I said."

He walked to the horses. "And can you meet me here again? The day after tomorrow?"

Lona hesitated. "Why should I? I don't know what you are talking about! These are all riddles and I have no idea why you say I may need friends, or why I should trust this new puncher! Or why I should either trust or listen to you!"

The Rider took a breath. "I don't blame you for that, but you must listen. You don't know it yet, but you're in trouble. Your marriage to Frank Mailer was planned a long time ago, Lona, before you ever heard of him, and it's bad! Plumb bad!

"Something else I want you to do," he added. "I want you to think about the times when you were a youngster, before you ever went away to school. Every minute from now on I want you to think about that wagon trip. The way it started, everything that happened. The more you try to remember, the more it will come back. It's very important to you." He hesitated. "You see, I knew your mother."

"What?" She turned on him, wide-eyed. "You knew . . . ? But why didn't you tell me?" Then suddenly she hesitated. Her eyes were suddenly frightened. "You . . . what did you know about her?"

"That she was a mighty fine woman, Lona. You look a lot like her, too. Yes, she was mighty fine. One of the sweetest, finest women I ever knew. I knew your father in those days, and he was a fine man."

"Why don't you come to see him, then?" she said, frowning at him.

He hesitated. "Lona, that man is not your father. He is no relation to you at all. There never was a 'Poke' Markham! Isiah Markham was your father. That man down there is Poke Dunning, a onetime gunfighter and outlaw from the Big Bend country. I don't know what it is he's doing here, but I aim to find out! Your father was once a friend to me when I needed him. That's why I, now, am a friend to you."

CHAPTER 2

At the corral bars she slid from the saddle as if stunned, then stood for a long time, staring at the far blue line of the cliffs from which she had just come.

Poke Markham was not her father!

The thought stood stark and clear in her mind, written across her consciousness in black, staring letters.

After the first minutes of stunned disbelief had come the uneasy memories which she had put aside and tried to forget. They came flooding into her mind. Little things and haunting details that had made her unhappy and puzzled.

The vague memories of her father before she went away to school had always been confused. Somehow she'd never been able to sort them out, to shape them into any plain picture. She knew now the reason for that confusion; it was that the memories of two individuals, two separate men, had mingled in her mind. This was why whenever she looked back to those years, the face of her father was always blurred, never sharp and clear.

The strange rider had said he was her real father's friend, that her mother had been a fine, sweet woman.

It was that last that flooded her mind with relief, for always when she had asked Poke Dunning about her mother, he had put her aside, evaded the issue, and so finally she had come to believe there was something shameful in her past, something in her story of which her father did not wish to be reminded. Lona had come to believe that her mother must have done something that had hurt and disgraced them both. Now she knew that was not true.

She knew?

Lona stopped at the thought, testing it, turning it over. Yes, she did know. The Rider was a stranger to her, and yet his voice had in it the ring of truth, and it was not only because she wanted so much to believe that her mother had been a fine, splendid woman, but simply because she knew it was the truth.

Now that the thought was there, a thousand minute details of the past came flooding back. Now she no longer had to fight the idea that she detested the man she had believed was her father. Always she had made excuses for him, avoided the question of his character and his little cruelties. Now she could face it, and she could wonder that she had ever believed him to be her father.

She remembered how few his letters had been, how she had never had from him any of the love or affection she wanted or that other girls had, how she had returned home on her first vacations with eagerness and then with increasing reluctance.

Stripping the saddle from the mare, Lona turned her into the corral. It was already past mealtime, and the hands were gone again. Rusty Gates was nowhere around, nor did she see Poke or Frank. She walked to the house and looked into the kitchen. Old Dave Betts looked up and his red face wrinkled in a smile. "You're late, ma'am, but come on in. I saved you something and kept it hot for you."

"Thanks, Dave."

He put out the food on the kitchen table. He was already preparing the evening meal, getting a few things ready in order to save time later. He glanced at Lona. "You aren't sick, are you?" he asked anxiously.

"No, Dave. Just thinking." She started to eat, but despite the long ride in the fresh, clear air, she was not hungry. "Dave," she asked suddenly, "how long have you worked for . . . Father?"

If he noticed her hesitation, he gave no sign or it made no impression. "Most of six years, ma'am. I come up to this country from Silver City. Went to Cimarron first, worked in a eatin' place there, then went back to punchin' cows for the XIT, then drifted back west an' come here. Poke Markham needed a cook, so I hired on. I was gettin' too stove up for ridin' much."

"Was Frank with him then?"

"Mailer?" Betts's face became cautious. "Well, no. No, ma'am, he wasn't. Frank didn't show up until shortly before you come home from school. He rode in here one day with Socorro an' they both hired on. Mailer, though, he'd knowed your dad somewhere else. That's why he hired him on as foreman."

"Is he really a gunman?" Lona looked up at Dave.

Betts swallowed uneasily and, stepping to the door, peered into the dining room, then outside. "I reckon there's no mystery about that. He sure is. Mighty bad . . . I mean, mighty good with a gun. So's Geslin." He looked at her quickly. "You better not ask many questions about him, ma'am. Mailer's right touchy about that. He don't like folks talkin' about him."

There was a sound of approaching horses and Lona glanced out the open door. Gordon Flynn and Rusty Gates had ridden into the yard and were swinging down. Flynn glanced toward the door, and when he saw her, he waved, then said something to Rusty and walked toward the house.

"Howdy, ma'am!" he said, his boyish face flushing a little. He had removed his hat and stood there, his wavy hair damp along his forehead where the hat had left a mark. The admiration in his eyes was obvious. "See you had been ridin' some. Why didn't you come over to the north range to see us?"

"Just riding," she said. "It was a pretty day for it and I wanted to think."

"I reckon there's no better way," he agreed. "It sort of just *makes* a body think, ridin' slow across the hills with lots of distance around you." He stepped into the room. "Dave, you got more of that coffee? Rusty an' me . . . ?"

"It ain't grub time," Dave said testily, "but you pull up a chair. I reckon I can do that for you, but I doubt if the boss would like either of you bein' here right now."

Rusty came into the room and took a quick, sharp look at Lona. He seemed satisfied with what he saw, and turned to Dave. "We have to go down to Yellow Butte after some cows and this was on our way. Drink up, Gord, and don't sit there looking calf-eyed at Miss Lona."

Flynn blushed magnificently. "Who's lookin' calf-eyed?"

he demanded, blustering. "Can't a man speak to a girl without folks sayin' things like that?"

Gates turned a chair back to the table and straddled it, grinning from one to the other. "Don't know's I blame you," he said. "She's a right pretty girl, and believe you me, if I was as good-looking as you are and not so durned bowlegged, I'd sure say my piece, too!"

Flynn's face was grim. "You're new around here," he said. "Miss Lona is engaged to the foreman."

Gates shrugged and looked pointedly at Lona. "When did a man ever let a thing like that stand between him and the girl he wanted? It sure wouldn't stop me!"

"Don't you be advisin' that sort of thing!" Betts turned irritably to Gates. "You don't know Frank Mailer! Anybody who steps on his toes or tries to move in on his girl had better be fast with a gun! He durned near killed one of the hands with his fists and boots just for talkin' to her!"

"Then I'll be careful," Gates said. Gulping his coffee, he shoved back from his chair and got up. "I just wouldn't let him catch me. But if I wanted a girl, I wouldn't stand by and see her go to another man, unless I was right sure she wanted that other man." He turned on his heel and walked out, letting the door slam behind him.

The kitchen was silent. Flynn was staring into his cup, and Lona's heart was pounding, why she could not have said. Glancing up, she could see the stubborn, angry look on Flynn's face and the sharp disapproval on the face of Dave Betts. After a minute Flynn swallowed his coffee and ducked out without saying another word.

Lona gathered the dishes and placed them on the drain board, stealing a glance at Betts's face from the corner of her eyes. "You be careful," Dave said suddenly, without turning. "You don't know Frank Mailer like I do. Don't you let no fool puncher talk you into trouble."

Lona hesitated. "What's the matter, don't you think Gordon is a nice fellow?"

Dave Betts turned sharply. "I sure do, ma'am. Flynn's one of the finest boys I know, an' he's a top hand, too. He's worth any four like Geslin or Starr, but he's too nice a boy to see shot to doll rags, ma'am, or to see stomped to bloody ruin like I've seen men stomped right here on this ranch!"

The canyon where Lona had come upon the Black Rider had several branches, all box canyons. There was, however, a trail to the rim if one knew the way and rode a good mountain horse. Not far up this steep trail there was a ledge that made a sharp turn around a jutting corner of rock. Here, in an almost hidden corner of rock, was a wide shelf, all of fifty yards across and something more in length. It was concealed from the canyon below by piñons, so that from below one would believe the cliff was unbroken. From above, due to a steep slide that broke off in the sheer drop, there was no way of approaching the ledge or looking down into the rocky niche.

Here, in this secret place, was good green grass and a thin trickle of water from a spring. At the back end of the niche was a deep undercut in which cliff dwellers had built several houses, walling part of the undercut with stone. In this hidden place the Rider had his retreat.

Dismounting, he stripped the saddle and bridle from the horse and let it go on a long picket rope. There was grass enough here, and water. From the look of the place, it had never been visited since the Indians had gone, yet one never knew. No better hiding place could be found, and here, he hoped, he was secure.

His rides over the country had given him a fair knowledge of the lay of the land, and he had been watching the Blue Hill ranch through his glasses and knew the daily procedure, yet despite the progress he had made that day in his talk with Lona Markham, he was restless, and he knew why. He wanted to see Nita.

She should never have come here, he knew. He had tried to convince her that the job was his alone, but she would have none of it, and in the end he had given in. He was pleased now that he had, for his restlessness was in a sense appeased by knowing her nearness. Once it had been decided that she was to come, Brigo, of course, had come, too. Jaime Brigo had been asked by Nita's father to watch over her, and that was an oath he had never broken.

Cain Brockman, the bartender, doubled Nita's protection, and it had been simple enough for Rusty Gates to hire out to the ranch, which put one of their own men in the enemy's camp. Yet there was much to be done, even now.

That somehow Poke Dunning had taken Markham's place, taken his ranch and usurped his position as father was obvious. Yet what had become of Markham? And what had become of his wife, Lona's mother? Where did Poke fit in? Also, was there any evidence that the ranch actually belonged to Lona other than Markham's statement to her? It seemed that the mere fact that Dunning was carefully deceiving this young girl showed that he was convinced that the ranch he had been running all these years actually belonged to her. It also seemed that Poke Dunning had somehow gotten control of the ranch by posing as her father, an act made all the easier by the fact that no one in these parts had known the original Markham. For all anyone knew, Dunning was the man who had given her the property, but now he was planning on transferring legal control to Mailer by having the girl marry him. Once the wedding took place, Dunning would not have to worry about his charade, and if something happened to Lona, Mailer would inherit the ranch simply by being her husband.

Dunning would say nothing to Lona about her mother. Was that because he did not know? And Lona had said her father had told her that her mother had died before they came on west, but was that statement made by her real father, or by Dunning?

Before facing Dunning, it was necessary to learn how title to the ranch was placed, and to have something substantial to go on. In so many years Dunning had had time to shape stories and the papers that would give him title, yet why, if that was true, had he kept the girl?

Collecting dry sticks that would make no smoke, he built a fire, and squatting above it, the Rider prepared his evening meal. He was a tall man, and his eyes were green; a sharp, straight look came into them at times that disturbed those he looked at, and at times changed quickly to easy humor and a ready smile.

Shadows were long and his meal was finished when he heard a distant sound. He straightened swiftly and, hitching his guns into place, moved swiftly from the side of the cliff dwelling across the green sward of the ledge. His horse was standing with his head up and his nostrils wide. "Easy, Buck!" he said gently.

Through the junipers he could look down into the canyon, and as he looked he heard a tapping of metal on metal. He listened a moment, then grinned and spoke aloud, knowing his voice would carry in the still air. "Straight ahead and left around the boulder."

In a few minutes he heard the horse, and then Rusty Gates appeared. It was dusk, yet light enough to see, and the cowhand stared around him in astonishment. "Now, how in the ever-so-ever did you find this place?" he demanded. "A man would sure never guess it was here!"

"It's well hidden. Come on back, I've put more coffee on."

When they were squatted over the small fire, Gates grinned across the coals at him. "Kilkenny," he said, "you have the damnedest nose for hideouts of any hombre I ever knew!"

The tall rider shrugged. "Why not? Lots of times I need 'em. It gets to be an instinct."

"You talked to Lona?"

"Uh-huh. I didn't tell her much, only that Poke was not her father."

"I thought so. She was walkin' in a trance when she got back to the spread. By the way," he added, "there's a hand on that ranch that's so much in love with her he's turnin' in circles. Name of Gordon Flynn. Nice lad."

"Well, they can work that out by themselves. I'm goin' to see she gets justice, but I'll be durned if I'll play Cupid."

Rusty chuckled. "Leave that to me! I already put a bug in their ears." He pushed a couple of sticks on the fire. "Lance, something is building down there, but I don't know what. Mailer has been doin' a lot of talking, strictly on the private, with Geslin, Starr, and Socorro. I think they've got somethin' up their sleeves."

"Not Dunning?"

"No, the old man isn't in on it. They are very careful not to get bunched up when he's around."

"What do you think of Mailer, Rusty?"

"Damned if I know!" Gates looked up, scowling. "Good as Geslin is, he listens to him. So does Starr. I guess they knowed each other before comin' to Blue Hill, too. That Socorro came in with Mailer."

"How's Nita?" Kilkenny asked, looking up.

"I was wonderin' when you'd get around to that. She's fine. Man"—he chuckled—"that girl is good! She's got brains aplenty, but, Kilkenny, she's got troubles, too! Frank Mailer is makin' a strong play for her."

Lance Kilkenny got to his feet. "Mailer?" He was incredulous. "I thought he was due to marry Lona?"

Gates looked cynical. "How much difference would that make to a man like Mailer? He's mostly interested in that ranch, I'm thinking, as far as she's concerned, anyway. But he's red-eyed over Nita."

"Has there been trouble?"

"Not yet." Gates told what had happened at the Fandango and how Nita had handled it. "So he wound up spending thirty bucks he hadn't figured on. But that won't be the end of it."

"How do Dunning and Mailer stand?" Kilkenny asked thoughtfully.

"I've been thinkin' about that. From what I hear, they trusted each other at one time, but I think a break is due. One thing: when it comes down to it, the old man will be standing all alone. The boys are all with Mailer; that is, all but Flynn, the cook, an' me. We're on the outside of that fuss."

Gates got to his feet. "I'd better get out of here before the moon comes up." He turned to go, then hesitated. "Lance, you make no mistake, Frank Mailer is dangerous."

"Thanks. I'll remember that." He grinned over the fire at Rusty.

"Hope we beat this deal without a shootin'," Rusty said.

"Me, too," Kilkenny said, almost wistfully. "Especially with that girl around, that's a tough crowd down there."

Long after Rusty Gates was gone, Lance Kilkenny sat

over his lonely fire. There had been too much of this, too much of hiding out in the wilderness, yet it was this or be recognized, and when he was recognized, there was always some wild-eyed puncher who wanted the reputation of killing Kilkenny.

He had never intended to gain a reputation, but his own choice of keeping himself anonymous had helped to begin the stories. He had become a strange, shadowy figure, a drifting gunfighter whom no man knew, until suddenly, in a blasting of gunfire, he wrote his name large across yet another page of Western history.

Long ago he had taken to haunting the lonely places or to roaming the country alone under an assumed name. He would drift into a new country and for a time he would punch cows or wrangle horses or hire out as a varmint hunter, and then trouble would come, and Kilkenny, who had rarely drawn a gun in his own battle, would fight for a friend, as he was fighting now.

This time, for the first time, he was not fighting alone. He had friends with him, good friends, and he had Nita Riordan, now using the name Howard, for there were those who knew that Nita Riordan was connected with Kilkenny.

Alone over his fire, he studied the situation. What was in the mind of Frank Mailer? What did he plan? How much opposition could Poke Dunning offer, if it came to that? If it came to a fight over the ranch? Kilkenny was enough of a strategist to appreciate the fact that in a gunfight, Dunning and Mailer might eliminate each other and so save him the trouble. Once they were out of it, he could face the others or they would leave.

What he needed to know now was how Dunning had come into possession of the ranch. When Markham had started west so long ago, he was going to this ranch, which he had acquired sometime before. Hence, Dunning had to have come into the picture after Markham left Santa Fe. Also, he must learn whether Markham's statement to Lona that the ranch was now hers was merely an idle comment or whether he had actually given the girl the title.

Yet there was on him something else, a driving urge to see Nita. He got to his feet and walked the length of the ledge, speaking softly to the buckskin, and then he walked back. The fire was dying, the embers fading. Maybe now was the time, if he could slip into Salt Creek quietly and get to the Fandango without noise. He turned the idea over in his mind, contemplating every angle of it. At last he shook his head, and replenishing the fire, then banking the coals, he crawled into his blankets and was soon asleep.

Old Poke Dunning got restlessly to his feet. He was alone much of the time now. Lona had been keeping to her quarters and he missed her. Scowling, he thought of that, and his eyes narrowed as he remembered the time of her marriage was coming nearer. That marriage was a deal that he had cooked up with Frank Mailer. But since that time he had come to distrust the man. Soon after he made his offer to guarantee them clear title to Blue Hill, Frank had started acting like he owned the place. Suppose Mailer made up his mind to go it alone? He, Dunning, would have no status, nothing that would stand up legally. Of late, Mailer had been making decisions without consulting him.

If he had it out with Mailer, he decided, he would need

an edge. Only a fool would take chances with Mailer. The man was too big, too tough. He looked as hard to stop as a bull elephant.

That Rider. The presence of the Rider might not bother Mailer, but it did bother him. He was suspicious and could find no reason for the man's continual evasion of contact with anyone.

The Black Rider must have provisions. How did he obtain them? The logical place was Salt Creek. Poke nodded; that was it. He would have a spy watching in Salt Creek, and then when someone resembling the Rider appeared, he would trail him. After that he would have a line on the man.

It was late, but he would ride into Salt Creek now and he knew just the man. The road was white in the moonlight, but Dunning rode swiftly on a powerful gray. He had not seen Mailer, and no doubt the man was again in town, and the boys with him.

Although well past fifty, Dunning was a strong and rugged man in the peak of condition. Age was no problem to him as yet, for his outdoor life and the rough, hardy food of the frontier had kept him in fine shape. He had made vast improvements on the ranch and it had provided a welcome cooling-off place for men on the dodge, as he once had been.

He had always insisted that the boys not pull any jobs while they "worked" for him, and while he paid all his men monthly, those on the run had handed back far more than their salaries in private. He also insisted that his hands not spend any of their ill-gotten gain in town or do anything that would indicate who and what they actually were. The kickbacks and free labor he had availed himself of over the years had helped make Blue Hill a profitable enterprise. Poke Dunning took great pride in the ranch. There was just Mailer and that matter of the girl and the confounded deed!

Salt Creek was a rough-looking town of some three-score buildings of which most were homes and barns. Along the one street of the town, a dozen or more buildings stared at each other, and the express office and Fandango were the biggest buildings in town. The Express, as it was known, was much more than its name implied. It was a general store as well as the post office and office of the justice of the peace, and had a small bar where drinks were sold, mostly to the older men in the community.

Up the street only two doors was another saloon, this one run by Al Starr, a brother of Sam, and beyond it another store and the livery stable, and beyond that the Fandango. It was ablaze with light when Poke Dunning rode the gray into town, but he stopped at the Express and shoved through the door.

Aside from Mr. Lisa, the Portuguese proprietor, only three men were in the Express. A couple of oldsters who were dry-farming near town, and the man Dunning sought, a hanger-on known about town as Kansas.

Kansas was more than a loafer, he was a man of unknown background and capacity. What his life had been in the years before he arrived in Salt Creek, nobody knew. He had a wife, and the two lived in a small cabin on the edge of town. It was nicer inside than most houses, for Kansas seemed to have a knack with tools, and he had even varnished the furniture and there were curtains in the windows and neatness everywhere. Moreover, Kansas had a dozen books, more than the rest of the town combined.

Yet he was a loafer, a short, heavy man with a round face and somewhat staring eyes who did odd jobs for his money. He smoked a corncob pipe, blinked like an owl, and had a faculty for knowing things or knowing how to find out. He had been in the War Between the States, and someone said he had once worked on a newspaper in the East. His conversation was more varied than customary in Salt Creek, for he knew something more than cows and the range. In fact, he knew a little of everything, and was nearly as old as Dunning himself.

"Howdy, Kansas!" Dunning said affably. "Have a drink?"

"Right neighborly of you, Poke! B'lieve I will!" He let the dark-faced Lisa pour his drink, then looked over at Dunning. "We don't see you much anymore. I guess you leave the business mostly to Mailer."

"Some things," Dunning agreed. It was the truth, of course, that Mailer had been doing the business, yet it nettled him to hear it said. "Any strangers around town?" he asked casually.

To Kansas, the question was not casual. He could not recall that Poke Markham had ever asked such a question before, and he was aware that the conversation of people will usually follow certain definite patterns. Hence it followed that the remark was anything but casual and that Markham was interested in strangers, or some particular stranger.

"Not that I know of," Kansas replied honestly enough. "Not many strangers ever come to Salt Creek. Being off the stage route and miles from the railroad, it doesn't attract folks. Were you expecting somebody?"

"No," Dunning replied, "not exactly." He steered the conversation down another trail and let it ride along for a while before he opened up with another question. "I expect like ever'body else you've seen that Black Rider they talk about," he suggested.

"Can't say I have," Kansas replied. So old Markham was forking that bronc, was he? What was on his mind, anyway? There was a point behind these questions, but Kansas could not place it.

"I've got my own ideas about him," he added, "an' I'd bet a little money they are true."

"What sort of ideas? You know who he is? Why he's here?" Poke was a little too anxious and it showed in his voice. Kansas needed some extra money and this might be the way to get it.

"Oh, I've been studyin' on it."

The two oldsters had started for the door and Lisa was opening a barrel of flour. Poke Dunning leaned closer to Kansas. "You find out who he is and I'll make it worth your while."

"How much is my while worth?" Kansas asked.

Poke hesitated, then dug into his jeans. "Twenty dollars?"

It was a talking point, but Kansas decided he might get more. He never accepted a man's first offer. "Make it fifty," he said.

"Too much." Poke hesitated. "I'll give you thirty."

Kansas sighted through his glass. "All right," he said, "I'll find out for you."

"What was your hunch?" Dunning wanted to know.

Kansas hesitated. "You seen this Nita Howard over to the Fandango?"

"Not yet."

"You take a good look. I think she's Nita Riordan."

The name meant nothing to Dunning and he said as much. Kansas turned his head toward Dunning. "Well, Nita Riordan is associated with Kilkenny. He met her down on the border during that wire war in the Live Oak country. Then she was with him over to the Cedars in that ruckus."

"Kilkenny . . ." Dunning's eyes narrowed as he half

spoke, half gasped the word. Now there was a thought! Why, if he could hire Kilkenny . . . ! When the split came with Mailer, it would pay to have the mysterious gunman on his side.

He scowled suddenly. "Why would he be here? What would he be doin' here?"

Kansas shook his head. "What he's doing here, I don't know. But Kilkenny keeps to himself like this Rider does. Moreover, the Howard woman at the Fandango calls her bartender Cain, an' Cain Brockman was with Kilkenny in that last fuss."

Dunning peeled a couple of twenties from a buckskin-wrapped roll of them and slapped them in the man's hand. "If you can get word to him, I'll give you another thirty. I want to see him on the quiet, an' don't let it get around, you hear?"

Kansas nodded, and Poke Dunning walked out and stopped on the step.

Kilkenny! If it were only he! But maybe he wouldn't take the job; there were stories that Kilkenny's gun was not for hire. That was sure nonsense, of course, any man's gun could be hired for enough money, and he had the money. To be rid of Mailer it would be worth plenty.

Lona was up at daybreak, having scarcely slept a wink. She had followed the Rider's instructions and tried to recall all she could of the ride on the wagon, but it was little enough. She recalled the town where the fat lady had been so nice to her and where she had given her maple sugar brought out from Michigan in a can. There had been Indians there, and a lot of people. She was sure that town was Santa Fe.

She waited until the hands were gone and then got a hurried breakfast from Dave Betts. "Rusty?" Betts asked. "Sure, I know where he went. He went south, down to Malpais Arroyo. Mailer sent him down there to roust some stock out of that rough country an' start it back this away."

Zusa was ready and eager to go, and Lona let the mare run. She was curious to talk to Gates again, for she was sure now that he knew who the Rider was. Though he seemed young, the Rider had known her father. Maybe Rusty would know.

She found him by as fine a flow of profanity as she had ever heard. He was down in the brush fighting an old ladino who had Rusty's rope on his horns but who had plunged into the brush even as the rope snagged it, and at the moment it was a stalemate, with Gates venting his irritation in no uncertain terms.

"Hi!" she called. "Having trouble?"

He shoved his hat back on his sweaty forehead and grinned at her. "That goll-durned, ornery critter!" he said. "I got to get him out of here, and the durned fool wants to stay! You just wait, I'll show him!" Rusty eased his horse sideways and then loosened his rope from the saddle horn. Before the steer could back up any farther into the brush, he whipped the rope around the stub of an ancient tree and tied it off. "There!" he said. "We'll just let him sit for a while."

Rusty walked over to her, his eyes curious, but if he had a question, Lona beat him to the draw. "Rusty, who is the Black Rider?"

Gates wrinkled his nose at the fancy name. "He'll tell you, ma'am, when he's ready, and he's the one to do it."

"But how could he have known my father?"

Rusty looked up quickly. "Ma'am, how he knew your

father, I don't exactly know, only it seems to be your pa helped him when he was a kid and havin' it tough. I guess your pa talked a good bit about his plans. He only found out a short time ago that your pa was dead an' that there might be trouble here. Naturally, bein' the man he is, he had to do somethin' about it."

The sound of a horse made them both look up, and Lona felt herself grow pale as she saw Frank Mailer!

"Lona!" His voice was hoarse with anger. "What's goin' on here? What are you doin', meetin' this puncher down here?"

"I'm talking to him!" she flared. "Why shouldn't I? He works for me! And it might be a good idea," she added with spirit, "for you to remember that you work for us, too!"

Frank Mailer's face stiffened and his eyes narrowed. "You seem to forget that you are the girl I'm to marry," he said, in a tone less harsh. "Naturally, I don't want you around like this."

"Well, until we are married," she said coldly, "it happens to be none of your business! If you'd like to change your mind, you may. In fact, I don't like your bullying tone and I think I've changed *my* mind!"

Frank Mailer was furious. He glared, struggling for speech. When he did speak it was to roar at Gates. "Get that steer out of that brush, you blamed farmer! Get it out an' you get them cows back to the ranch, pronto!"

Rusty Gates calmly went to work freeing the steer. Lona and Zusa started out of the arroyo. "Wait!" Mailer shouted. "I want to talk to you!"

She turned in her saddle. "Until you learn how to act like a gentleman, I haven't got a thing to say!"

Touching a spur to the mare, she was gone like a streak.

Frank stared after her, then swearing bitterly, he reined his horse around and rode away, ignoring Gates.

CHAPTER 3

Frank Mailer was in a murderous mood when he returned to Blue Hill. He left his saddled horse to Flynn and went up the steps to the house. Poke Dunning was standing in front of the fireplace when Mailer stormed into the room.

"Poke!" Frank said. "I've had about enough out of that girl! She threw her weight around too much today! Let's fix that marriage for next week!"

Dunning was lighting his pipe and he puffed thoughtfully, his eyes on the flame. Here it was, sooner than he wanted it. Well, there was more than one way to stall.

"What's the matter? What did she say?"

"I found her down at Malpais with that new puncher. I told her I didn't like it and she told me it didn't matter whether I did or not, that I worked for her! For her!"

Dunning chuckled. "Well, in a way she's right!" he said slyly. "This here is her ranch. And you're the foreman."

Mailer's eyes narrowed vindictively and he felt hot rage burning inside him. There were times when he hated Dunning. He glared at him. "I'm a damn sight more than any foreman!" he flared.

"Are you?" Dunning looked up under shaggy brows. His hands were on his hips, whether by accident or design, but his eyes were cool and steady.

Frank Mailer felt everything in him suddenly grow still. He turned on Dunning, and with a shock, he realized something he had been forgetting, that Poke Dunning was a gunman himself, and that he was not, by any means, too old. Right now he looked like a fairly dangerous proposition, and Mailer found that he did not like it, he did not like it one bit. He felt sure he could beat Poke, but he might get a slug in the process, and tomorrow they would be leaving on that job.

No fight . . . not now.

"What's the matter, Poke? You on the prod?"

Dunning recognized the change in Mailer's tone and it puzzled him. He knew the big man too well, yet here, with an even break between them, or almost an even break, for Dunning all but had the butts of his guns in his hands, Mailer was avoiding the issue. It puzzled Dunning, and worried him. He had known Mailer too long not to know the man was a schemer.

"No, Frank, I'm not," he said quietly. "Only here lately you've been taking in a little too much territory. We have our plans, but we can't ride into this roughshod. That girl has a mind of her own, and suppose she lights out of here to Salt Creek and raises hell about bein' forced to marry you? It might stir up some talk, an' we can't afford that.

"You've got to play it smart, Frank. You can't push Lona around; she's got too much fight in her. Take it easy, win her over. You can't handle a woman by shouting at her; they need soft talk."

There was truth in what Dunning said, and Mailer knew it. He was, he admitted, bullheaded. And he had been taking on a lot of weight around here. Anyway, first things come first, and there was that bank job to be handled. There would be time enough to take care of Dunning when that was off his hands. Geslin and Starr both wanted the money they would get from that job, and if he expected to keep them around, he must keep them busy, give them a chance to make a few dollars.

"Maybe you're right," he agreed. "It's a shame that Markham had to fix things that way."

"He did, though," Dunning said. "We don't dare take over until you marry her, then her property is legally yours an' we can do what we want."

"Sure, you've explained that," Mailer agreed grudgingly. He turned toward the door. "By the way, Poke," he said, in more affable tones, "I'm takin' some of the boys on a little trip tomorrow. I heard about some cattle and want to look them over. We'll be gone two days. Flynn and Gates will handle things on this end."

Dunning nodded absently. "All right. Good luck on the trip."

Outside on the porch, Frank Mailer stared angrily into the darkness. "We'll need it," he muttered. "And once I've married that girl, you'll need it!"

One thing he knew. The time was coming for a showdown. He would wait no longer. That Spanish woman, now . . . if he were owner of the Blue Hill, she would pay attention to him. She liked him, anyway, but was just stalling. That was always the woman's way, any woman. The fact that he would be married to Lona would matter but little. He would have things in his hands then, and he would know how to handle matters. Poke Dunning had to die.

Lance Kilkenny was riding to Salt Creek. Despite his desire to remain unknown, he had missed Nita so much that he could no longer stay away. Also, with his instinct for trouble and his knowledge of the situation in Salt Creek and on the ranch, he knew the lid was about to blow off. It was high time that he appeared on the scene.

Yet reaching town, he did not ride immediately into the street, but studied it carefully. He could see the lights of the Fandango, and nearer, the lights of Starr's Saloon and the Express. He rode the buckskin into the street and swung down in front of the Express.

He stepped up onto the boardwalk, feeling all that tightness he always knew when appearing for the first time in a strange town. His eyes slanted down the street, studying each building with strict attention. Every sense was alert for trouble, for a man who had used a gun as he had would have enemies, and in a strange town one never knew whom one would see.

The street was empty and still, its darkness alleviated only by the windows of the four or five lighted places in Salt Creek. He turned and opened the door to the Express and walked in.

Down the left-hand side was a row of boxes and sacks backed by a wall of shelves filled with various articles of cutlery and other tools. On his right were shelves of clothing, a few wide hats, and nearer the counter at the end was the ammunition, and beside it the bar. There were groceries and several opened barrels. Near a stove, now cold, sat two old men. At the bar Kansas was talking to Lisa.

Kilkenny walked down the right side of the long room whose middle was also stacked with boxes and barrels. As he approached the near end of the bar, Kansas looked up. In that instant the gunfighter knew he was recognized.

"Rye, if you would," Kilkenny said quietly. His eyes turned to Kansas, alert, probing. "What are you drinking, friend?"

Kansas's mouth was dry. He started to speak, swallowed, and then said, "Rye. Mine's rye, too, Lisa."

The Portuguese noticed nothing out of the ordinary, and put the glasses on the bar. His quick glance, however, noticed that the gray shirt was new and clean, the flat-brimmed hat was in good condition, and Kilkenny was clean-shaven. He left the bottle on the bar. He knew when a man could pay for his drinks.

Kansas recovered himself slightly. Here was his chance to do that job for Poke, dropped right in his lap. Luck seemed to be with him, but he reflected uneasily that Kilkenny did not have a reputation as the sort of man who would hire his gun. "Driftin' through?" he said.

"Maybe."

"Nice country around here."

"Seems so."

"There's jobs. Mailer, he's foreman out to the Blue Hill, he took on a hand the other day." He dropped his voice. "Poke Markham was talkin' to me. Seems he's huntin' a particular man for a very particular job. From the way you wear those guns, you might be just the man."

Kilkenny looked into his glass. Now, what was this? A trap? Or was Dunning looking for gunmen? "We might talk about it," he said. "I just might be interested."

Kansas was pleased and disappointed at the same time. He had heard much of Kilkenny, and while if he did this job for Poke, it might mean more money, which he could always use, he was sorry that Kilkenny would consider such a thing.

"Many folks in town?" Kilkenny asked quietly.

"A few. Mailer's here, if you're interested, but better not talk to him about this Markham job. I had the idea Markham was hiring someone confidential."

Kilkenny nodded. . . . So? Was there a break there? If so, it might work out very well for him. And Rusty had said Mailer was planning some move in which Dunning was not concerned. Maybe Poke knew more than Mailer realized.

"This Mailer," he said carelessly, "what sort of hombre is he?"

"Mighty big an' mighty bad," Kansas replied honestly. "He's hell on wheels with a gun an' ready to use one on the slightest provocation, but he would rather use his fists and boots. Sometimes I think he likes to beat a man." There was animosity in Kansas's voice, and Kilkenny noticed it at once.

"Where's he from?"

"You've got me," Kansas admitted. "Folks around here have done a lot of wondering about that. Where he came from or what he was, I don't know. Somebody did say they saw him talking to Port Stockton over to Bloomfield once."

Port Stockton was a name Kilkenny knew. Boss of the Stockton gang, marshal of Bloomfield, and formerly in the Lincoln County War in the faction opposed to the Tunstall-McQueen outfit that had Billy the Kid. Stockton was no honest man, by all accounts, and a dangerous one. It was worth looking into, that angle.

He straightened. "You tell Markham I'll talk to him. I'll get in touch with him myself within the next couple of days." Turning, he walked to the door, scanned the street briefly, and then stepped out.

The Fandango was ablaze with lights, and Kilkenny did not hesitate; he walked at once to the doors and pushed them open. The place was crowded. Nita had a faculty for knowing the sort of place the range people liked, and she gave them lots of light and music. A half-dozen card tables were going now, and the long bar was lined with booted and spurred men.

A few men in business suits mingled with the roughly dressed cowhands, but one and all they were wearing guns. The first person who saw him was Jaime Brigo, and the big Yaqui did not smile, merely reaching back with his knuckles and tapping a signal on the door.

Nita Riordan heard that signal. She was at her mirror, and for a minute she stared at her reflection. She had known Kilkenny now for more than three years, and had loved him every minute of them, but after one of these absences it never failed to leave her breathless when she heard his voice, his step, or heard the signal that signified his presence.

Kilkenny had walked to the end of the bar, and Cain Brockman moved at once to him and placed a glass and a bottle there. His head moved ever so slightly, and Kilkenny's eyes followed the movement. He saw Frank Mailer towering above the crowd, his face red and flushed from drinking, his glassy-blue and slightly protuberant eyes bold and domineering as they surveyed the crowd around him.

The slender hatchet-faced man would be Geslin, of course. Starr was there, and the sallow, dark-haired Socorro.

Mailer, Kilkenny observed, kept turning his head to glance toward the door where Brigo sat. Kilkenny studied him without seeming to, watching the man with the side of his glance. The fellow was a bull, but big as he was, there was no evidence of fat. Even his thick neck looked like a column of muscle; there was cruelty in the man's eyes and in his thin lips, and there was brutality showing all through him. Even without knowing who he was and why he was here, Kilkenny would have felt the same animal antagonism for the man.

Suddenly Nita was in the room. He knew it without turning his head. He would always know it, for there was that between them, that sharp, strong attachment, something physical and yet more than physical. He turned and their eyes met across the room and he felt something well up within him. She smiled, ever so slightly, and turned to the nearest card table, speaking to one of the players.

Frank Mailer had seen her, too, and he turned abruptly away from the bar. "So there you are!" he boomed. "Come and have a drink!"

"I don't drink. I believe I have told you that."

"Oh, come on!" he insisted, reaching for her arm. "Don't be foolish! Come on an' have a drink with me."

Suddenly Nita Riordan was frightened. Kilkenny had moved away from the bar; he was coming toward them.

"I'm sorry," she said coldly. "I'll not drink with you. Why don't you join your friends?"

Kilkenny was beside her now, but Mailer had eyes for nobody else. He had been waiting for this woman to come out, and he had been drinking, thinking of her, wanting her. He told himself she wanted him, and there had been enough of foolishness. "Come on!" he said roughly. "I want to talk to you!"

"But the lady does not want to talk to you!" Kilkenny said. Frank Mailer turned his big head sharp around. For the first time he saw Kilkenny. "Get lost!" he snarled. "Get . . . !"

What he was going to say never came out. He was seeing Kilkenny, really seeing him for the first time, looking into those hard green eyes, level and dangerous now, into the bronzed face of a man that he instinctively recognized as being something different, somebody new and perhaps dangerous. "Who the hell are you?" he demanded.

"The man who tells you the lady does not wish to talk to you," Kilkenny said. He turned, "Miss Howard, do you wish to go to the bar?"

She turned instantly and started to go off with him.

Mailer found himself left in the middle of the floor alone, and he had made his brags about this woman and himself. They had an understanding, he had hinted. In fact, he had convinced himself it was true. Somebody snickered, and Frank Mailer blew up.

Lunging, he grabbed at Nita's shoulder, but knowing his man, Kilkenny had been watching. He moved swiftly and thrust the hand aside. Instantly, Frank Mailer struck. He struck with his ponderous right fist that had already lifted with the violence of his grab at the girl, but Kilkenny rolled his head and smashed a left and right to the body.

Lance Kilkenny knew the manner of man he was facing and knew that if ever he had been in for a battle, he was in for one now. He struck fast and he struck hard, and the blows smashed Mailer back on his heels. Before he could catch his balance, Kilkenny hooked high and hard with a left and the blow knocked Mailer crashing to the floor.

He hit hard, in a sitting position, knocked back all of four feet, and as he hit he knew he had been struck with such force that all the other blows he had taken seemed mere child's play. He hit the floor drunk and raging, but he came up with a lunge, and cold sober.

Skilled in the rough-and-tumble style of barroom brawling, Lance Kilkenny knew what he was facing, yet he had more than that sort of skill on which to draw, for long ago in New Orleans he had studied the art of boxing and become quite proficient at it.

Mailer came up with a lunge and charged, swinging. Kilkenny nailed him on the mouth with a straight, hard left and then smashed another right to the ribs before the sheer weight of the rush smashed Kilkenny back against the bar. Mailer blazed with fury and confidence. Now he had him! Against the bar!

One hand grasped Kilkenny's throat, pushing his head

back. Then he jerked up his knee for Kilkenny's groin. Yet Kilkenny's own knee had lifted an instant quicker and blocked the rise of Mailer's drive. At the same time Kilkenny struck Mailer's left hand away from his throat by knocking it to the right, and he lunged forward, smashing the top of his skull into Mailer's nose and mouth.

Blood streaming from his smashed lips, Mailer staggered, pawing at the air, and Kilkenny let him go, standing there, breathing easily, and waiting. The crowd had been shoved back, he saw, and Jaime Brigo was standing beside Nita with drawn gun. Over the bar behind him he heard Brockman speak, Brockman whom he had once fought in just such a battle, before they were friends. "Don't worry, boss. Nobody butts in!"

Mailer recovered his balance and stared at Kilkenny with malignant eyes. With the back of his hand he mopped the blood from his lips, staring at Kilkenny. "Now," he said, his voice low and dangerous, "I'm goin' to kill you!"

He moved in, his big fists ready, taking his time now. This man was not going to be smashed down in a couple of driving rushes. Mailer was not worried. He had always won, no man could stand against him.

Mailer moved in, feinted, then lunged. Kilkenny did not step away or retreat; he stepped inside and his legs were spread and he smashed wicked, hooking drives to the ribs that jolted and jarred Mailer. Frank shortened his own punches and caught Kilkenny with a mighty right that knocked him to the floor. With a roaring yell, Mailer sprang into the air and leaped to come down on Kilkenny's body, but Lance rolled over and sprang to his feet like a cat, and Mailer, missing, lunged past him against the bar. Kilkenny smashed a wicked right to the kidney, and as Mailer turned and grabbed for him he swung the man over his back with a flying mare.

Mailer came up fast and rushed and they stood toe-to-toe, swapping punches. Shifting his feet, Kilkenny was caught with a foot off the floor and he went back into the bar. The big man lunged and grabbed Kilkenny around the waist with both mighty arms.

Growling with fury, he tightened that grasp, but Kilkenny, caught with his hands down and inside that mighty hug, jerked both thumbs into the lower abdomen, low and hard. Mailer jerked back from the thumbs, and instantly Kilkenny turned his hips inside the hollow left between their bodies, and grasping Mailer's right sleeve with his left hand, he slid his right arm around his waist, and jerking down with the left, he swung Mailer across his hip and crashing to the floor with a thud that shook the building. He sprang back then, getting distance between them, and mopping the blood and sweat from his eyes. Frank Mailer got to his feet, throttling rage in his throat mingled with something else, something he had never felt before, the awful, dreadful fear that he might be beaten!

He lunged, and Kilkenny stepped into him. The gun-fighter was utterly savage now. Watching, Cain Brockman cringed with the memory, for Kilkenny's fists cracked like ball bats on Mailer's face. It was a driving, utterly furious attack, that smashed Mailer back with solid blow after solid blow. Mailer lunged, grabbed him again, and jerked him clear off the floor, hurling him down. Kilkenny hit hard, and one of his guns went scooting, but Nita stooped quickly and caught it up.

Kilkenny was on his back and Mailer lunged for him. Kilkenny swung a boot up and caught the oncoming man in the solar plexus and the drive of the rush, and the moving boot carried the big man over like a catapult and he hit the floor beyond, his fall broken by the crowd that could not move fast enough.

Kilkenny rolled over and was on his feet. Punch-drunk, Mailer came up, and Kilkenny let go with both hands. Mailer sagged and his knees buckled and Kilkenny threw an uppercut with all the power that was in him. It lifted the big man from his feet and turned him over, and Frank Mailer hit the floor on his shoulder blades, out cold!

Kilkenny drew back, feeling for his gun. The right gun was still with him and he faced the crowd, his eyes desperate, blazing with cold fire. He swept the crowd until he found Geslin and Starr. Their eyes met and he stood there, his chest heaving with the struggle for air, sweat streaming down his face, his shirt in rags about him. He stood there, and suddenly Nita spoke. "In your holster!" and he felt his left-hand gun slide home. For a minute he held their eyes, steady, waiting.

Nobody moved, nobody spoke. He straightened then and glanced down at the beaten and bloody man who sprawled on the floor. "Tell him all the roads are open, but they run one way . . . out of town!"

It was a silent, grim bunch of men who took the trail that night back to Blue Hill, but while they rode slowly, and Frank Mailer slumped heavily in his saddle, his great head thudding with a dull ache, there was a man ahead of them who rode very swiftly indeed. It was Kansas, and he was riding to be the first to report to Dunning. This was something Poke would want to know, something he needed to know.

After Kansas was gone, Poke Dunning paced the floor alone. Frank Mailer whipped! It was unbelievable! Had the earth opened and gulped down the Blue Hill, the ranch and its neighboring peak, he could have been no more shocked. That Mailer might be beaten with a gun, he knew. But with fists? In a rough-and-tumble fight? It was impossible!

But it had happened. Mailer was beaten. Despite his satisfaction, Dunning was worried. He turned in late, but he did not sleep, lying there and staring up into the darkness. He had worked a long time for this ranch, and he meant to keep it. He would kill anybody who endangered his possession of the ranch. Even Lona. Even Lona, the girl he had reared.

Kilkenny awoke early the following morning. He had returned at once to his hideout, but now he was awake. His hands were swollen and battered, and in the mirror he carried, he could see one eye was swollen almost closed. There was a welt on the corner of his mouth and a blue swelling on his cheekbone. He heated water on the fire and soaked his hands; carefully he cleaned the cuts and scrapes on his head and arms.

He was still tending to his injuries at noon when Gates appeared. He swung down and crossed to Kilkenny with jingling spurs. "Man! Did you beat that big lug! He was still punch-drunk when they left this morning!"

Kilkenny looked up sharply. He didn't feel too good himself. "They left? How many of them?"

"Mailer himself and four hands. Geslin, Starr, Socorro, and a mean-faced hombre with a scar that I've not seen around much."

"Thin? Stoop-shouldered with yellowish eyeballs?"

"That's him, who is he?"

"That's Ethridge, one of the Stockton gang." Kilkenny got to his feet, drying his hands. "That gives me a hunch, now. I think I know who Mailer is. If I'm not wrong, he's one of a bunch that operated out of Durango. Used a flock of names. One of them was Lacey or something like that."

"Yeah, I've heard of him."

Kilkenny studied his swollen hands. "Look," he said presently, "we're going to wind this up. Lona should come to see me today, and I've got to go see Poke Dunning. He left word with Kansas down at Salt Creek. He's got a proposition for me."

"Watch yourself."

"I will. But I want to see him. The lid's set to blow off anyway, and we might as well start the ball rolling while Mailer is gone."

"He said he'd be gone two days."

"All right, that gives us some time. I'll talk to Lona, then I'll ride down and see Dunning. You be ready, and you talk to Flynn and that cook."

After Gates was gone, he thought it over again. Kilkenny had taken care to learn something about the extent of the Blue Hill holdings, and the ranch was vast in area and in stock. There were thousands of head of cattle, and in the breaks to the west there were sheep. It was a big stake, truly.

How had Mailer worked into the deal? He was sure that Poke had started it alone . . . in fact, in his own mind he was sure that Dunning had killed Markham. But somehow Mailer had come into it.

He was thinking about that when he heard Lona ride into the amphitheater below, so he got to his feet and swung into the saddle.

She smiled brightly when she saw him, then gasped as she saw his face. "Oh, what happened to you? You're hurt!"

Kilkenny chuckled. "No, not really. I had a fight last night. Didn't you hear about it?"

"No . . . how would I hear?"

He took off his hat and swung down to a seat near her on a boulder. "It was your man Mailer I was fighting."

She came to her feet. "You . . . fought Frank Mailer?"

He smiled, painfully. "If you think I look bad, you should see him!"

"You . . . whipped him?" Lona was amazed. The more she looked at the tall young man on the rock, the more impossible it became that this man could have beaten Mailer.

Kilkenny grinned. He didn't like to brag, and yet . . . well, what man doesn't like to have a pretty girl think well of him? "Well, to tell you the truth, I did, and if you'll pardon my saying so, I did a bang-up job of it. Not that I didn't catch a few!" He felt with delicate fingers of the lump on his cheekbone.

"He'll kill you now." She was very positive. "He'll never let you get away alive."

"It's going to get to that point anyway," Kilkenny said. "I'm going to make sure that ranch is in your hands, all free and clear, with Poke Dunning and Mailer both out of the picture. Do you believe now that Dunning's not your father?"

She looked at him seriously. "I . . . I never really doubted that. He was always funny around me, and he would never tell me anything about my mother. I remember a lot of little things now."

"Anything about that wagon trip?" he asked quickly.

"Not much. I remember a town where there were Indians, and from all else I recall, it must have been Santa Fe. There was another man with us then. And we came west from there."

"You remember nothing after that?"

"Well . . . sort of. It's not very clear, not at all, but I have a memory of a place . . . of coming up a long canyon with a small stream in the bottom. We came up it for a long, long way, it seems to me. Once we climbed out of it and I remember Father pointing at a great peak or mesa that was far away. He . . . I remember that because he said something about an orphan at the time, and I pestered him to tell me what an orphan was. I guess it wasn't long after that I became one."

Kilkenny nodded. "That helps. We're getting places now. I would bet fifty dollars that the long canyon was Canyon Largo. The Orphan makes sense. You see, that's the name of a mesa over in the desert near Largo. They call it El Huérfano . . . the Orphan, because it stands alone."

"Isn't that funny?" she said. "I never connected the mountain and the orphan, at all! Now, let's see, there was something else, too. Last night I was thinking about it and I dreamed something about a night when there was a fire and I woke up and I could see the light dancing on a rock wall. I've thought about that real often. You know how it is, you forget so much and then two or three things sort of stick in your mind? It was that way with this. . . . I remember waking up and being afraid because I could see that Father was not in his blankets, but when I called to him, he spoke to me from far off and told me to be quiet. I went back to sleep then."

Kilkenny squinted his eyes at her. "You remember anything else about that?"

She shook her head. "No, only I think it was the next day that we got here and the old Indian woman took care of me. I didn't see Father again for a long time."

"Probably you never saw him again, not actually."

Kilkenny got to his feet. "You know, I've a hunch that night you woke up was the night your father was killed, and if you got to the ranch the next day, it could not have been far from here."

"Oh, but I can't be sure!" she objected. "It's been so long, and telling it this way makes it seem a lot more real than it actually was! It's pretty vague."

"Nevertheless, I think I'm right. Before I see Dunning today, I'm going to have a look."

"But how could you find it after all this time?" she asked.

"I'll have to be lucky," he admitted. "Mighty lucky. But there aren't many trails across this country from Santa Fe, and I don't believe he ever brought the wagons on much further than that. He may have burned them, and if he did, they may still be there, or the rims may. I'll have a look, anyway."

"But why? What's to be gained?"

"I don't know," he confessed. "Maybe nothing. I'd like to get something on Dunning, though. Something definite. And there might be a clue."

She nodded, looking out past the screen of pines toward the distant hills.

Then suddenly, almost as she turned her head, he was gone from the rock! She stared, then started to her feet. Where in the world . . . ?

"Lona!" She whirled. It was Gordon Flynn. "What in the world are you doin' way back here?" he asked. He was sitting a dun pony that he often rode, and he looked around wonderingly. "An' how did you ever find this place? I'd never have guessed it was here."

"I found it."

Kilkenny stepped from behind a clump of piñon, and Flynn gulped. "You . . . you're Kilkenny?"

Lona's eyes flew open and she gasped, "Kilkenny!"
"Yes, ma'am," he replied, "that's my name."

CHAPTER 4

The hamlet of Aztec Crossing was born of a broken axle and weaned and reared on Indian whiskey. For three weeks the town was a covered wagon and three barrels of whiskey, but by that time "Hungry" Hayes, onetime buffalo hunter and freighter, had built a dugout roofed with poles and earth.

With those three barrels of Indian whiskey to prime the pump of prosperity, and a Winchester to back the priming, Hayes turned his broken axle and the river crossing into a comfortable fortune. Indian whiskey is a simple concoction of river water, not strained, straight alcohol (roughly two gallons to the barrel), three plugs of chewing tobacco, five or six bars of soap (very strong lye soap), one half pound of red pepper, and a liberal dose of sagebrush leaves. To this is added two ounces of strychnine, and the resulting brew is something to make a mummy rear on his hind legs and let out a regular Comanche yell. This recipe was not, of course, original with Hungry Hayes. He merely adopted the formula in use throughout the Indian country, the ingredients varying but little.

The first two settlers of Aztec Crossing halted because of proximity to the source of supply, yet neither proved as hardy as the durable Hayes. The first to pass on was helping Hayes mix the whiskey and decided that he preferred it straight, without the addition of the river water. The following morning Hayes planted him on the bank of the river with due ceremony. The second settler departed this world after a brief but emphatic altercation with four Apaches. His mistake was entirely due to a youthful disdain for mathematics, for having slain three Apaches, he straightened up from his protecting buffalo wallow to leave, and took an arrow through his chest. He was buried, after an interval of sunshine and buzzards, by Hayes, taking with him a surplus of arrows but considerably less hair.

Yet, as time passed, Aztec Crossing grew. Ranching began, and the town acquired a general store, four saloons, a livery stable, a bank, and various other odds and ends of business enterprise. Hungry Hayes, fat with money, departed for the East and settled down in a comfortable Kentucky homestead, where people forever after regarded him as a liar for telling what was actually less than the truth.

The latest institution, and from Frank Mailer's viewpoint, the most interesting, was the Aztec City Bank.

With a dozen ranches nearer to Aztec than any other town, the bank was at times fairly bulging with coin. This fact had not gone unnoticed, and the five hard-bitten gentlemen who drifted into Aztec on the bright and sunny morning in question had decided to give some attention to this money.

Aztec was drowsing in the sun. The weather-beaten boards of the walk in front of the Aztec Saloon supported the posteriors of four old settlers, talking of great deeds against the warlike Comanche. In front of the livery stable, half-asleep, old Pete chewed tobacco in drowsy content. In the store, his glasses as far down on his nose as possible, Storekeeper Worth studied a month-old newspaper. A dun pony flicked a casual tail at a fly who buzzed in deep bass, and the morning was warm, pleasant, and sleepy.

Frank Mailer, mounted on a blood bay, walked his horse down the main street with the saturnine Socorro beside him. Reining in at the bank hitching rail, he swung down, and Socorro did likewise, and stayed between the horses, fussing with some saddle gear, his carbine close at hand.

Geslin and Starr came down from the opposite direction, and Geslin drew up, taking time to light a smoke while his slate-gray eyes studied the street with a cold, practiced gaze. Starr chewed tobacco, and sat his horse, his thick thighs bulging the cloth of his jeans. Ethridge walked up from behind the bank and stopped at the corner of the building. He carried a Henry rifle, and with Socorro faced one way and he another, they could cover the street with ease.

Mailer, his face swollen and ugly, jerked his head at Geslin. Starr followed. Geslin was worried, for he had never seen Mailer as he was today. Always brutal, the man was now in a vicious mood, his whole manner changed. The beating he had taken had aroused all the ferocity innate in his being. He pushed open the door and walked in and toward the office of the president. Geslin went to one window, and Starr to the other. Starr took the man who was standing there and spun him sharply, smashing a Colt down over the man's skull.

"All right," he said, "sack it up!"

The cashier looked, paled, gulped, and reached for a sack. Mailer had the president out, and with three men under their guns and the fourth on the floor out cold, they proceeded to strip the bank.

Across the street Johnny Mulhaven was coming out of the saloon, and Johnny Mulhaven had more nerve than brains. He saw the sudden collection of horses, he saw two men facing the street with rifles, and he let out a shrill Texas yell and went for his gun.

Ethridge dropped the rifle on him and fired . . . the shot was too quick and too high. It hit Johnny in the shoulder and he dropped his gun, but caught it in the air with his left hand and snapped a quick shot at Ethridge. His shot was quick but lucky. Ethridge caught the bullet where his ribs parted and dropped his rifle.

The old Comanche fighters dove for shelter, two of them under the walk, one behind a watering trough; another dashed for the saloon. Without doubt he was headed for a drink to ballast his shocked nerves, but he was doomed to die thirsty. He caught a slug from Socorro's rifle and went down on the very step of his goal, and in a matter of seconds the street was laced with gunfire, stabbing, darting flames.

Young Johnny Mulhaven was still on his feet, carrying enough lead for three men to die, and he was still firing left-handed. Scar Ethridge had made one attempt to get up, but Johnny made sure of him with a bullet through the skull. One of the horses sprang away, and then the bank door burst open and three men charged into the street.

Mulhaven took the full blast of their fire and went down hard, blood staining the gray boards of the walk. A rifle spoke from the livery stable, another from the store. Three men were unlimbering guns from within the saloon. Old Pete, at the first shot, had come erect with a lunge, swallowed his chewing tobacco, and methodically pulled his old pistol, aimed, shot, and put a slug into Kane Geslin.

And then, suddenly as it had begun, it was over. Five men had come into town, and four rode out. Two of them were wounded.

It was only then that the full story was known. Within the bank, the slugged man told it. He had come out of it just in time to see Mailer strike the banker down, then unlimber his pistol and kill all three of the men within the bank. Wisely, he lay still and lived.

Four men were dead, but Johnny Mulhaven, miraculously, was still alive, but with nine wounds.

Headed east and riding fast were the four remaining outlaws. Geslin had a flesh wound and Socorro had come out of it with a bloody but merely burned shoulder. All four were ugly, despite the success of their venture, and three of them were worried. They had known Mailer for a long time, but not the Mailer in the bank. They were all men who had killed and would kill again, yet those three killings were cold-blooded, unnecessary, and dangerous to their safety. Dangerous because while many a Western town might overlook a bank robbery, they would never overlook a cold-blooded killing.

They swung north, leaving the trail for the rough country, and circled west, heading for a crossing above White Canyon. They had good horses, and doubted if a pursuit would immediately get under way. Silent, brooding, and bloody, the four men crossed the Rio Grande and headed up Pajarito Canyon, crossed to Valle de los Posos, and headed for the Rio Puerco.

Nobody talked. Geslin had lost blood and felt sick and sore. The movement of the horse hurt him. Sweat smarted the burn on Socorro's arm and his mood became vile. Steadily, they pushed on under a baking sun, their shirts stained with blood and sweat, their horses plodding more wearily. Behind them there might be pursuit, and they could easily be followed. There were Indian trackers at Aztec Crossing.

No clouds marred the faint blue of the sky where the sun hung brassy and broiling. Nothing moved but the sage, and there was no wind, only a heavy, stifling heat. Sam Starr alone seemed unaffected, but from time to time his eyes turned toward the huge sullen figure of Frank

Mailer. Mentally, he told himself he was through. When I get mine, he told himself, I'm pullin' stakes.

Alkali dust lifted in soft clouds and dusted a film over their clothing. Socorro cursed monotonously and Geslin stared ahead with bleak, desperate eyes, his lips dry, his body aching for rest and water. Frank Mailer, indomitable and grim, rode on ahead. Starr stared phlegmatically before them, his eyes squinting against the intense white glare of the sun. He watched his horse carefully, keeping it to good ground whenever possible, knowing how much depended on it.

At last the night came and shadows reached out and touched them with coolness. In a tiny glade on the Rio Puerco, the men swung stiffly from their horses. Starr eyed the sacks thoughtfully, and Socorro with greedy, eager eyes, watchful eyes, too, for they shifted vaguely to the night, and then with more intentness on the men close by.

Bulking black against the starry sky, looming almost above them, were the rugged San Pedro Mountains. Starr got some food together, and nobody talked. Geslin bathed his wound and bandaged it; Socorro did likewise. Mailer stared into the flames, hulking and dangerous.

"Will we make it back tomorrow?" Socorro asked suddenly.

"No," Geslin replied, "there isn't a chance."

"Let's split the money now," Socorro suggested.

Starr wanted nothing more than that, but he was hesitant to agree. His eyes shifted to Mailer and they all waited for him to speak, but he said nothing. Starr had seen men like this before when killing was on them. There was only one end to it. Death. They killed and killed until they themselves were slain. He wanted no part of it. He wanted to get away. He also wanted his money.

Dawn found them pushing northeast, heading up Capulin Creek. With the San Pedros to the south and the bulk of Mesa Prieta to the north, there was no way to see if there was any pursuit or not. Geslin was willing to bet there was, and Starr agreed. They told each other as much during a moment when they had fallen behind.

It was dusk when they drew up at a spring and slid from their horses. "We'd better stop," Geslin said. "My arm's givin' me hell!"

Mailer turned on him. "What's the matter?" He sneered. "You turnin' into an old woman?"

Geslin's face whitened and for an instant they stared at each other. "Go ahead!" Mailer taunted. "Reach for it!"

Sam Starr stepped back, his eyes watchful. Geslin was in no shape for this. The man's nerves were shot, he was weakened from loss of blood, and beaten by the endless riding.

"What's the matter?" Mailer said. "You a quitter? You yellow?"

Geslin's hand flashed for his gun, and Frank Mailer swung his pistol up with incredible speed. An instant it held, then the shot bellowed, thundering between the cliffs. Geslin went down, his gun spouting fire into the dirt, shot through the heart.

Socorro touched his lips with his tongue, and Sam Starr stood very still, staring at Mailer. The man was fast; he was chained lightning.

Mailer's eyes went to Socorro, then sought Starr, but Sam had his back to darkness and shooting at him would have been a poor gamble. "Anybody sayin' anything?" Mailer demanded. He waited while one might have counted five, and neither man spoke. Then he turned away. "No time for loafin'. We're ridin' on."

.   .   .

Three days before, Lance Kilkenny had set out on the trail of what he suspected was a thirteen-year-old murder. Following Lona's vague memories of the journey to the Blue Hill ranch and his own knowledge of the best route to that area from Santa Fe, Kilkenny cut across country to a spot he hoped would intersect the path the Markham wagon had taken. By morning he was in Canyon Largo, headed west, with the sun at his back. Lona had told him that she had gone on only one more day after she'd been told that her father had traveled on ahead. That meant that the site of that last camp and possibly the site of the killing was relatively close to the ranch. By going a good sixty miles farther east than would seem necessary, Kilkenny hoped to follow the best path for a wagon and therefore have some hope that he might discover the exact way that Markham, Lona, and Poke Dunning had approached the ranch. He was covering ground faster than any wagon could have, not bothering to look for any true clues of the Markham family's passing, just getting a feel for the slope of the land, watching for deep arroyos and trying to think like a man would when driving with a heavy load.

By noon he had stopped at a place where the stream had eddied back on itself and made a good watering hole. From the growth of trees and brush, Kilkenny figured that it was a place that had remained unchanged for many years and was not the creation of some recent alteration in the flow of water.

He got down and, leaving Buck to graze on whatever grass he could find, scouted around on foot. In twenty minutes he had discovered nothing, so he mounted up and headed off again figuring that he'd cross and head on out north of Angel's Peak. He had not gone a score of yards when he saw it.

He drew up staring at a crude drawing scratched on the rock wall of Largo Canyon. It was scarcely three feet from the ground and was a crude, childish representation of a girl with stick legs and arms. An Indian drawing? he wondered. But no Indian had ever made a drawing like that!

He rode straight up now, his eyes searching the canyon walls and the sandy bed. Although he had found no campsite, and Lona had not mentioned making this drawing, he was sure that he had stumbled onto their route.

The following morning, scarcely ten miles from the ranch, he watered his horse and rested on the east side of Thieving Rock. Idly wandering about, Lance Kilkenny suddenly saw a charred wheel, then some bolts.

Near a sheltering overhang, half-hidden by brush, were the old remains of a large fire. Here a few stones had been huddled together and blackened with soot. He dropped to his knees and dug in the sand, feeling around to see what he might turn up.

At the bottom of the inner wall, the water or wind of some bygone age had scoured out a small crevice in the stone. It was partly covered, but his eye caught a glimpse of something more than sand, and stopping, he prodded at it with a stick. It moved and he saw that it was an iron box!

Kneeling, he grabbed the corner, and brushing away the sand, he pulled out the box. It was ancient and badly rusted, so picking up a stone he struck at the lock.

Another blow and the box broke open. Within it were a few silver pieces, black with age, and a handful of papers. Carefully, he picked them up. A birth certificate for Lona! Markham's marriage certificate! A last will and testament! And the deed to the ranch, placing it in Lona's name, along with the old original deed given him when he himself acquired the ranch!

Probably he had been afraid of Dunning and had concealed this box each night to prevent it being found by him if anything happened.

That evening Kilkenny had ridden down the Old Mormon Trail to Blue Hill. Rusty Gates was mending a bridle and he glanced up at him as he rode in. Gordon Flynn was working around the corral and Lona saw him coming and smiled nervously as he swung down. "I'm hunting Poke Markham," Kilkenny said loudly. "Is he around?"

Dunning appeared in the door. He was wearing two guns, Kilkenny noticed, whereas he had worn but one heretofore. "Come on in!" Poke said, and turned and walked back into the room.

Lance followed him across the porch, then stopped, closing his eyes for an instant so he would see better inside away from the sunlight. He took in the room with one quick glance. A glance that gauged the distance to all the doors and placed the main articles of furniture. A lot might happen before he left this room.

"You wanted to see me?"

Poke Dunning looked up from under shaggy gray brows. His eyes were hard, measuring. "You're Kilkenny?"

"That's right."

"You whipped Frank Mailer the other evening. You reckon he will take it lyin' down?"

"He can take it as he chooses."

"He'll meet you with a gun, Kilkenny, and he's fast as greased lightnin'."

Kilkenny waited, saying nothing. This old man wore his guns with the butts well forward. Some gunmen liked them that way.

"You can't get away from meeting him unless you run,

an' you don't set up like a running man. I want you to meet him right away. Soon as he comes back."

"Where's he gone?"

"How'd I know? Don't care, neither. He's a bad hombre, that one, and he's got to be killed. You got to kill him, anyway, but if you hunt him down or kill him as soon as he gets back, any way you like, I'll give you five hundred dollars!"

The way he said it made the sum sound big . . . but was it big enough? What were the stakes to Poke Dunning?

"No. I'll meet him when I have to. I won't hunt him down." Kilkenny pulled out his tobacco and began to build a smoke. "Nice place you've got here. Had it long?"

Dunning tightened up inside. The old fear was always on him. "Quite a spell," he replied. "Been some changes made."

"I heard it belonged to your daughter, to Lona."

"Well, you're right. I gave it to her when she was just a child."

"You going to start another place someday?" Kilkenny touched the tip of his tongue to his cigarette, then placed it in his mouth. He dug out a match and lit up, glancing through the first smoke at Dunning. "Let her have her inheritance?"

"Maybe," Poke said flatly. "Someday." Poke Dunning stared at Kilkenny. What was this, anyway? He had the man out here to try to hire him, and now he was asking questions. Too many questions.

"I was wondering. . . . Why is it that they call you 'Poke,' Mr. Markham? What was your given name?"

He faced Kilkenny. "What's it to you?"

"Just curious."

"Too durned curious! You ain't takin' me up on Mailer?" Poke wanted to change the subject.

"No." Kilkenny moved a step toward the door. "But I'll be back to see you, 'Poke.' " He stopped at the door. "You see, Ike Markham was a friend of mine!" As he spoke he stepped quickly back into the shadows, dropped a hand to the porch rail, and vaulted it neatly. "Buck!" he called.

The horse came to him, holding his head high and to one side so as not to step on the trailing bridle reins. Catching them up, Lance Kilkenny wheeled the horse and vanished into the darkness.

He need not have hurried. In the big room of the old ranch house, Poke Dunning was standing where Kilkenny had left him, his face ashen, his cheeks sunken and old.

For all these years he had been afraid of just this. A dozen times he had thought of what he might do if ever faced with somebody who knew Markham, and now the moment had come and gone, and he had let the man get away. He should have killed him! But why, if someone had to come, did it have to be Kilkenny, of all people?

Alone in his room, he paced the floor. After all these years! Why, there had to be a way out! There had to be! There was no justice in it!

Mailer! If he could only steer Mailer into Kilkenny! They might kill each other off, or at least make it easy for him to kill the survivor. In that case, there might still be a chance.

He paced the floor, cursing Mailer's absence as once he had blessed it, eager for the man to return.

It was this fear that had caused him to keep the gunmen on the payroll even after he had given up banditry and rustling. This fear that someday, someone would come over the Old Mormon Trail who knew the truth. He had made a bold play, that long-ago night in the dark shadow of Thieving Rock. . . . Markham had been a friendly man when they met, and he had talked cheerfully of the ranch he had for his young daughter, and little by little Poke had worked the information out of him, that his wife was dead, that he had no near relatives but Lona. Poke Dunning could see his big chance, and in the following nights he sat across the fire from the man who was carrying him west, and waited for his chance. It came, finally, only a day's drive from the ranch itself. It came when he was growing desperate with anxiety, and he knew that Markham had begun to suspect him, that the man moved his bed at times, shifting it from one place to another after they had turned in.

Yet, in the accomplishment, it had been easy. He had tossed a stone into the darkness near the horses, and Markham, seeing him lying there, apparently asleep, had risen and walked out to the horses, fearful that a mountain lion might come down on them. Poke Dunning had slid out of his blankets and followed him in his sock feet. He had used a pick handle, and it was only after the third and last blow had fallen that little Lona called from her blankets and he had replied that everything was all right, keeping his voice low.

The next day he told the child her father had gone on ahead to make ready for them. Later he told her that he was off doing business for the ranch and made arrangements to send her to school. Once she was gone, he had gambled that she would not remember after the years. He had even gone so far as to change his own ways, to use gestures and mannerisms the father had used, and even grow a beard in the same style as her father. It had been a bad moment when she returned on her first holiday, but after eleven years the memory had dimmed, and although he saw doubt in her eyes, he soon managed to make her forget those doubts. When she finally came home after many years, the memories from when she was five or almost five had been erased but for a few moments. The rest was a shadowland where memory and fantasy mingled, where the face of her father was never quite distinct.

Poke Dunning had made his big gamble, and he had won. Now he might lose. He would lose if something was not done. For years he had built up the ranch. Though Lona was the actual owner, in his mind the ranch was his and his alone. And now he was threatened.

When she had first returned from school, Poke had been worried and he had started planning how to take back control without raising a lot of questions. Frank Mailer had been his first hope.

He had hoped that Frank Mailer, the outlaw that owed him for so much, would be a fitting partner in the ranch. But now he was increasingly sure that Frank had his own plans and that Poke Dunning did not figure in them. Mailer could be handled, but somehow he must stall him on marrying Lona until after Kilkenny was out of the way. Then he could take care of big Frank, and he would enjoy doing it. He was going to make sure that Mailer died. He was going to make sure that Kilkenny died. And now that his long-held plan to legally wrest ownership of the ranch from Lona had fallen apart, he would kill her, too. If she died, wouldn't he, as her only surviving relative, inherit the ranch? After all, wasn't he supposed to have given it to her?

Only *Lona's* death had to look like an accident. Gunmen like Kilkenny and outlaws like Mailer were always dying violently. He could shoot Mailer himself, and if he carefully revealed what he knew about the big man's outlaw past and various aliases, no one would think twice about it. But killing a woman, a girl, was another thing entirely.

As if his murderous fantasy was echoing in his mind, Dunning suddenly heard her voice. She was in the kitchen talking to old Betts, and something was said about coffee.

At this hour on nearly every night Dave Betts made coffee for the two of them. Dunning suddenly heard a new voice, Flynn's, making some laughing comment.

Poke's eyes narrowed. What was going on here? What was Flynn doing in the house so late at night? The hands rarely came for coffee this late unless working cattle close by, and they were not now. He turned and started for the kitchen.

Voices suddenly stilled as he opened the door. He glanced at Lona, her face bright with laughter, the light catching in her auburn hair, and then at Flynn. Dave had drawn back near the big cooking range, his face drawn.

"What's goin' on here?" Dunning demanded. "Flynn, you should be in bed asleep. Ain't nothin' for you at the house this time of night."

"I was just palaverin'," Flynn replied.

"We was havin' coffee," Betts offered. "You want a cup?"

"Yes, won't you have some?" Lona looked up at him, and there was something level and hard in her eyes that he had never seen there before. "I like to talk to Gordon."

"So it's Gordon, is it?" He glared balefully at the puncher. "Get out!" he growled.

Flynn hesitated, and Dunning's gun flashed in his hand. He was thinking that something else had been going on behind his back, that this Flynn . . . "Get out!" he said quickly.

Gordon Flynn backed to the door. Never before had he seen the old man go for a gun, and on his best day he could not have come within twice the time to match that draw. He was no gunfighter. On the other hand, his eyes met Lona's. "Go, Gordon. I'm all right." She spoke softly and he opened the door and backed out, his face white.

Poke Dunning stood very still, first glaring at Dave,

then at Lona. "You come in here!" he said. "I want to talk to you!"

"All right." Lona got to her feet. She felt a queer, frightened sensation inside her, yet in another sense she was perfectly calm, her thoughts working carefully.

Kilkenny had come to see Dunning. The man might know his secret, kept for so long, was now about to be exposed. What would he do? What would he try?

She stepped past him into the big room and walked past the long dining-room table in the huge old parlor of the ranch house. She crossed to the fireplace, and stood there straight and looking suddenly taller than she was as she awaited him.

Poke Dunning slammed the door behind him and crossed the room. He dug his pipe into a can of tobacco and tamped it home. Then he looked up, his eyes bitter and hard, like flecks of steel under his shaggy brows. "We've got to have a talk. Sorry I got sore out there. Don't like to think of you wastin' time on those cowhands. You're too good for them."

"But you approve of Frank Mailer?" she asked coolly.

He looked up then, measuring her with his glance. "No," he said flatly, "and you ain't goin' to marry him. That was a bad idea."

"I agree." Lona waited, wondering.

He rubbed his chin. "Lona," he said hesitantly, "I got a confession to make. When Mailer first come down here, I figured him a right upstandin' young feller. Lately, he ain't seemed so much what he should be; in fact I been hearin' some things from up Durango way."

"Things?" She looked at him, puzzled. "What do you mean?"

"Stories. Stories of robberies and such. When he comes back I may have to fire Frank Mailer."

At that moment they both heard a shout, then a sound of running horses, and Mailer's hard voice, talking to Socorro.

Dunning turned on the girl. "Get to your room!" he said. "An' Lona, you keep your mouth shut to what we've been talking about!"

CHAPTER 5

Miles back, along the trails north and west of Aztec Crossing, there rode a small, grim-faced group of men. In the van were three men on gray horses, three men who answered to the names of Jim, Pat, and Terry Mulhaven, the brothers of Johnny, who was alive but badly shot up back in Aztec.

There were eight of these men in all, headed by an Apache tracker, and these were the men who had built the Crossing from nothing to a fairly stable little outpost. Storekeeper Worth, answering to the name of Bill, was among them, his old Sharps across his saddlebow.

The peace and contentment of their town had been violated and good citizens had been done to death, so the attitude of the posse, self-appointed, was harsh and determined. A dozen times they had lost the trail, and a dozen times they had found it again. Their progress had been slow, but it was relentless.

Most often, it was the distinctive tracks of the blood bay ridden by Mailer that they found. They knew this horse by sight, and they knew his tracks.

"I wonder how much further?" Worth asked.

"We got all summer," Jim Mulhaven replied shortly. "This is one trail I ain't leavin' until those hombres stretch hemp."

A good day and a half behind the outlaws, they had

come upon the body of Kane Geslin. The sign made evident what had happened here. "Killed by one of his own men," Worth commented.

"One less for us," Pat said grimly. "Let's be ridin'!"

They rode on, into the hot, still afternoon, their eyes grimly upon the trail.

At Blue Hill, Mailer had wasted no time in facing Poke Dunning. He went at once to the ranch house, opened the door, and closed it, looking at the older man across the big room. "Poke, let's get this over with. Come Saturday, I'm marrying Lona!"

He could see that something had happened—what, he did not know—but Mailer was a changed man, not suddenly insistent, demanding, but with some deeper, more deadly change.

"I don't think so, Frank. She doesn't want to marry you. And now I agree with her."

Frank Mailer looked at old Poke Dunning through narrowed eyes. "You double-crossin' me, Dunning?" he asked.

"It could be I'm protectin' myself from a double cross. An' don't think that I'm scared of you telling people who I really am. I've been here for years and most of those that haven't forgot who Poke Dunning was are dead."

"What if you died, mighty sudden," Mailer suggested, his eyes holding Poke's, "an' I married Lona?"

Dunning shrugged. "The trouble with that is"—he spoke carefully, knowing how slender was the thread along which their course was holding, a thread that might snap with a burst of gunfire at any moment—"that Kilkenny knows."

"Who?" Mailer started at the name. "Kilkenny? Is he here?"

"Who do you think whipped you, Frank?" Dunning asked. "That was him, all right. Kansas tipped me off."

"Kilkenny!" All thoughts were suddenly gone from Mailer's mind but the one. It was fantastic. He had heard of the gunfighter for years, but had never seen him. Remembering the description that Gates had given in the saloon the first night they met, he knew Poke was telling the truth. Despite himself, he was awed and worried.

Had anyone suggested that the name frightened him, he would have scoffed at it. He had never been frightened of anything, but one could not hear the countless stories surrounding that name without it taking on an almost magical quality. He felt a strange, deadly chill within him. Kilkenny! And the man had beaten him with his fists, but perhaps with a gun . . . ?

"Look," Poke said softly, "we've had our troubles, Frank. We both have it in for each other, but it ain't necessary. We started in this deal an' we can do all right with it yet. I can't let you marry Lona yet . . . not until I can trust you. We can settle this; the only thing in the way is this Kilkenny. We've got to get rid of him."

"We?" Mailer looked at Dunning, trying to assemble his thoughts. The knowledge that Kilkenny was in this deal disturbed him.

"Sure! Look, alone neither of us can win. Together we can. As long as Kilkenny is in the picture, we stand to lose, so what we've got to do is get him out of it. Then we can settle this deal between us, or work partners on it. Our first job is to be rid of him."

"Maybe you're right," Mailer agreed grudgingly, "but that won't be so easy. Got any ideas?"

"Sure. I've been thinking about it. Look, he came over to the ranch once, so we can get him here again. He was a friend of Lona's father. All right, we send him a message

from her. He'll come, an' when he does, we'll be waitin'
for him. Geslin, Starr, Socorro, an' us."

"Not Geslin. He's dead."

"Dead?"

"Yeah." Mailer's cold eyes shifted to Dunning's. "We
had some words an' he tried to draw on me. I killed him."

Poke Dunning absorbed that and didn't like it. He had
known Mailer was good, but if he was good enough to get
Geslin and not even collect a slug in the process, then he
was even more dangerous than Poke had believed.

"Ethridge is dead, too." Mailer was rolling a smoke.
"We took that bank at Aztec Crossing."

Rage boiled up inside of Poke Dunning. He had refused
to allow anything of the kind. This was going directly
against his orders. For an instant he was about to give vent
to his fury, but he throttled his anger. "That's no matter. We can use Socorro an' Starr. It will be easy enough.
You an' me an' Starr will be out of sight. We can have
Socorro mendin' a saddle or something. Kilkenny rides in,
an' we take him in a cross fire. Four guns. He won't beat
that."

"All right," Mailer agreed. "It's a good plan. Can you
get word to him?"

"Sure. Through Kansas or that Spanish girl."

"You're right, there's something between them."

"Yeah"—Dunning nodded—"we should have guessed
it. She's that Nita Riordan who was with him on the border and at the Cedars. Remember? We heard about her."

So that was it? Kilkenny's girl? But after Kilkenny died?

"Poke," Mailer said suddenly, "I think I'm goin' to like
this. You get word to Kansas or the girl. Let's get started
on this an' get it over with."

. . .

Sam Starr walked into the bunkhouse and pulled off his boots. Behind him Socorro followed, and Rusty Gates opened his eyes and looked at them in the darkness. He could see only vague outlines, but he heard Socorro's muttered curse, then Starr's low question. "How do you feel?"

"Bad," Socorro said. "My whole arm and shoulder are so stiff it hurts to move."

"You feel better than Geslin."

Socorro did not say anything for a minute. Then he said, "Frank should have buried him. If there's a posse, they are liable to stumble on the body."

Rusty Gates was wide-awake now. What went on here? To speak would cause them to clam up, and he wanted to hear more. He lay still and listened.

"There *will* be a posse," Starr said. "Aztec is a tough place. I knew that kid who opened up on us. He was one of the Mulhaven boys, an' there's four or five more."

"Gunfighters?"

"No, but tough hands, and clannish as all get out. You can bet we've got a Mulhaven on us now, somewhere."

"What you plannin' to do?"

Sam Starr let that question slide. It was not that he did not know, but Socorro was pretty thick with Mailer. Starr planned to get his share of the loot and light a shuck for Texas. But fast.

A long time after, Gates saw Gordon Flynn come into the room, get something out of his bunk, and leave again. Mailer still had not come in. When he did he undressed and fell right into bed.

After Mailer left him, Dunning moved swiftly. He had to prepare for battle on two fronts. The trap had to be set for Kilkenny and he needed to be ready for Mailer's next move, whether they'd done in Kilkenny or not. He crossed the patio and rapped lightly on Lona's door. "Who's there?" she asked.

"It's me . . . Pa. Get your clothes an' come out of there. You sleep in the back room tonight. Beside Dave Betts."

Lona thought quickly. Why Dunning wanted her to move she could not guess, but being close to Dave would make her feel much safer. She knew the old man's affection for her, and his loyalty. "All right," she said after a minute.

"You'll be all right there. Mailer's back."

She said nothing but went to the room mentioned, barred the door, and climbed into bed. Poke Dunning walked into Lona's bedroom and sat down on the empty bed with his six-shooter in his hand.

His hunch might be wrong, but Lona was the pawn in the game now. Possession of her person was as important as possession of the ranch itself, even more important, as things stood. If Mailer came . . . it was almost daylight when he heard the soft rustle of grass, then heard a low voice. "Lona!"

He sat very still, and then a head and shoulders loomed at the open window. "Lona!" the voice called.

Poke Dunning fired.

Mailer, Gates, and Starr came awake on the instant. Starr thought first of a posse, Gates and Mailer were thinking of Kilkenny. Gates kicked off the blankets and reached for his boots. Mailer stared at him, then leaned back in bed. Going out into that yard was something he had no idea of doing right now. Firing a pistol and then waiting might be just the trick Poke Dunning would try. "See what it is," he said, and sagged back in his bunk.

Rusty Gates walked out into the yard, but there was no

sound and no movement. He waited, then crossed the hard-packed earth of the ranch yard toward the house. He heard a faint stirring and turned toward the wing of the house. Someone had lighted a lantern, and he rounded the corner to see the dark figure of a man bending over another one on the ground.

Rusty had his gun out. "Who is it?" he demanded.

Dunning turned, saw Gates, and saw the gun. "It's Flynn," he said. "He tried to get into Lona's window and got shot."

"Shot? Lona shot Flynn?" Gates could not believe that. He bent over the cowhand. "Dead?"

"No, he ain't, but he's bad hurt. Let's get him inside."

Poke was cursing his luck, for when he fired he was sure that it was Mailer he had under his gun. But why was Flynn here? Had Lona planned to escape?

When they put the boy down on Lona's bed, Gates worked over him, and Dunning watched. "Where do you stand in this, Gates?" Poke asked suddenly.

Rusty looked up. He had wondered if he would be asked. "Now, that's a good point, Dunning. I don't know where I stand. I don't know what the fuss is all about. However," he added, "this is a deal where I'd look to see where the money was."

"I've got it. You work for me an' you can make yourself a fast stake."

"That sounds good to me. What do I do?"

"Saddle a horse an' see that girl at the Fandango. Tell her Poke Dunning wants to see Kilkenny tomorrow at three. Then you get back here and stand ready to side me . . . against anybody."

"What does it get me?" Rusty knew the question was expected.

"Two-fifty for five days. Double if you have to fight."

. . .

Rusty saddled up and rode out of the ranch but he did not ride more than a half mile before he swung off the road and headed for Monument Rock. He would ride directly to Kilkenny. Whatever this meant he did not know, but Kilkenny could make his own decision after he apprised him of the facts.

Kilkenny heard him out in silence. The return of three men to Blue Hill when five had gone out, the shooting of Gordon Flynn. "No," Gates said, when asked, "he's not dead. But he's got a bad wound and lost a lot of blood. When I left, Dave was takin' care of him, and old Betts is a good hand with a gunshot."

Kilkenny got to his feet and paced nervously beside the fire. It was daylight now, but the morning was still cool. They wanted him there at three o'clock, and between now and three many things could happen, and Gates was here. "You get back to the ranch," he said. "You watch your chance, and if there is one, get that girl out of there. If there isn't, watch her close. Maybe it's just best to do that."

"Are you comin' at three?"

"I think so."

"It may be a trap."

"Could be. Anyway, tell him I'll be there."

He watched Rusty go with misgiving. Dunning, Mailer, Starr, and Socorro would be there to meet him, yet there seemed to be no suspicion of Rusty, and it would be only a matter of hours until he would go himself.

Over his coffee, he considered the whole setup at Blue Hill, remembering every detail of the ranch and its layout.

This was to be a showdown, he knew that. Whether or not Poke Dunning wanted to talk business, Kilkenny knew very well that if he did not agree to whatever Dunning demanded, he would have to fight his way out. Knowing this, he made plans to stay in. Dunning was going to deal the cards, but he would play his own hand the way that suited him best.

The killing of Geslin interested him. Frank Mailer was fast, for Geslin had been very fast and an excellent shot. And Mailer had killed him.

From what Gates said, they had been in some sort of a gun battle, for Ethridge, too, was dead. They had brought back sacks stuffed with money, and that might mean a holdup at any one of a dozen places.

Shortly before noon Kilkenny mounted the buckskin and left his hideout, but he did not ride out into the flatlands toward Blue Hill; instead he crossed Salt Creek Wash and rode up the canyon that opened opposite Monument Rock and ran due north. Emerging from the canyon at a place just west of Popping Rock, he struck an old trail across the highlands back of the cliffs that formed the northern boundary of the Blue Hill range. It was a trail he had used before, and one he well knew. Within an hour of easy riding, he was on the point of rocks opposite Blue Hill, and here, after concealing his horse among the piñons, he found a place on the crest of the cliffs and began to make a systematic study of the ranch through his glasses.

His point of observation could scarcely have been better, for he was at an altitude of some six thousand feet, while the ranch itself was all of five hundred feet lower and scarcely a mile away. From his vantage point in the clear mountain air, he could easily see the figures and, knowing them, could distinguish one from the other, even though features would not be discernible. Yet after fifteen minutes of careful study, he saw no one.

Becoming increasingly anxious, Kilkenny moved down

a little lower and somewhat closer to the edge of the cliff, and studied the terrain still more carefully. A few of the buildings were concealed by the bulk of the nearer peak, but the house and the bunkhouse he could plainly see, and there was still no movement.

He got up at last and rode west. He had a ride of at least two miles before there was a way down from the rim, and when he made it, he was on the Old Mormon Trail. Worried, he studied the trail, but there was no evidence of any recent travel. Turning off the trail, he chose a way that would keep him close against the cliffs, where he would have the partial cover of desert brush, piñon, and fallen boulders until he could reach a point that would put the bulk of the peak between himself and the ranch buildings.

From time to time he halted and studied the ranch anew through his glasses, and there was still no movement. The place might have been deserted for years; it lay silent and crystal clear in the bright noonday sun.

Far away across the desert the heat waves danced weirdly, and the towering shoulders of Monument Rock were purple against the sky, while between rolled the salmon, pink, and shadowed magenta of the desert, flecked with islands of cloud shadow. The air was so still that one felt as if a loud voice might shatter it to fragments, or dissolve the whole scene like something reflected in the rounded surface of a soap bubble.

Uneasily, Kilkenny pushed back his hat and mopped the perspiration from his brow and face. It was very hot. No breath of wind stirred the air. He dried his palms on his handkerchief and stared thoughtfully at the silent ranch, then let the buckskin pick his way forward another hundred yards. He hesitated again, every sense alert for danger, and he loosened the guns in their holsters and squinted his green eyes hard against the glare.

He studied the ranch again, near enough now to discern the slightest movement, but there was none. Removing the glasses from his eyes, he wiped them off, then studied the ranch again. If he went much farther, he would have to ride out in the open, and a marksman atop the peak would have him in easy shooting distance. For a long time he studied the rim of the nearer peak, then the buildings and corrals of Blue Hill, yet he saw nothing.

Something was radically wrong. Something had happened, and it must have happened since Rusty left the ranch . . . or after Rusty returned, for there was no sign of him, either.

If it were indeed a trap, it had been set much too soon, for he was not due for almost an hour. Furthermore, they would have left somebody in sight; they would have had some natural, familiar movement to lull his suspicions. Yet there was nothing; for all the movement, the scene might have been painted on glass.

Far away over the range a lonely steer moved, heading for water, miles away. Above, the heat-dancing air, where a buzzard swung on lazy, waiting wings. Kilkenny shoved his glasses back in the saddlebag and rode forward, clinging still to the cliff shadow and its slight obscurity. Now he slid his Winchester from the scabbard and, turning the buckskin away from the cliff, rode directly across to the shadow of the peak opposite.

When he could ride no closer without presenting too large a target, he swung down from the buckskin, and speaking to it softly, he moved forward. Always light on his feet, he moved now like a wraith, then halted, scarcely forty yards away from the ranch house, to look and listen. He waited there while a man might have counted a slow fifty. There was no sound, no movement. A flat, uneasy stillness hung over the place.

What had happened?

Kilkenny arose swiftly from behind the shrub and moved with swift, silent strides to the wall of the building and along the wall to Lona's window, from which he had seen the girl's shadow on that first day before she emerged to wave to him. The window was open, and the lace curtain hung limp and lifeless in the dead, still air.

Inside the room a mirror hung on the wall, and from the side he could see it, and it gave him a view of most of the inside of the room. There was nothing. He had left his Winchester with the horse, but now he slid a Colt into his hand and stepped quickly past the window to get the view from the opposite side. The room was empty. He stepped over the sill and stood inside.

There was some blood on the sill where Flynn had been shot the previous night. The door was open on the silent, sunlit patio. Kilkenny returned his gun to his holster and crossed to the door, studying the patio.

Under the eaves of the porch hung an *olla*, its sides dark with the contents of clear, cold water. Several strings of peppers hung from the eaves across the way and a spring bubbled from the ground into a tiny pool in the center of the patio, then trickled off through a stone pipe to empty into the water trough away at the corral.

Listening, he heard nothing. Yet within any one of the half-dozen windows or two doors, a gun might wait. Back inside the window where he would be invisible, either Dunning or Mailer might stand, gun in hand. A gourd dipper hung near the *olla* and another at the spring. Kilkenny's mouth was dry and he longed for a drink. His ears straining with the effort to hear some sound, he waited a moment longer, then stepped out into the patio, and crossed it, to the door opposite. As he walked he glanced sharply right toward the open side from which he could see the corrals and the stable. All was bright and still.

The kitchen was empty. He placed a hand on the coffee-pot, and it seemed to be vaguely warm. Lifting the lid of the stove, he saw a dull red glow among the few coals atop the gray of ashes and the grate. He stepped past the stove and walked into the dining room, and then he stopped.

In a doorway on his left a hand was visible, lying flat and lax, palm down on the floor. It was an old hand, worn and brown.

Stepping quickly around the table, Kilkenny saw the man who lay there, his bald head rimmed with a fringe of graying hair, his shirt dark with blood, and the floor beneath him stained with it.

A six-shooter lay near his hand and he still wore the apron that marked him for who and what he was. Dave Betts was dead. He had been shot twice through the chest.

Stepping quickly past him, Kilkenny looked into the room from which Betts had apparently emerged. It was definitely bachelor quarters. Turning to the room beside it, he found a mussed bed, and bending over, he sniffed the pillow, detecting a faint perfume. This, then, was where Lona had spent the night, but where was she?

And where were they all?

Stepping past the old man's body, Kilkenny moved the length of the long table and stepped through the open door into the large living room.

No one. This, too, was empty and still.

Somewhere, thunder rumbled distantly, mumbling in the far-off hills like a giant disturbed in his sleep. A faint breath of wind coming alive stirred out over the desert, and he heard the rustle of the peppers on their strings in the patio, and the curtain stirred faintly as though moved by a ghostly hand.

Kilkenny mopped his face of sweat and moved carefully across the room. The wind stirred again, and suddenly he heard another sound, a sound that sent a faint chill over him, making his shoulders twitch with the feeling of it. It was the sound of a strained rope, a rope that hung taut and hard, creaking a little, with a burden.

He stepped quickly to the door, his mouth dry. As though drawn by foreknowledge, his eyes went to the stable, whose wide-open door he could now see. From the cross beam over the high door, made high to admit racks of hay, he saw a long and heavy form suspended by a short rope.

Nearer, sprawled upon the ground in the open, lay an outstretched body. Gun in hand, Kilkenny stepped quickly outside, his eyes shooting right and left, then he ran across to the stable. One glance at the face, and he straightened, sorely puzzled. The man was a total stranger!

Crossing to the barn, he found where the rope was tied and unfastened it, lowering the man who had been hanged. His spurs jingled as the dead man's heels touched the ground. One glance at the blue face and he knew. It was Socorro.

Walking to the bunkhouse, he hesitated, for the steps were bloodstained. Then he moved inside. On the floor before him lay another stranger, his body fairly riddled with bullets, and against the end of the room sat Sam Starr, his head hanging on his chest, guns lax near his hands, and his shirt and trousers soaked in blood.

Crouching beside him, Kilkenny lifted Starr's chin, and miraculously, the man's lids stirred, and his lips worked to form words. "Shot . . . me," he whispered, his lips working at the words he could not shape, "Mulhavens."

Kilkenny motioned to the dead man inside the door. "Is that a Mulhaven?"

Starr indicated assent. "Tough," he said, "plenty . . . tough."

"Where's Dunning?"

Starr shook his head.

Kilkenny grasped the dying man's shoulder. "Tell me, man! Where's that girl! Where's Lona? Dammit, speak up!"

Starr's eyes forced themselves open and he struggled to speak. "D . . . d . . . don't know. Poke, he . . . away."

"Poke Dunning has her," Kilkenny said. "Is that it?"

Starr nodded. "Mailer's craz . . . y. Plumb gone bats . . ." Sam Starr's voice trailed away, and he fainted.

Carefully, Kilkenny eased the man to a prone position and grabbed a pillow for his head from the nearest bunk.

Swiftly, he worked over the dying man, doing what he could to ease his position and his pain. Then he hurried from the bunkhouse and made a quick survey of the ranch.

He found no one else. Four dead men and the dying Sam Starr. Dunning, Mailer, Lona, Rusty Gates, and Gordon Flynn were all gone.

Hurrying back with a bucket of cool water, he found Starr conscious. Holding a gourd dipper to the man's mouth, he helped him drink. Starr looked his gratitude. "Mailer's gone after . . . after your girl," he gasped. "He's crazy!"

"My girl?" Kilkenny was dumbfounded. "At Salt Creek?"

Starr nodded weakly. "An' . . . an' the Mulhavens are after G . . . G . . . Gates."

"What?" Kilkenny sprang to his feet. "But he wasn't an outlaw!"

"You try tellin' 'em that!" Starr's face was turning gray.

Kilkenny stood flat-footed and still above the dying man. Frank Mailer, kill-crazy and full of fury, was gone to Salt Creek after Nita. Somewhere, Poke Dunning was escaping with Lona, and his friend Rusty Gates, the man who had come into this only to help him, and probably with a wounded man for company, was riding to escape a blood-hungry posse whose reason had been lost in a lust for revenge for the killing of their own friends and brothers!

Kilkenny knew of the Mulhavens. A family of tough Irishmen, three of them veterans of the Indian wars. Hard, honest, capable men. He knew, too, the men of Aztec Crossing, and they were not men to take the bloodletting Mailer had visited upon them without retaliation. If they had trailed those men to this ranch, they would regard all upon it as tarred with the same brush and would make a clean sweep. Two of their group had died here, and that would make matters no easier.

Leaving Starr, he dashed outside and stopped in the sunlight. Where to go? Nita was in danger. Rusty was being pursued by a hanging mob, and Lona . . .

Kilkenny forced himself to coldness. Brigo was at Salt Creek with Nita, and so was Cain Brockman. He would have to gamble that they were protection enough. Lona, wherever she was, must wait, for it was not immediately apparent what danger she might be in. Rusty had evidently taken Flynn and somehow managed an escape, knowing that the wounded Flynn would certainly be taken as one of the outlaws. Rusty had come into this only to help him, and to have him hanged by mistake would be a horrible responsibility.

He took swift strides toward the corral, glancing over the remaining horses. Rusty's mount was not there.

Turning, he whistled shrilly, and in a moment saw Buck come trotting around the building toward him.

Again in the saddle, Kilkenny began a painstaking sweep of the ranch, yet his job was in a measure simplified by knowing that Gates must make his escape by some route that would take him from the rear of the buildings. Forcing himself to take his time, Lance Kilkenny soon found the tracks of Gates's horse and another. He studied the hoofprints of this other horse carefully, then mounted and worked the trail out of the brush and rocks to a shallow dip south and west of Blue Hill.

Apparently, Rusty was heading for the rough country of Malpais Arroyo, and walking his horses. Was that because of the wounded Flynn? Or to keep from attracting attention?

He was something over a mile south of the ranch when a bunch of tracks made by hard-running horses came in from the north. Lance felt his stomach turn over within him. The Aztec posse! They had seen them and were in pursuit. Touching a spur to the buckskin, he went into a lope, then a run. The tracks were easy to follow now. The wind whipped at his face, and thunder rumbled over the mountains beyond Monument Rock. The brim of his hat slapped back against his skull, but the buckskin, loving to run, ate into the distance with swiftly churning hooves.

The trail dipped into the arroyo and led along it, and heedless of ambush, thinking only of his friend, Kilkenny rode on, his face grim and hard. He knew mobs and how relentless and unreasoning they could be. There would be no reasoning with this bunch. If he met them, it could well be a payoff in blood and bullets. He had never, to his knowledge, killed an honest man, but to save his friend he would do just that.

Suddenly he saw that the pace of the horses he followed had slowed, and he drew up himself, walking his horse, and listening. Then, carried by the echoing walls of the arroyo that had now deepened to a canyon, he heard a yell. Soon somebody called, "Boost him up here, durn it! Let's get this job over with!"

The voices were just around a bend in the rocks ahead. His stomach muscles tight and hard, his mouth dry, Kilkenny slid from his horse. His hands went to walnut-butted guns and loosened them in their holsters, then he moved around the bend and into sight.

There, beneath a huge old cottonwood, stood Rusty Gates, and beside him, Gordon Flynn. The wounded man was being held up by a man who stood directly in front of him. There were seven men here, seven hard, desperate men.

Flynn's eyes went past them and he saw Kilkenny.

"Kilkenny!" he yelled.

As one man, the posse turned to face the owner of that dread name.

He spoke, and his voice was clear and strong. "Step back from those men, damn you for a lot of brainless killers! Get away, or I'll take the lot of you!"

CHAPTER 6

Surprise held the men of the posse immobile, and in the moment of stillness Kilkenny spoke again. His voice was sharp and clear. "You've got the wrong men there! While you try to string up a couple of honest cowhands, the real killers are gettin' away!"

"Oh, yeah?" Terry Mulhaven's voice was sharp. He had suddenly decided he was not going to be bluffed, Kilkenny or no Kilkenny. "You keep out of this! Or maybe," he added, his voice lowering a note, "you're one of them?"

Kilkenny did not reply to him. Instead, he asked quickly, "Did any of you see the holdup? Actually see it?"

"I did," Worth said sharply. "I saw it."

"All right, then. Look again at these men. Were they among those you saw?"

Worth hesitated, glancing uneasily at Terry Mulhaven. "The redhead wasn't. I saw no redheaded man, but we wounded two of them, anyway, and this man is wounded." He gestured at Flynn. "That's enough for me."

"It's not enough!" Kilkenny returned crisply. "If all you want to do is kill, then kill each other or try killing me. But if you want justice, then try thinking rather than stringing up the first men you meet!"

"All right, mister. You tell us how we should be thinking. You talk quick, though."

"That man was shot by Poke Dunning when he tried to help a girl get away from that bunch of outlaws." Kilkenny spoke swiftly, for he had them listening now, and he knew Western men. Quick to anger and quick to avenge an insult or a killing, they were also, given a chance, men of good heart and goodwill, and essentially reasonable men. They were also men of humor. Such men had been known to let a guilty man go free when he made some humorous remark with a noose around his neck, or under a gun. They respected courage, and given a chance to cool down, they would judge fairly.

He had them talking now, and he meant to keep them talking. "The men who rode to the Crossing were led by Frank Mailer, the worst of the lot," he continued rapidly, arresting and holding their attention by his crisp, sharp speech and the confidence of his knowledge. "With him rode Geslin, Sam Starr, Socorro, an' Scar Ethridge.

"Ethridge never came back. You hanged Socorro and killed Starr at the ranch. You also killed an honest man, Dave Betts."

"We got Ethridge at the Crossin'," Mulhaven said, "but if that honest man was the hombre on the floor inside the house, we didn't kill him. He was dead when we got there!"

This was news to Kilkenny. Apparently Dave had given his life in trying to protect Lona Markham. Dunning had evidently carried her off.

"Mailer's still loose and I'm after him myself," Kilkenny added. "These two men were the only honest hands on the place aside from that old man you found dead."

Bill Worth walked over to Flynn and took the noose from his neck, then he removed the loop from Rusty's neck. "Glad you showed up," he said shortly. "I tried to tell these hombres that redhead wasn't among 'em!"

Kilkenny had no time for conversation. "Rusty," he said swiftly, "get Flynn back to the ranch. I'm ridin' to Salt Creek after Mailer. Then we'll have to hunt Poke Dunning."

Turning abruptly, he swung into his saddle, and with a wave at the posse and his friends, he was off at a dead run.

Terry Mulhaven stared after him, then mopped his brow. "Man!" he said. "When I turned around an' looked into them green eyes, I figured my number was up for sure!" He glanced at Rusty. "Is he as fast as they say?"

"Faster," Gates said wryly.

Bill Worth looked at the Mulhavens. "Let's pick up the bodies," he said gently, "and head for home. The folks will be worried."

"Yeah"—Terry nodded—"we better." He glanced sheepishly at Rusty and Flynn. "No hard feelin's?"

Gates stared at him, then his red face broke into a grin. "Not right now," he said, "but a few minutes ago I was some sore!"

In a tight knot, the posse headed north for the ranch, and later, with the bodies of the two fallen men across their saddles, they started toward home. They rode slowly and they talked but little, and as a result they were startled by a sudden grunt from their Apache tracker. "Look!" he said. "Big red hoss!"

They looked, and the tracks were there. Terry Mulhaven glanced at this brother, then at Worth. "Well," he said, "we know that track. We followed it all the way from Aztec. Let's see what we find this time!"

Grimly, they turned their horses down the trail made by Frank Mailer's horse. This time somebody would pay the cost of the heavy burden the two lead horses carried, the burden left upon them by the murdered men in the bank.

Due east of Monument Rock and the hideout used by Kilkenny was an old prospector's cabin. This adobe shelter had been used by drifting cowhands, by rustlers and sheepherders as a temporary shelter, but for some years now it had been passed by and forgotten. It was huddled in a tight little corner of rock far down one of the southern-reaching tentacles of Salt Creek Wash, and here Poke Dunning had taken Lona Markham.

She had not gone willingly. In the confusion of the Blue Hill ranch gun battle, Poke had made his move. His first thought had been to try to put a bullet in Frank Mailer, but as he moved to the window that faced the bunkhouse and the ongoing fracas, rifle in hand, he'd spotted big Frank sliding down the side of the wash that ran across one side of the ranch yard. He had a set of saddlebags over his shoulder and was out of sight before Dunning could shoot. Poke figured that the saddlebags probably held the loot from Mailer's robbery.

Realizing that no matter what happened during the shoot-out, he'd still have Mailer to deal with, Dunning headed for Dave Betts's room and Lona. Knowing that he had only moments before the posse turned its attention on the main house, he plunged into the room.

"Out the window, quick!" he snapped. "We're gettin' out of here."

"You go. I'm staying here." Lona had made the mistake of thinking that Kilkenny had come, and although she had been afraid because of all the shooting, she was now sure that if Poke was running, then Kilkenny must be winning.

"Dammit, girl!" He grabbed her by the arm and dragged her toward the window.

"You hold up there, Mr. Markham!" Dave Betts was frightened by the fear he saw in Lona's eyes . . . something was wrong here. He grabbed Poke's shoulder.

Turning, Poke drew his right-hand gun and shot Dave twice in the chest; then, as Lona opened her mouth to scream he knocked her unconscious with a diagonal swipe of the barrel. He shoved her out the window, and then dropping out after her, he headed for the corrals.

In the remote cabin, never visited in these days by anyone, he left Lona tied securely.

He had not been able to escape the ranch on either his or Lona's personal mount. Her horse, Zusa, was essential to his new plan. He was tired of playing games with Mailer and Lona and everybody else. Lona was going to die. The two of them escaped the confusion back at the ranch. Frank Mailer would be revealed to be the vicious bank robber that he was, but in their escape there would be a tragic accident . . . a riding accident. His daughter would pass away and no one would ask any questions about his continuing to live on the ranch. There might eventually be some documents to be filed, but the right kind of lawyer could handle that.

He was headed now for Blue Hill, intending to arrive there just after dark. With this idea in mind, he cut an old trail south and rode on until he was in the tall shadow of Chimney Rock. He drew up and got stiffly from the saddle.

This place was lonely and secure. He would wait here until almost dark, then he was going to sneak in and get Lona's horse . . . once he'd done that, he could take her out, kill her with a blow to the neck, and fake the fall. Seating himself on the ground in the shadow of the Chimney, he filled his pipe and began to smoke.

It bothered him to contemplate the idea of murdering the girl that had lived as his daughter for so many years. She'd always been a tool, but he would admit that he was fond of her. For a few minutes he considered taking the money he'd hidden away and starting over somewhere else, but there wasn't quite as much as he'd have liked, and after all, he'd never been a quitter.

Nearby, a huge old cottonwood rustled its leaves and he leaned back, knocking out his pipe. There would be a couple of hours to kill, and he was in no hurry. He would sleep a little while. His lids became heavy, then closed, his big hands grew lax in his lap, and he leaned comfortably back among the rocks. It was a joke on Mailer that he had taken the big bay, Frank's favorite horse. The cottonwood had a huge limb that stretched toward him, and it rustled its leaves, gently lulling him to sleep.

He did not hear the slowly walking horses, even when a hoof clicked on stone. He was tired, and not as young as he once had been, but no thought of murdered men behind him, or of the girl, bound and helpless in a remote cabin, disturbed him. He slept on. He did not awaken even when the silent group of men faced him in a crescent of somber doom. Silent, hard-faced men who knew that blood bay, and carried with them the burden of their dead. It was the creak of saddle leather when Terry Mulhaven dismounted that awakened him.

Five men faced him on horseback, another on foot. Still another had thrown a rope over that big cottonwood limb, and Poke Dunning, who had lived most of his adult years with the knowledge that such a scene might be prepared for him at any moment, came awake suddenly and sharply, and his hand flashed for a gun.

He was lying on his side, his left gun beneath him, and somehow, in stirring around, his right gun had slipped from the holster. Not all the way, but so far back that when he grabbed it, he grabbed it around the cylinder, and not the butt.

The difference might seem infinitesimal. At this moment it was not. At this moment it was the difference between a fighting end and a hanging. Pat Mulhaven's rifle spoke, and the hand that held the gun was shattered and bloody.

Gripping his bloody hand, Poke Dunning stared up at them. "What do you want me for?" he protested. "You've got the wrong man!"

"Yeah?" Pat Mulhaven sneered. "We heard that one before! We know that horse! We know you!"

"But listen!" he protested frantically. "Wait, now!" He got clumsily to his feet, his left hand gripping the bloody right. Great crimson drops welled from it and dripped slowly from his finger ends to the parched grass and sand beneath him.

He started to speak again, and then something came over him, something he had never experienced before. It was a sense of utter futility, and with it resignation. Roughly, they seized him.

"Give me a gun," he said harshly, "with my left hand! I'll kill the lot of you! Just my left hand!" he said, his fierce old eyes flaring at them.

"Set him on his hoss," Bill Worth said calmly, "behind the saddle."

Sometime later they rode on, turning their horses again toward home, and walking slowly, their task accomplished, with the feeling that their dead might ride on toward that dim cow-country Valhalla, attended by the men who had handled the guns.

Behind them, the shadow of Chimney Rock grew wider and longer, and the leaves of the cottonwood rustled gently, whispering one to the other as only cottonwood leaves will do, in just that way. And among them, his sightless eyes lifted skyward as if to see the last of the sunlight sky, and the last of the white clouds, looking through the cottonwood leaves, was Poke Dunning.

The point shadows of night had infiltrated the streets of Salt Creek when Lance Kilkenny came again to the town. The long-legged buckskin entered the dusty street with a swinging trot and did not stop until it reached the hitching rail of the Fandango. Yet already Kilkenny knew much. He knew that nothing had happened here tonight.

Before the Express, Lisa, the Portuguese, was sweeping the boardwalk, and he glanced up to see Kilkenny ride in; then, unaware of his identity, he returned to his sweeping. Before Starr's Saloon, Al Starr smoked his pipe, unaware that his brother was at this moment lying dead and chock-full of Aztec Crossing lead on the bunkhouse floor at Blue Hill. At the Fandango, Cain Brockman was arranging his stock for a big night.

All was sleepy, quiet, and peaceful. Although it was early, a lamp glowed here and there from a cabin window, and there was a light in the Express. The advancing skirmishers of darkness had halted here and there in the cover of buildings, gathering force for an invasion of the street. Lance swung down, spoke softly to the buckskin, and stepped up onto the boardwalk. There he turned again, and swept the street with a quick, sharp, all-encompassing glance. Then he pushed through the swinging doors into the almost empty saloon.

Brockman looked up quickly and jerked his head toward the door where Brigo sat, but Kilkenny walked directly to the bar, waving aside the bottle that Cain immediately lifted. "Has Mailer been in?"

Cain's eyes sparked. "No, ain't seen him. What's up?"

"Hell to pay!" Swiftly, Kilkenny sketched out what had happened. "He was headed for here," he added.

"Let him come!" Cain said harshly. "I've got an express gun loaded with buckshot."

Brigo was on his feet and coming over. Leaving Cain to tell him what had happened, Kilkenny went swiftly to Nita's door and rapped. At her reply, he opened the door and entered.

She stood across the room, tall, lovely, exciting. He went to her at once and took her hands, then stood and held them as he looked at her, his heart swelling within him, feeling now as no other woman had ever made him feel, as none ever could, none but this Spanish and Irish girl from the far borderlands. "Nita, I've got to find Lona and Frank Mailer . . . then I'm going to come back, and when I do, we're going to make this a deal. If you'll have me, we'll be married. We'll go on further west, we'll go somewhere where nobody's ever heard of Kilkenny, and where we can have some peace, and be happy."

"You've got to go now?"

"Yes."

It was like her that she understood. She touched him lightly with her lips. "Then go . . . but hurry back."

He left it like that and walked back into the saloon. Brigo and Cain turned to look at him. With them was a tall, sandy-haired cowhand.

"This fellow says he saw Dunning and Lona riding east. He was some distance off, but he said it looked like she was tied. He lost them in the canyons of Salt Creek."

"All right. We'll have a look." Kilkenny took in the sandy-haired hand with a sharp, penetrating glance. This was a good man, a steady man. "You want to ride to Blue Hill and tell Rusty? Then if you want, have a look. That girl's in danger."

"I'll look," Sandy said. "I've heard about the fightin' this mornin'."

"You be careful," Kilkenny warned. "Poke Dunning is handy with a gun."

"I know him," Sandy said shortly. "We had trouble over some strays, once. He's right handy with a runnin' iron, too."

Where to look for Lona was the next thing. While he

was looking for her he had to be cautious not to run afoul of Mailer. The man was dangerous, and he would be doubly so now.

"Night and day," Kilkenny told Cain and Brigo, "one of you be around. Never let up."

In the morning Kilkenny mounted the buckskin. He returned to the house at Blue Hill and scouted around, but the profusion of tracks told him nothing. Working the trail a bit farther out proved helpful in that he found the tracks of several riders. They seemed to be scouting around some and he figured they were out looking for the lost girl, same as he was. Their tracks had obliterated the original trail and so he followed them quickly, covering ground as fast as possible.

He had stopped at a well due west of Chimney Rock when he saw a rider approaching. It was Sandy. His face was drawn and gray. "Been ridin'," he said. "Rusty is out, too. An' that Flynn."

"How is he?"

"In no shape, but he won't quit. Head poundin' like a drum, I can tell. Pale around the gills. We tracked Poke as far as Monument Rock, then lost him. Other tracks wiped his out."

"The posse, maybe?"

"I reckon." Sandy wiped his chin after a long drink. "Maybe they got him."

"If they found him, somebody is dead." Kilkenny knew the men. "They didn't like it even when I stopped them hanging the wrong men. They wanted an eye for an eye."

"Dunning won't be taken easy," Sandy said. "Where you headin'?"

"Northeast. Look," he added, "why don't you swing back and follow the posse tracks? If they turn off the route back to Aztec, you've got a lead."

Sandy turned his bronc. "See you," he said, and cantered off.

Kilkenny wiped the back of his hand across his mouth. His eyes were dark with worry. Someplace in these bleak hills that girl was with Dunning. Someplace Mailer lurked. Neither was pleasant to think of. He swung into the saddle and glanced northeast. The tower of Chimney Rock loomed against the sky, beyond it the mountains, and there was a trail into them by that route. He turned the buckskin.

He rode with a Winchester across his saddle, his eyes searching every bit of cover, his ears and eyes alert. He saw nothing, heard nothing.

On a point of rocks near Eagle Nest Arroyo, Frank Mailer, his face covered with a stubble of coarse black beard, watched Kilkenny riding north through his glasses, and he swore softly. Twice, the gunfighter had been close to him, and each time Mailer had held off rather than dare a confrontation. Being on the dodge had him worried, for too long he'd lived the easy life at Blue Hill, taking off to do jobs outside the territory but always with the safety of Dunning's ranch to return to if things got bad. He had learned of what had happened, knew of the end of Sam Starr and Socorro. He had found the body of Poke Dunning, lynched for the crimes that he, Mailer, had committed, but strangely he felt depressed. There was the man that he had wanted dead, and he was dead. He had the nine thousand dollars from the Aztec bank, a good horse, and a beltful of ammunition. But the good old days were gone. The hanging of Poke Dunning affected him as nothing else had; there was an inevitableness about it that frightened him.

Frank Mailer, six feet five in his socks and weighing over two hundred and fifty pounds, walked back to his gray horse. He stood with a hand on the pommel, and something was gone out of him. For the first time since he was a youngster, he was really on the dodge. He was running.

Poke had run, too, and it hadn't done him any good. Dunning had beat the game for years, and now look at him. Somehow it always caught up with you. Frank Mailer heaved himself into the saddle and turned his horse across country.

The sight of Dunning's body had even driven the lush beauty of Nita Riordan from his mind. He rode on, sullen and dazed; for the first time he had a feeling of being hemmed in, trapped.

Kilkenny was hunting something; was it him? Now there was something he could do. He could seek out a showdown with Kilkenny and beat him. There was a deep, burning resentment against the man. If he had stayed out of it, all would have been well.

A mere half-dozen miles north, Kilkenny rounded a sandstone promontory and saw just beyond a horseman picking his way over the rounded gray stones and gravel of a wash. The man looked up and waved. It was Sandy again. "Found her," he said when they were closer. "Flynn found her. She was tied in a shack back in the hills. Dunning left her there with water and a little grub. Never saw nothin' like it. She was tied in the middle of the 'dobe with ropes running around her body an' off in all four directions. She couldn't move an inch one way or the other, an' couldn't get free, but she had her hands loose. Those ropes were made fast in the walls an' windows, knots so far away she couldn't reach 'em. She picked at one of the ropes until her fingers were all raw, tryin' to pull it apart."

"She's all right?"

"I reckon so. They took her to Blue Hill." Sandy eyed him thoughtfully. "Dunning left her the day before yesterday. You ain't seen him?"

"No. Nor Mailer."

"I'm headin' home." Sandy was regretful. "The boss will be raisin' hell. See you." He turned his horse, then glanced back. "Luck," he said.

Kilkenny sat his horse for a moment, then turned and started south again. Now he was hunting Mailer, not to kill him, unless he had to, but to make sure he was gone, out of the country before he relaxed his guard.

"He will want to see," Kilkenny told Buck. "If he's on the dodge but hasn't left the country, he'll have headed for the ridgelines."

Shadows grew long and crawled up the opposite wall of the mountains, and Kilkenny turned aside, and in a hollow in the rocks, he bedded down. He built no fire, but ate a little jerked beef and some hardtack before crawling into his blankets.

He was out at dawn, and had gone only a few miles when he saw the tracks of a big horse cutting across his trail. A big horse . . . to carry a big man. Kilkenny turned the buckskin abruptly. He had no doubt that this was Frank Mailer's horse. It was rough terrain into which the trail was leading, country that offered shelter for an ambush. Yet he followed on, taking his time, following the sign that grew more and more difficult. A bruised branch of sage, a scratch on a rock, a small stone rolled from its place, leaving the earth slightly damp where it had rested but a short time before. Once he saw a scar atop a log lying across the trail where a trailing hoof had struck, knocking the loose bark free and leaving a scar upon the bark and the tiny webs in the cracks beneath the bark.

It was a walking trail. Whether Mailer knew he was tracked or not, once in the mountains he had been exceedingly careful, and it could not be followed at a faster pace than a walk. Sometimes Kilkenny had to halt, searching for the line of travel, but always there was something, and his keen eyes read sign where another might have seen nothing, and they pushed on.

Kilkenny drew up, and sitting his horse close against a clump of piñon, he rolled a smoke. His mouth tasted bad and his hair was uncombed. He squinted his eyes against the morning glare of the sun and studied the hills before him. He put the cigarette in his lips and touched a match to it, feeling the hard stubble of beard on his chin as he did so. His shirt felt hot and had the sour smell of stale sweat from much riding without time to change. He felt drawn and hard himself, and he worked his fingers to get the last of the morning damp out of them.

Then he rode out and he met the hard, flat sound of a rifle shot and felt the whip of it, barely ahead of his hat brim. He left the saddle, Winchester in hand, but there was no further shot. Staring up at the rocks, his eyes hard and narrow, he waited. There was no sound.

The warm morning sun lay lazily upon the sandstone and sage; a lizard came out from under a rock, and darted over another rock that was green with copper stain and paused there. Lying where he was, Kilkenny could see the beat of its tiny heart against its side. Then something flickered and he saw a vanishing leg and fired quickly, the .44 thundering in the depths of the canyon.

Chips flew from the rock where the leg had vanished and from the opposite side of the rock where his second shot had struck. Then he heard the sound of a running horse, and he came out and climbed into the saddle.

In a few minutes he had found the trail. A big horse carrying a heavy man and running swiftly. He moved after it, riding more warily now, knowing that Mailer knew he was on the trail, and that from now on it would be doubly hard.

He forded Coal Mine Creek, carrying little water now, and headed for the five-hundred-foot wall of the Hogback, a high, serrated ridge biting with its red saw teeth at the brassy sky. Then, suddenly, as though in a painting, horse and man were outlined sharp against the sky. An instant only, but Kilkenny's rifle leaped to his shoulder and the shot cracked out, echoing and reechoing from the wall of the Hogback. Kilkenny saw the horse stumble, then go down, and the man spring clear. He fired again, but knew he had missed.

Coming up through the brush, he dismounted near the fallen horse and returned his rifle to its boot. The Hogback reared above him in a brown and broken-toothed height that offered a thousand places of concealment. Kilkenny dug into his saddlebags and got out his moccasins. Leaving his boots slung on the pommel, he moved out after Mailer on foot.

There was no way of telling how he had gone, or where. Yet Kilkenny moved on, working his way in among the boulders. Then, at a momentary pause, he saw some birds fly up and directed his course that way, but working to get a little higher on the cliff. He was on a narrow ledge, some seventy feet above the jagged rocks below, when he heard a low call. Startled, he looked up, to see Mailer on a ledge some fifty yards higher ahead of him.

The man was smiling, and as he smiled he lifted his pistol. Kilkenny drew left-handed and snapped a shot. It was a fast draw and the shot was more to move Mailer than with the expectation of a hit. Mailer lunged sidewise and his own shot clipped the rocks above Kilkenny and spat dirt and gravel into his face.

A small landslide had scoured out a hollow in the mountain, and Kilkenny started up it. The climb was steep and a misstep might send him shooting all the way to the bottom, but the soft moccasins gave him a good toehold. When he reached the higher ledge he was panting and winded.

The sun was blazing hot here, and even the rocks were hot under his hands. The burned red sandstone was dotted with juniper and it broke off in a steep slope. Steep, but not a cliff. He moved up behind a juniper and studied the mountain carefully. All was hot and still. Sweat smarted his eyes and he rubbed them out, then mopped the sweat from his brow and cheeks.

Overhead, an optimistic buzzard circled in widening sweeps. Far away over the valley that lay in the distance, was Blue Hill. Almost due west was Salt Creek. A thin trail of smoke lifted near the town. Below, the terrain was broken into canyons and arroyos, and the color shaded from the deep green of the juniper to the gray green of sage, and from the pale pinks and yellows of the faded sand to the deep burned reds and magentas of the rock.

Some thirty yards away a tree had died and the dry white bones of its skeleton lay scattered in a heap. Nearby a pack rat had built a mound of branches in a clump of manzanita. Kilkenny pulled his hat brim down to shade his eyes and moved out cautiously, walking on his cat feet across the mountainside.

Ahead of him a startled jackrabbit suddenly sprang from the ground and charged full tilt right at him. Kilkenny whirled aside and felt the blast of a bullet by his face. He started forward, running swiftly, and saw Frank Mailer spring up, gun in hand. Mailer fired and missed, and Kilkenny's shot blasted . . . too quick, but it cut through Mailer's shirt and then the man dove for him.

Kilkenny fired again, but whether he scored or not he had no idea, for he sprang forward and smashed a driving blow to Mailer's face. The punch was a wicked one and it caught the big man lunging in, caught the corner of his mouth and tore the flesh, so that Mailer screamed. Then he wheeled and grabbed Kilkenny's throat, wrenching him backward. Lance Kilkenny kicked his feet high and went over with Mailer, the sudden yielding carrying the big man off balance. Both went down and Mailer came up, clawing for his pistol, and Kilkenny drew his left-hand gun and fired. Mailer went to his knees, then grabbed wildly and caught Kilkenny's ankle. As Lance came down he lunged to his feet and dove for shelter in a nest of boulders. Flat on the ground, Kilkenny crawled to retrieve his gun, then loaded the empty chambers. Then he saw blood on the ground, two bright crimson stains, fresh blood!

A shot kicked dirt in his teeth and he spat it out and shot back, then lunged to his feet, his own position being too exposed, and sprang for the rocks and shelter.

He lit right into Mailer and the big man came up with a grunt and chopped for Kilkenny's skull with a pistol barrel. Bright lights exploded in his head and he felt his knees melting under him and slashed out with his own pistol, laying it across Mailer's face. He hit ground, heard an explosion, and Mailer fell on him.

Panting, bloody, and drunk with fury and pain, Frank Mailer leaped to his feet and stood swaying, a thin trickle of blood coming from a blue hole under his collarbone. He lunged at Kilkenny.

Exhausted, beaten, and punch-drunk himself, Kilkenny swung wildly and his fist connected with a sound like a rifle shot striking mud, and Mailer stopped, teetered, and fell.

Kilkenny backed up, his chest heaving, his lungs screaming for air, his skull humming with the blow he had recently taken. He caught up a gun and turned just as Mailer rolled on his back, a gun also in his hand. Both guns bellowed at once, and Kilkenny was knocked back on his heels, but as he staggered he pulled his gun down and fired again.

Where Mailer's ear had been there was blood, and the big man, seemingly indestructible, was getting up. With a wild, desperate kind of fury, Kilkenny flung himself on the rising man, and he heard guns bellowing, whether his own or Mailer's or both, he did not know, and then Mailer rolled free and fell away from the boulders. Slowly, ponderously, at each roll seemingly about to stop, the big man's body rolled over and over down the slope.

Fascinated, Kilkenny stared after him. Suddenly the man caught himself, and then, as if by magic, he got his hands under him. Something inside of Kilkenny screamed, *No! No!* and then he saw Mailer come to his feet, still gripping a gun.

Mailer swayed drunkenly and tried to fire, but the gun was empty. His huge body, powerful even when shot and battered, swayed but remained erect. Then, fumbling at his belt for cartridges, he began, like a drunken man trying to thread a needle, to load his gun. Kilkenny stared at him in astonishment, his own mind wandering in a sort of a sunlit, delirious world. Mailer faced him and the gun lifted, and Kilkenny felt the butt of his own gun jump and Mailer's hips jerked back grotesquely and he went up on his tiptoes. Then his gun spat into the gravel at his feet and he fell facedown on the slope.

When Kilkenny opened his eyes again, it was dark and piercing cold. A long wind moaned over the mountaintop and he was chilled to the bone. He was very weak and his head hummed. How badly he was wounded he had no idea, but he knew he could stand little of this cold.

Near the pack rat's nest he found some leaves that crackled under his touch. And shivering with such violence that his teeth rattled and his fingers could scarcely find the matches, he struck and pushed the match into the leaves. The flames caught and in a moment the nest was crackling and blazing.

He knew he had been hit once, and perhaps twice. He had a feeling he was badly wounded, and how long he could survive on this mountaintop he did not know. He did know that it was in view of Salt Creek, if anyone happened to be outside. The flames caught the gray, dead wood and blazed high and he lay there, watching the inverted cone of flame climbing up toward the stars, filled with a blank cold and emptiness.

Finally, as the fire died and its little warmth dissipated, he turned and crawled back among the boulders and lay there, panting hoarsely and shivering again with cold.

When he got his eyes open again, the sky was faintly gray. He could distinguish a few things around him and there were here and there a few scattered sticks. He got them together with a handful of grass and put them on the coals of last night's fire, then cupped his hands above the small flame. He felt a raw, gnawing pain in his side and his face was stiff and his hands were clumsy. Overhead, a few stars paled and vanished like moths flying into smoke, and he added another small stick and felt for his gun. It was gone. He moved, scraping the fire along until he was beneath the dead tree. Slowly he built up the fire around its dried-out trunk, and as it caught he rolled backward, away from the flames. He lay there as the white branches went up in a rush of smoke and flame, and as he passed out he prayed for help.

His eyes flickered open again at a sun-brightened world and he saw a huge turkey buzzard hunched in a tree not fifty yards away. He yelled and waved an arm, but the buzzard did not move. It sat there, waiting, and then its head came up, and it launched itself on lazy wings and floated off over the desert.

Kilkenny lay still, staring up into the brassy vault of the sky, his mind floating in a half-world between delirium and death. Out of it floated a voice, saying, "Here's a hat!"

And then another voice. "They can't be up there! It ain't reasonable!"

There was a long silence, and suddenly his eyes flashed open. That was no delirium! Somebody was searching! Hunting for him! He tried to call out, but his voice would muster no strength, and then he gathered himself, and picking up a small stick from near the fire, he threw it.

"He's got to be here. You saw all that smoke an' that's Buck down there, an' where you find that horse he ain't far away!"

"Do you see him?" The voice was unfamiliar, sarcastic. "I don't."

Then the other. "I'm goin' on top!"

"You're crazy!"

A long time later a loud whoop and then running feet. "Here's Mailer! Hey, would you look at that? Man, what happened up here, anyway?"

He tried to call out again, and this time they came hurrying. Cain Brockman, Rusty Gates, Gordon Flynn, his head bandaged and his face thin, and with them several men from town. "You all right, Lance?" Gates pleaded, his face redder still with worry.

"What do you think?" Kilkenny muttered.

And when he opened his eyes again, he was lying in darkness between clean white sheets and he felt vastly relaxed and comfortable. And Nita came in, walking softly, and sat down beside him. "Everything all right?" she asked.

"Yes, ma'am," he whispered. "As long as when I'm well we're goin' to California to sit by the sea."

She smiled, "There's a little port town called San Pedro, and I expect the railroad workers and dock men will want a gambling hall as much as anyone." She kissed him gently. "When I see you're better, I'll have Cain start packing the wagons."

Afterword

by Beau L'Amour

This book contains the last of Louis L'Amour's unpublished western stories, the history of which I set down in the introduction to *West of Dodge*. It also marks the end of an era for the western genre. For fifty-seven years Louis L'Amour's westerns have been published, first in pulp magazines, then in paperback originals, and now in hardcovers. Louis grew up in the time just after the closing of the frontier; born on the North Dakota plains in 1908, his world as a child was one of wheat farms and cattle ranches, Civil War veterans and aging Indian warriors. At the time of his death, Louis may have been the last writer of western fiction to have actually met the kinds of characters that he often wrote about. In his youth he occasionally had the opportunity to sit and listen to the likes of Buffalo Bill Cody, Bill Tilghman, Jeff Milton, Chris Madsen, Elfageo Baca, George Coe, Tom Pickett, Frenchy McCormack, Deluvina Maxwell, and a hundred other less historically notable men and women who remembered the days when the West was wild. Although his vision of the frontier was essentially that of an author of romantic entertainment, Louis L'Amour was, in reality, one of our world's last links to the nineteenth century.

This book that you hold in your hands rounds up the last stragglers in the Kilkenny, Bowdrie, and Cactus Kid series. It contains an additional tale of the Utah Blaine character, whom Louis may have once planned a series around, and the last Talon story. We still have a couple more collections to be published, so keep a lookout in the late spring for the next several years for more books of Louis's classic adventure, detective, sports, and the last few western stories from the old pulp magazines. There are still several adventure and mystery stories that have never been published before and quite a few that were only published back in the 1940s or '50s.

The Louis L'Amour biography continues. A more complete list of the names of people that I am trying to learn about can be found on pages 254 to 261. It is a fantastic experience for me when someone who knew Louis or knew about him writes in. Many people have been a great help and I have learned many new facts and a few lessons. . . .

One of those has been the responsibility of dealing with history and my perception of what history is. In a recent radio interview in Jamestown, I made some premature and ill-advised conjectures about my grandparents' state of mind at the time they left North Dakota. My opinion had been based on some evidence that I had discovered earlier that day, but that evidence was far from all-inclusive. A few weeks later I got a letter from some members of my father's family, some of whom knew my grandfather and grandmother. They expressed their displeasure with my statements and informed me of several aspects of my grandfather's nature that I should have been able to deduce but had not taken into consideration when my tongue slipped and poured the contents of my mind into a microphone and out over much of the upper Midwest. I vowed that the contents of this letter and anything else that I learn would be fully digested by the time I write this book. I am sure that there will always be someone somewhere who will not agree with whatever it is that I finally write, but in this case I realize that I didn't agree with myself!

The material to be included in this biography may have occurred in the past but it is not disconnected ancient history. There are still many of you out there to whom the story or parts of the story are personal and the more of you who can write in the better, for the more information I have the better and more accurate a book it will be.

This book also marks the tenth anniversary of Louis's death in June of 1988. Both my family and all the people at Bantam Books wish to extend our gratitude to all of you who have continued to follow the work of Louis L'Amour for so long after he left this earth. I think that Dad would be amazed at his continuing popularity and proud that he will be continually published even after the year 2000.

Thank you all for your continued readership.

Here are the names of the people that I would like to contact. If you find your name on the list, I would be very grateful if you would write to me. Some of these people may have known Louis as "Duke" LaMoore or Michael "Micky" Moore, as Louis occasionally used those names. Many of the people on this list may be dead. If you are a family member (or were a very good friend) of anyone on the list who has passed away, I would like to hear from you, too. Some of the names I have marked with an asterisk (*); if there is anyone out there who knows anything at all about these people, I would like to hear it. The address to write to is:

Louis L'Amour Biography Project
P.O. Box 41183
Pasadena, CA 91114-9183

Marian Payne—Married a man named Duane. Louis knew her in Oklahoma in the mid-to-late 1930s. She moved to New York for a while; she may have lived in Wichita at some point.

Chaplain Phillips—Louis first met him at Fort Sill, then again in Paris at the Place de Saint Augustine Officers' Mess. The first meeting was in 1942, the second in 1945.

Anne Mary Bentley—Friend of Louis's from Oklahoma in the 1930s. Possibly a musician of some sort. Lived in Denver for a time.

*Pete Boering**—Born in the late 1890s. Came from Amsterdam, Holland. His father may have been a ship's captain. Louis and Pete sailed from Galveston together in the mid-1920s.

Betty Brown—Woman whom Louis corresponded with extensively while in Choctaw in the late 1930s. Later she moved to New York.

*Jacques Chambrun**—Louis's agent from the late 1930s through the late 1950s.

Des—His first name. Chambrun's assistant in the late 1940s or early 1950s.

*Joe Friscia**—One of two guys that joined Hagenbeck & Wallace circus in Phoenix with Louis in the mid-1920s. They rode freights across Texas and spent a couple of nights in the Star of Hope Mission in Houston. May have been from Boston.

*Harry "Shorty" Warren**—Shipmate of Louis's in the mid-

1920s. They sailed from Galveston to England and back. Harry may have been an Australian.

Joe Hollinger*—Louis met him while with Hagenbeck & Wallace circus, where he ran the "privilege car." A couple of months later he shipped out with Louis. This was in the mid-1920s.

Joe Hildebrand*—Louis met him on the docks in New Orleans in the mid-1920s. Then ran into him later in Indonesia. Joe may have been the first mate and Louis second mate on a schooner operated by Captain Douglas. This would have been in the East Indies in the later 1920s or early 1930s. Joe may have been an aircraft pilot and flown for Pan Am in the early 1930s.

Turk Madden*—Louis knew him in Indonesia in the late 1920s or early 1930s. They may have spent some time around the "old" Straits Hotel and the Maypole Bar in Singapore. Later on, in the States, Louis traveled around with him putting on boxing exhibitions. Madden worked at an airfield near Denver as a mechanic in the early 1930s. Louis eventually used his name for a fictional character.

"Cockney" Joe Hagen*—Louis knew him in Indonesia in the late 1920s or early 1930s. He may have been part of the Straits Hotel–Maypole Bar crowd in Singapore.

Richard LaForte*—A merchant seaman from the Bay Area. Shipped out with Louis in the mid-1920s.

Mason or Milton*—Don't know which was his real name. He was a munitions dealer in Shanghai in the late 1920s or 1930s. He was killed while Louis was there. His head was stuck on a pipe in front of his house as a warning not to double-cross a particular warlord.

Singapore Charlie*—Louis knew him in Singapore and served with him on Douglas's schooner in the East Indies. Louis was second mate and Charlie was bosun.

He was a stocky man of indeterminate race, and if I remember correctly, Dad told me he had quite a few tattoos. In the early 1930s Louis helped get him a job on a ship in San Pedro, CA, that was owned by a movie studio.

Renée Semich—She was born in Vienna (I think) and was going to a New York art school when Louis met her. This was just before WWII. Her father's family was from Yugoslavia or Italy, her mother from Austria. They lived in New York; her aunt had an apartment overlooking Central Park. For a while she worked for a company in Waterbury, CT.

Aola Seery—Friend of Louis's from Oklahoma City in the late 1930s. She was a member of the "Writer's Club" and I think she had both a brother and sister.

Enoch Lusk—Owner of Lusk Publishing Company in 1939, original publisher of Louis's *Smoke from This Altar*. Also associated with the National Printing Company, Oklahoma City.

Helen Turner*—Louis knew her in late 1920s Los Angeles. Once a showgirl with Jack Fine's Follies.

James "Jimmy" Eades—Louis knew him in San Pedro in the mid-1920s.

Frank Moran—Louis met him in Ventura when Louis was a "club second" for fighters in the later 1920s. They also may have known each other in Los Angeles or Kingman in the mid-1920s. Louis ran into him again on Hollywood Boulevard late in 1946.

Jud and Red Rasco*—Brothers, cowboys, Louis met them in Tucumcari, NM. Also saw them in Santa Rosa, NM. This was in the early-to-mid–1920s.

Olga Santiago—Friend of Louis's from late 1940s Los Angeles. Last saw her at a book signing in Thousand Oaks, CA.

Jose Craig Berry—A writer friend of Louis's from Oklahoma City in the late 1930s. She worked for a paper called the *Black Dispatch*.

Evelyn Smith Colt—She knew him in Kingman at one point, probably the late 1920s. Louis saw her again much later at a Paso Robles book signing.

Kathlyn Beucler Hays—Friend from Choctaw, taught school there in the 1930s. Louis saw her much later at a book signing in San Diego.

*Floyd Bolton**—A man from Hollywood who came out to Oklahoma to talk to Louis about a possible trip to Java to make a movie in 1938.

Lisa Cohn—Reference librarian in Portland; family owned Cohn Bros. furniture store. Louis knew her in the late 1920s or early 1930s.

Mary Claire Collingsworth—Friend and correspondent from Oklahoma in the 1930s.

C. A. Donnell—Man in Oklahoma City in the early 1930s who rented Louis a typewriter.

*Captain Douglas**—Captain of a ship in Indonesia that Louis served on. A three-masted auxiliary schooner.

*L. Duks**—I think that this was probably a shortened version of the original family name. A first mate in the mid-1920s. I think that he was a U.S. citizen, but he was originally Russian.

Maudee Harris—My aunt Chynne's sister.

*Parker LaMoore and Chynne Harris LaMoore**—Louis's eldest brother. Parker was secretary to the governor of Oklahoma for a while, then he worked for the Scripps-Howard newspaper chain. He also worked with Ambassador Pat Hurley. He died in the early 1950s. Chynne was his wife and she lived longer than he did, but I don't know where she lived after his death.

Mrs. Brown—Who worked for Parker LaMoore from the 1930s to the 1950s.

*Haig**—His last name. Louis described him as a Scotsman, once an officer in the British army in India. Louis said he was "an officer in one of the Scottish regiments." Louis knew him in Shanghai in the 1930s; we don't know how old he would have been at the time. He may have been involved in some kind of intelligence work. He and Louis shared an apartment for a while, which seems to have been located just off Avenue King Edward VII.

Lola LaCorne—Along with her sister and mother, she was a friend of Louis's in Paris during World War II. She later taught literature at the Sorbonne, had (hopefully still has) a husband named Christopher.

Dean Kirby—Pal from Oklahoma City in the late 1930s who seems to have been a copywriter or something of the sort. Might have worked for Lusk Publishing.

Bunny Yeager—Girlfriend of Dean Kirby's from Oklahoma City. Not the famous photographer for *Playboy*.

Virginia McElroy—Girl with whom Louis went to school in Jamestown.

Guardsman Penwill—A British boxer in the period between the mid-1920s and the mid-1930s.

Arleen Weston Sherman—Friend of Louis's from Jamestown, when he was thirteen or fourteen. I think her family visited the LaMoores in Choctaw in the 1930s. Her older sister's name is Mary; parents' names are Ralph and Lil.

Harry Bigelow—Louis knew him in Ventura. He had a picture taken with Louis's mother, Emily LaMoore, at a place named Berkeley Springs around 1929. Louis may have known him at the Katherine Mine, near Kingman, AZ, or in Oregon.

Tommy Pinto—Boxer from Portland; got Louis a job at Portland Manufacturing.

Nancy Carroll—An actress as of 1933. Louis knew her from the chorus of a show at the Winter Garden in New York and a cabaret in New Jersey, where she and her sister danced occasionally, probably during the mid–to–late 1920s.

Judith Wood—Actress. Louis knew her in Hollywood in the late 1920s.

Stanley George—The George family relocated from Kingman, AZ, to Ventura, CA, possibly in the late 1920s.

Francis Lederer*—Actor whom Louis knew in the late 1920s in Los Angeles. I'm looking for anyone who knew him in Hollywood between 1926 and 1931.

Lieutenant Rix—Who served in the 3622 Quartermaster Truck Co. in Europe in 1944–45.

Pablo De Gantes*—Ex-soldier of fortune who occasionally wrote magazine articles for *Lands of Romance* in the 1930s. This man used several names and I believe he was actually a Belgian. He lived in Mexico at one time.

Lieutenant King—Who traveled all the way from Camp Beale, CA, through Camp Reynolds, PA, and on to England with Louis when he was shipped overseas in early 1944.

K. C. Gibson or his two nephews—Louis met them when they picked him up hitchhiking in October of 1924. They were crossing New Mexico and Arizona bound for Brawly, CA.

Wilma Anderson—A friend of Louis's from Oklahoma who worked in the Key campaign headquarters in 1938.

Johnny Annette—A boxer with whom Louis fought a bout in Woodward, OK (or KS), in the 1930s.

Harry Bell—A boxing promoter Louis worked with in Oklahoma City in the 1930s.

Joe Bickerstaff*—Also an occasional boxing promoter. He knew Louis in Klamath Falls in the late 1920s.

Pat Chaney—Friend of Louis's from Choctaw, OK, in the late 1930s.

*Mr. Lettsinger**—An older man whom Louis knew in Klamath Falls, OR, in the late 1920s. I think he was from the Midwest or South.

*Tommy Danforth**—A boxing promoter from Prescott, AZ, in the mid-1920s. Was using the VA hospital at Ft. Whipple.

*Ned DeWitt**—Knew Louis in Oklahoma in the 1930s, also a friend of Jim Thompson.

Austin Fullerton—Who sold tickets for athletic events in Oklahoma City in the late 1930s.

Martha Nell Hitchcock—A friend from Edmond, OK, in the 1930s.

*Joe Hollinger**—Who ran the "privilege car" for the Hagenbeck & Wallace circus and shipped out to England in the mid-1920s.

*Tommy Tucker**—Boss Stoker on British Blue Funnel ships from the mid-1920s to mid-1930s.

*Dynamite Jackson**—An African-American fighter that Louis helped promote in Oklahoma in the 1930s.

Orry Kelly—Designer in Hollywood, Louis knew him in the late 1940s.

Dorothy Kilgallen—A newspaper columnist who worked in L.A. in the 1950s.

Henry Li—Whom Louis knew from 1943 when he was at Camp Robinson, AR.

*Savoie Lottinville**—Of the University of Oklahoma.

Julio Lopez—Whom Louis worked for very briefly in Phoenix in the mid-1920s.

Joe May—A rancher Louis boxed with in Ft. Sumner, NM, in the 1920s.

Ann Mehaffey—Friend of Louis's from the time he spent at Camp Robinson, AR.

Sam Merwin or Sam Mines*—Who once worked with Leo Margulies at Standard Magazines/Better Publications.

Jack Natteford—Screenwriter who worked with Louis in the 1950s.

Joe Paskvan—Once part of the Oklahoma Writer's Project; Louis knew him in the late 1930s.

Billy Prince—Who went to sea in the late 1930s on the *Wallace E. Pratt*, a Standard tanker.

Countess Dulong de Rosney (Toni Morgan)*—Whom Louis knew in France in the mid-1940s.

Dot and Truitt Ross—Brother and sister whom Louis knew in Oklahoma in the 1930s.

Mary Jane Stevenson—A friend of Louis's from L.A. in the late 1940s.

Orchid Tatu—Who lived in Sparta, WI, in the mid-1940s.

Florence Wagner—Wife of Rob Wagner of Rob Wagner's Script.

Doris Weil—A roomer in the flat where Louis lived in the late 1940s.

Sandra Widener—Who wrote an article on Louis called "The Untold Stories of Louis L'Amour."

Anyone who served on the *S.S. Steel Worker* between 1925 and 1930. In particular Captain C. C. Boase, second mate Ralph Jones, third mate Raymond Cousins, radio operator Stanley Turbervil, carpenter George Mearly, bosun H. Allendorf, chief engineer C. B. Dahlberg, first assistant engineer O. E. Morgan, second assistant engineer W. Haynes, third assistant engineers George G. Folberth and William Stewart, oilers A. Chagnon and A. Kratochbil, firemen William Hohroien, J. Perez, Manfrido Gonzales, John Fennelly, and E. G. Burnay, wipers A. Sanchez, J. J. Dalmasse, and F. Clifford, steward J. Shiel, messmen Dean Bender,

William Harvey, and J. H. Blomstedt, able-bodied seamen Ernest Martin, Chris Moore, Karl Erickson, Steve Schmotzer, Michael Llorca, Louis Armand, Joseph Morris, Herbert Lieflander, William Reichart, and H. F. Waite.

Anyone familiar with Singapore in the late 1920s, the "old" Straits Hotel, and the Maypole Bar.

Anyone who is very knowledgeable about the military history, and/or politics of western (Shansi, Kansu, and Sinkiang provinces) China between 1928 and 1936.

I am also looking for seamen who served on the following ships: the *Catherine G. Sudden*, between 1925 and 1936; the *Yellowstone*, between 1925 and 1936; the *S.S. Steadfast*, between 1924 and 1930; the *Annandale*, a four-masted bark, between 1920 and 1926; the *Randsberg*, a German freighter, between 1925 and 1937.

Anyone who knows anything about an old square-rigged sailing vessel called the *Indiana* that was used in movies in the 1920s and 1930s. This ship was docked at San Pedro.

Anyone who knows anything about the following boxers: Jonny "Kid" Stopper, Jack Horan, "Kid" Yates, Butch Vierthaler (Bill Thaler), Ira O'Neil, Jimmy Roberts, Jimmy Russo, Jack McGraf, or Jackie Jones. Louis met these men in Arizona in the 1920s.

Anyone who knows anything about a fight (I assume with small arms) between two trading schooners that was stopped by a British warship near Pinaki in the South Pacific. This would have been between 1926 and 1932.

Anyone from the family or group that Louis guided around Egypt sometime between 1926 and 1937. Although he very much looked the part, Louis finally admitted that he wasn't a real guide and that he'd been using a tour book from a library to learn about the sites to which he led his group. They may have stayed at Shepherd's. Some or all of the party were Americans and there may have been as many as twelve of them.

Anyone who might know about a flight that Louis took across Africa with a French officer with stops at Taudeni and Timbuktu. This would have been between the mid-1920s and late 1930s.

Anyone familiar with an island in the Spratly group called Itu Aba.

Anyone who knows anything about a very short-lived magazine published in Oklahoma City in 1936 called *Uptown Magazine*.

Anyone who knows if Norman Foster and Rex Bell (George Francis Beldam) ever went to sea during the 1920s or early 1930s.

Anyone who knows where the personal and business papers of B. P. Schulberg (not Budd) and Sam Katz are archived. Both of these men worked at Paramount Publix Pictures. The period that I am interested in is the late 1920s to the early 1930s.

Anyone familiar with the Royal Government Experimental Hospital in Calcutta, India.

I would like to hear from men who served in the following military units: the 3622 Quartermaster Truck Company, between June 1944 and December 1945; the 3595 Quartermaster Truck Company, after October 1945 and before January 1946; the 670th Tank Destroyer Battalion, in 1943 at Camp Hood, TX; the 808th Tank Destroyer Battalion, at Camp Phillips, KS in 1943.

Soldiers or officers who: took basic training at Camp Robinson, AR, between September 1942 and January 1943; took winter training at Camp McCoy, WI, and near Land o' Lakes and Watersmeet on the northern Michigan peninsula between October 1943 and February 1944; remember Louis in early 1944 when he was staying at the St. Francis

Hotel and the Belleview in San Francisco. During this time he worked at the Oakland Air Base, and Fort Mason, CA. Later he was at Camp Beale, CA.

Anyone who worked with the Oklahoma WPA Writers Project.

Any recordings that anyone knows about of any of Louis's speeches.

About Louis L'Amour

"I think of myself in the oral tradition—as a troubadour, a village tale-teller, the man in the shadows of the campfire. That's the way I'd like to be remembered—as a storyteller. A good storyteller."

It is doubtful that any author could be as at home in the world re-created in his novels as Louis Dearborn L'Amour. Not only could he physically fill the boots of the rugged characters he wrote about, but he literally "walked the land my characters walk." His personal experiences as well as his lifelong devotion to historical research combined to give Mr. L'Amour the unique knowledge and understanding of people, events, and the challenge of the American frontier that became the hallmarks of his popularity.

Of French-Irish descent, Mr. L'Amour could trace his own family in North America back to the early 1600s and follow their steady progression westward, "always on the frontier." As a boy growing up in Jamestown, North Dakota, he absorbed all he could about his family's frontier heritage, including the story of his great-grandfather who was scalped by Sioux warriors.

Spurred by an eager curiosity and desire to broaden his horizons, Mr. L'Amour left home at the age of fifteen and enjoyed a wide variety of jobs including seaman, lumberjack, elephant handler, skinner of dead cattle, miner, and an officer in the transportation corps during World War II. During his "yondering" days he also circled the world on a freighter, sailed a dhow on the Red Sea, was shipwrecked in the West Indies and stranded in the Mojave Desert. He won fifty-one of fifty-nine fights as a professional boxer and worked as a journalist and lecturer. He was a voracious reader and collector of rare books. His personal library contained 17,000 volumes.

Mr. L'Amour "wanted to write almost from the time I could talk." After developing a widespread following for his many frontier and adventure stories written for fiction magazines, Mr. L'Amour published his first full-length novel, *Hondo,* in the United States in 1953. Every one of his more than 100 books is in print; there are nearly 230 million copies of his books in print worldwide, making him one of the bestselling authors in modern literary history. His books have been translated into twenty languages, and more than forty-five of his novels and stories have been made into feature films and television movies.

His hardcover bestsellers include *The Lonesome Gods, The Walking Drum* (his twelfth-century historical novel), *Jubal Sackett, Last of the Breed,* and *The Haunted Mesa.* His memoir, *Education of a Wandering Man,* was a leading bestseller in 1989. Audio dramatizations and adaptations of many L'Amour stories are available on cassette tapes from Bantam Audio publishing.

The recipient of many great honors and awards, in 1983 Mr. L'Amour became the first novelist ever to be awarded the Congressional Gold Medal by the United States Congress in honor of his life's work. In 1984 he was also awarded the Medal of Freedom by President Reagan.

Louis L'Amour died on June 10, 1988. His wife, Kathy, and their two children, Beau and Angelique, carry the L'Amour tradition forward with new books written by the author during his lifetime to be published by Bantam.